THE FOSSIL FOREST

STEVEN C. HARBERT JR.

authorHOUSE®

AuthorHouse™
1663 Liberty Drive
Bloomington, IN 47403
www.authorhouse.com
Phone: 1 (800) 839-8640

© 2017 Steven C. Harbert Jr.. All rights reserved.

No part of this book may be reproduced, stored in a retrieval system, or transmitted by any means without the written permission of the author.

Published by AuthorHouse 06/16/2017

ISBN: 978-1-5246-9704-4 (sc)
ISBN: 978-1-5246-9702-0 (hc)
ISBN: 978-1-5246-9703-7 (e)

Library of Congress Control Number: 2017909396

Print information available on the last page.

Any people depicted in stock imagery provided by Thinkstock are models, and such images are being used for illustrative purposes only.
Certain stock imagery © Thinkstock.

This book is printed on acid-free paper.

Because of the dynamic nature of the Internet, any web addresses or links contained in this book may have changed since publication and may no longer be valid. The views expressed in this work are solely those of the author and do not necessarily reflect the views of the publisher, and the publisher hereby disclaims any responsibility for them.

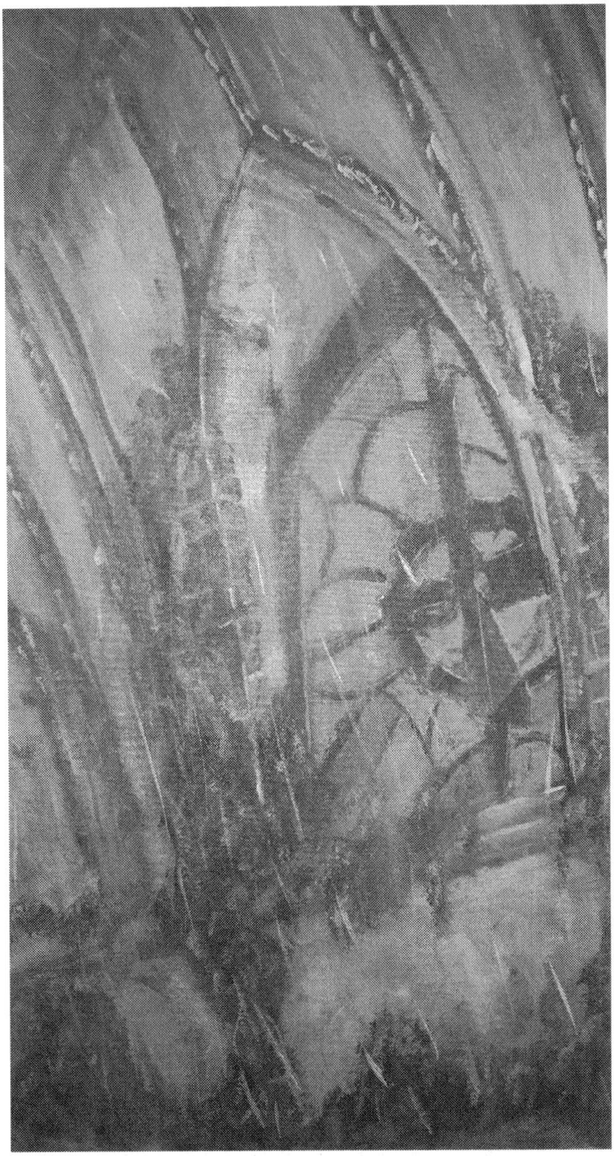

To all those I call family whose characters and personalities are the epitome of what human beings are meant to be. You were yourselves in a time where most can't remove the masks they've made. Thank you. All of you.

"We are but a teardrop in the eye of the Universe. And how she weeps so."

-Steven Craig Harbert Jr.

The Fossil Forest
Written by Steven Harbert
Story by Steven Harbert and Marcos Garcia
Artwork by Gerard McDermott
Edited By Kurt Bennamon and Sara Ebaugh

Chapter 1

No Quiet Night

The night was unusually dark yet warm. The cries and calls of creatures echoed off into the distance and darkness of the tall forest. The fog rolled in down below the great city walls. Above the wind howled, screaming, over the fortified walkway between two large towers that stand guard over the large wooden entrance. Several train tracks leading out of the Kingdom, rusted and unused since the war between societies, disappeared under the thick canvas of trees. The old vine covered lamps no longer lighting its way almost serving as grave markers along its old tracks. Their solace and darkness gave the way into the forest an eerie look of desolation. The thick dark clouds overhead began to bleed its heavy cries upon the land. Beating against the stone walkway all around the sentry as he looked off into the dark forest.

"Marcus." Scott called out to him through the pouring rain.

Marcus, standing in the rain, wearing a dark grey hooded poncho, dark blue military fatigues and plated boots. His large rifle barrel jutted out as it hung to his right side. His skin slightly tan suggesting his ancestors were of Latino descent. Turned leaning against the stone wall. His hat peeking out just past his hood beaded off droplets of rain as he looked over the kingdoms many small towns and cities. The lamps and street lights winding their way up towards the Kingdom's center. Large lights and burning torches lined the walls. Small prattles of gun fire from the nearest town to their gates. It was a peaceful night Marcus thought.

"Marcus?" Scott called again.

Scott emerged from the darkness to join his partner out on the wall to stand watch. Marcus was smoking a cigarette lost in his own thoughts. He didn't hear the tall man's calls to him until a heavy hand placed onto his shoulder shook him from his mental prison.

"What are you doing out here all by your lonesome, weirdo?", the man asked looking at his illuminated watch. "We still had ten minutes before we needed to relieve those fucks."

The rain had stopped suddenly and the sky broke with rays of moonlight.

Scott was older than Marcus, yet strong and oddly intimidating. He, maybe half a foot taller than Marcus, stood clenching his semi-automatic shotgun in his left hand. He was dragging a smoke with his right. The glow from the cherry lit up his stern face. Thick dark eyebrows, thin dark eyes illuminated in the orange glow behind the cigarette. Scandinavian descendant due to his light skin and demeanor. He was wearing dark green pants, plated boots, a thick heavy gun belt lined with shell carriers, a thick blade at the small of his back, and a black waterproof hoodie to keep him dry.

"I don't know man. I felt like just getting out here early and have a moment to myself."

"You sure, I'll go check on the other tower and leave you to your thoughts if you want, brother."

Marcus smiled slightly and returned glaring out into the night. "No, you're fine."

"Alright, brother." Scott replied squinting at his young partner. He produced from his shoulder pockets two cigarettes handing one to Marcus. Marcus flicked its finished butt over the side. They both lit their smokes as they listened to the screams and roars of the night from the forest before them.

"You ever wondered what it was like before all, this?", Marcus broke the silence.

"You ever wonder what is coming after all, this?", Scott replied.

The two looked at each other and chuckled for a moment.

"I mean; they had completely different animals and the food chain was in the Humans favor. Now we can't walk out there without being heavily armed. A basilisk could come from nowhere and fucking eat you. Hell, we are fucked if a Chimera shows up…"

Scott's glance cut through the night. Marcus caught himself immediately. "Sorry brother, I know you ran into one back during the War of Ascension."

Scott said nothing. he gazed out into the Jungle taking a long drag from his cigarette before flicking it over the side of the wall. "I'm going to check on the other tower. I'll be right back."

Scott walked with almost a sway in his step, feeling definitively older than he should as he made his way down the old brick and stone pathway on top of the great wall.

"Hey brother!", Marcus yelled to Scott.

He stopped and turned. "Yeah?"

"Wanna get drunk after this?"

"As we should, but… aren't we already drunk?", Scott gestured, shrugging his shoulders.

"Oh yeah," Marcus laughed.

A subtle whining, as if a turbine was powering up, called both their attention. Marcus picked his rifle up under his poncho. Searching for the origin of the noise. It was coming from the forest. Scott picked his weapon up slightly as he peered over the wall into the forest.

"Boss, this is tower one, our thermals just went white, you see anything out there, over?"

"Tower one, we got some humming noise, tower two, status, over.", Scott replies.

"Tower two, yeah we have the same shit as one, thermals are white, whatever the hell it is, it's burning out our sights, night vis has nothing, motion sensors are picking up normal patterns of life. Want us to send some lume?"

Scott squinted trying as hard as he could to see into the forest. "Yeah, send one from you and tower one, base of the tree line. Light her up."

"This is tower one, roger."

"Tower two, roger."

Scott and Marcus waited as the towers prepared to fire. The massive multi-barreled cannons rotated with heavy clunks as they locked into position.

"Prepare for shot, over."

Scott, clearly irritated, called over the net.

"Just shoot the mother fuckers, and call up to Post and have a mobile crew on standby."

Before anyone could reply, a red beam of intense heat fired out of the darkness of the forest. The thin light drew a line across the base of the second tower into the first tower. The beam was gone just as quickly as it appeared, Scott and Marcus looked down, and radio chatter begin to come over their net. The wooden gate caught fire, the stone started to grow brighter and brighter as it turned into a bubbling molten form. Scott reached for Marcus, the gate and towers exploded from the line from the red beam. The towers folded forward and fell. The door blew inward. Marcus and Scott were sent through the air only to slam into the wet grass as debris fell around them.

Scott picked himself up from the heavy indent he just made with his face, back, and whatever else decided to hit the ground as he landed. The sound of engines, turbine in nature, sophisticated and clean running quietly, hummed over the noise of hardening molten rock and the blaze of fire from the tall wooden gate that lay in pieces for several hundred meters. Alarms sounded all over the Kingdom. Scott could hear them over each other faintly.

"This is not a test, multiple attacks on fortified walls, Dragonares, Old Guard, Boltiers, Gun Walzer territories have been affected. War posture now in effect. War Posture now in effect…" The message continued with breaks in between sentences as the air raid sirens screamed out into the rapidly illuminating cities and towns.

"What in the fuck?", Scott grunted.

He was covered in mud, angrily wiping his hood back, checking his shotgun. He turned to see the damage caused by the beam. The towers lay in rubble towards the forest, like arms reaching out to embrace mother once again. The fires upon the remains of the door, looked like stars scattered across the sky. Scott drew in the air, and a grin split his face as he tossed both pieces of his broken weapon into the mud. Marcus grunted and moaned over exaggeratedly as he gets up to a knee leaning on his rifle.

"What the fuck was that?", Marcus groaned out.

"I have a feeling we are about to find out real soon", Scott said as he stood ready, searching with his eyes.

From the glow of the fire, silhouettes of almost mirages appeared bending the dull dancing light around them.

"Impossible…", Marcus whispered.

Scott said nothing, his head leaned forward as he widened his stance.

The rain began to pick up.

"You good?", Scott said jokingly with a grin on his face.

Marcus shifted his gaze to Scott.

"I'll survive."

"Then get up, you lazy fuck."

Marcus got onto his feet.

The mirages before them seemed to short out as the rain fell harder. Their images now clear as they walked towards Scott and Marcus. Seven of them, the smallest one in the middle facing Scott, two to his right and two to Marcus's left.

The hexagonal pattern flashes of images out of place from the forest behind them. The rain was affecting their ability to cloak. They all have sophisticated weaponry, long since forgotten. Side arms, heavy battle belts with a wench style system, a small cylinder possessing the power source for the cloaking suits they are all wearing.

"These defenses are amateur. A child could have gotten through here without a problem." The woman, as her voice suggested, said to the others.

"Your orders? We don't have much time, we'll have to feed again if we want to continue, your highness." Another female replied.

Before the leader could answer another, male from the tone of his growling deep voice.

"How can we be sure? They are the same species. Regardless of what uniform they wear, we cannot leave them alive… Or we should take them with us, they could be useful in many other ways."

The small one in the middle answered "Ha." She spouted. "Kill them both now. What we came here for is in the north."

Before any of the hooded figures could pick their weapons up Scott and Marcus fired. Razor sharp accuracy and blinding fire rates, they were empty in a second. Violently sliding to a wet stop only to realize that not one of their rounds had found their target. Their rounds had shattered in midair. Slamming into something unseen, the area around each of the individuals standing before Marcus and Scott had blurred ever so slightly.

"Infuckingpossible", Scott spouted as he reloaded both of his under barreled revolvers.

Marcus fired again, moving faster than humanly possible sliding to a stop behind ruble.

Scott walked out in front of the group.

"My Lady, these men are not normal, they are much more formidable than the last species we encountered", one of them stated.

"Take them with us, these are Gun Walzers, they could be useful after all." The leader ordered with the sound of astonishment in her voice.

Before any of them could move, Marcus opened fire, his magazine dropping to the ground. He was already reloading his third. The shells flipped and tumbled away as he dumped magazine after magazine of accurate blinding fire into each of the hooded figures.

Scott appeared right in front of the leader. One of the figures stepped into Scott's way. The world seemed slow down as all of the group attempted to react, but they were far too slow. Scott head butted the male that attempted to block him. The figure buckled, slamming into the ruble and sending small pieces of stone in all directions. Unconscious from the force of the blow, Scott's under barrel revolver was pressed against the hooded figure's head. His second revolver, without looking, was out trained on the closest one to his left. His dark eyes slid up, making contact with hers. And once they had met, he saw two beautiful glowing orange eyes, wide slits for pupils dilated to see in the dark.

Scott said nothing. She had anger and almost fear in her eyes. Marcus ran out of magazines and drew his two 1911 frame pistols and begin firing rapidly. The leader stepped forward and kicked Scott square in the chest sending him up several meters into the air. He fired rapidly as he rocketed away. The rounds bounced off the blurring sphere. He landed digging into the wet grass with his heavy boots. She met him with a heavy right hook. He took it as if it were nothing. Before she knew it, his strong left hand was gripping her throat.

The rest of the group of hooded figures rushed to her aid. Two broke away from the group firing machine guns at Marcus's position, pinning him down. Marcus tossed a grenade, landing perfectly to where the two were headed. The grenade exploded as their shields blocked the blast without issue.

"What the fuck are these assholes", Marcus spouted as he ran to another position.

Scott backhanded one of the attackers, the body flipped once, twice, and finally bounced off the ground rolling to a stop in the mud. The next met Scott's heavy boot in the chest; sending the attacker violently across the field. Scott blocked a wild haymaker from another flanking him, the leader broke free of his grip. His hands seemed to have disappeared, flickering into several body shots and finally a palm strike to the chest of another attacker. The figure launched from Scott's heavy attack, catching the corner of a jutting piece of stone and flipping over the remains of the wall. The screams fell silent as the figure hit the ground on the other side.

The leader now, the only one still left standing circled Scott like a predator. Scott pulled his blade from the large leather sheath belted to the small of his back. Its D-guard handle protecting his knuckles, its long cleaver style blade made him look like a butcher. She charged thrusting, his hands blurred, striking but once, shattering his blade into pieces. She leapt back several meters, he looked at his blade with disgust written on his face. A thud between his legs catches his attention. He looked. A grenade more than likely, but a design he did not recognize. He kicked it away. The grenade exploded in midair several meters away.

He continued moving towards her. She signaled one of the others, but Scott payed no mind. She is his target. She drew her pistol firing rapidly to no avail. Scott weaved in and out of every shot almost fading from her sight. Before she knew it Scott backhanded the weapon from her grip. She grabbed him by the hood and rolled back kicking upwards tossing him like a rag doll. He landed hard on his back rolling onto his stomach. He was on his feet ripping the ground up from his movements. Sliding as he cocked back for a heavy palm strike to the chest. She blocked with both her arms. The sound of heavy meat hitting bone smacked as she was sent tumbling across the field into a pile of rubble.

Scott landed over her pinning her down looking into her gorgeous eyes. His teeth grinding as she fought with all her might to push him off. Her skin was of green scales and brilliant blue markings. Her teeth sharp but white as could be. A barrel pressed to the top of his head. Heavy panting as the shaking weapon called his attention.

"Let's see you dodge this, you vile beast." The hooded figure with heavy breaths angrily proclaimed. She fired. Scott flickered and his image was gone, he was gone. He was seen sliding backwards like a dog digging into the ground with all fours. The hooded figure picked up their leader and they began to run.

Marcus fired again, his rounds sparking off the invisible shield. Scott took off, mud and patches of wet grass kicked up from his quick steps. The two chasing Marcus spotted him, one pulled a small cylindrical tube open and took aim. They fired, the rocket screamed for Marcus landing just on the other side of his cover right in front of him. The explosion sent him flying into the rubble. He bounced off and landed hard in front of Scott. Scott stopped. The group as now placed something in the rubble. Its blue lights counted down rapidly. Scott quickly moved to Marcus kicking him in the stomach sending him skipping across the wet grass like a stone across water. Marcus rolled to a stop still unconscious several hundred meters away.

She looked back, as their eyes met. She disappeared, the rain stopped, and the device went off. The blast sent a shockwave in all directions, Scott took the brunt of it. He hit the ground hard unconscious as he tumbled and rolled finally slamming into a large piece of the stone remains. He was out. The hooded figures have escaped. Dawn was breaking. And vehicles roaring engines grew louder.

An hour or so later.

"Hey…"

"Hey…" Her voice was familiar to Marcus.

"Wake the fuck up!" A loud slap.

Marcus shot up grunting. Eyes thin with pain from the sun. "I'm up, I'm up."

The medic was still slapping him just for enjoyment. He blocked with no help of his senses. The young medic was laughing, still trying to smack him playfully.

Another petite medic with short hair was sitting next to Scott. She was smoking a cigarette perched on a large stone piece of debris from the wall. Scott opened his eyes and with much pain got to his feet. With squinted eyes, he looked around leaning against the large stone. She handed him a cigarette and a rather large vial with an almost glowing green liquid in it. She lit his cigarette.

"You guys got fucked up last night."

He glared at her. "I've never seen anything with eyes like that. I swore I saw scales too. Whatever she was, she was not human. Not even like any Chimeras we've seen before, not a known species to me anyway."

As he took a pull from the vial she replied. "They beat you, so they are something we can't take lightly. In fact, The Kings Guard are here." She pointed.

"What the fuck is this shit Kris, you trying to kill me?", He asked as he hands her the vial. His face was twisted in disgust as he wiped his mouth.

"That's almost pure. Your wounds will heal. And you'll be unbalanced for a while. Don't drink anymore today. That will keep you well drowned."

He stood up. "What do those cocksuckers want?"

He turned to face her. She hopped off the rock. He towered over her by almost a foot and a half. She was well defined. Short sandy blonde hair. Blue eyes. Very defined even through her fitted fatigues.

"They want to talk to you and him once you're awake. They have a letter for you from the King himself."

He grunted. "Give me another smoke will you?"

She smiled handing one and lighting herself another. "You feeling any better, sunshine?"

"No more than normal, Moonlight. I'll see your gorgeous ass later." He walked away toward Marcus and his medic who were giggling. He was already feeling good from his physical nature and constantly apologizing.

"You good?", Scott pointed at Marcus.

"Yeah."

Marcus immediately stood up and followed Scott as he passed by. They walked over to the massive Amazonian almost Spartan-like woman. They were wearing their armor like always. The suits were a mix of mechanized machines and knights from the old age. Their great spears held in their massive hands. Scott and Marcus now were the smallest of the group, almost stretching their necks to make eye contact with the giant women.

"By order of the King…"

Scott took the scroll from the Golden Guard. He pressed his thumbprint on the biometrics pad at the center of the golden capped scroll. A small winding noise and fabric produced from the silver cylinder. He pulled it out reading it to himself looking up to the Knights. They patiently glanced back. He handed the scroll to Marcus. His expression of surprise showed through his composure. He handed it back to Scott. He looked down tugging on the fabric slightly and letting go, the fabric retracted back into the cylinder. He tossed the scroll as it ignited into a small intense ball of fire. It burnt up before hitting the ground.

As it sizzled in the background Scott pulled the smoke from his mouth. He looked around and then at Marcus. He looked up at Scott who was annoyed clearly. Heavy bellowing of smoke showed his irritation. Marcus saw the medics standing by their armored buggy talking amongst each other. He looked around seeing the hundreds of workers building up the wall. Clearing debris, putting out fires. Guards lined the rest of the wall with heavy guns and positions every 10 meters or so. It was unbelievable really to see how fast their ant hill secured its entrance.

"We have no choice?", Scott asked.

"No. You have 12 hours to prepare. You will meet here at dusk where the rest of your element will be standing by. Here…", the Golden Guard insisted, as she produced a small sack from her heavy utility belt.

"What's this?", Scott asked.

Marcus took the small bag. Opening it revealed to the two soot covered tattered men, at least 20 gold coins with the spear cross sword and axe symbols stamped into them. His surprise was just as obvious as the sun reflecting off the currency.

"There's a lot of money in here", Marcus laughed.

"And who will be joining us on this suicidal venture to meet our makers?", Scott demanded sharply.

"Others who had survived last night's attempt on our lands." The leader of the two replied.

Scott nodded and walked over to the Medics. The Golden Guard left on their long-armored jet bikes. The bodies resembled that of dragons. The wings, however, were fixed forward acting as a shield for the whole motorcycle and the rider.

"Scott?", Marcus asked.

"It said, 'if you fail; we will be exiled… and if we return, they will hang us in the Capital Square. But if we succeed, we will be given riches beyond our imagination.' What the fuck is that? We are just soldiers, when the hell do they send out Gun Walzers into the forest to the Southern Ruins?"

"I don't know. I wish I did. Even for us going beyond the wall, leaving at night since it's forbidden unless hunting or traveling along the railroads to the east. Something more serious is at work here, those cocksuckers that attacked us were looking for something. Something they believe was taken here. I wonder if all those rumors were true…"

Marcus was curious. "What rumors?"

"The sound of aircraft leaving from the Dragonares side. Some sort of stealth camouflage system. Can't be seen by the naked eye." Scott replied as he pointed to his own eyes.

Scott grunted as they approached the medical buggy. Kris was sitting on the hood. He leaned against the front fender over the large mud tires. With a heavy sigh, he discharged a commendable amount of smoke from his mouth. He pulled out his flask which was emptied from a piece of small shrapnel. Kris handed him her small flask. He took it without word, he knocked it back taking a hefty pull.

"Need a lift into town?", she asked taking a pull as well.

"Yeah. It's going to be a long day."

Marcus standing next to Kris's partner, all smiles, the two giggled amongst themselves taking another look around.

"Dude", he called Scott's attention. "We need new guns man."

"As we should", Scott replied.

"We going to get some chow?," Marcus asked.

"Yeah", Scott replied again.

Marcus walked over to Scott.

"What the fuck were they? They knew what they were doing, and they were using some tech I've never seen before. Those weren't make shift bombs. Those were military grade explosives. Ancient technologies, cloaking devices, their shields, they are using the best of the best."

"I know, I want to find the one with the orange eyes. She has the answers we need." Scott replied.

Marcus squinted at him. "Ohhhhhh…" He said nudging Scott with an elbow jokingly.

"You want more than just answers. Was she at least pretty?"

"Her eyes, mesmerizing as they were, have a deep sorrow within them. We'll find her."

"Then you can look into her eyes a little longer, eh…eh." Continuing with his nudging and giggling.

Scott chuckled and smiled. "If she'll have me."

Chapter 2

The Hate Among Allies

The bar had just opened. The heavy batwing doors made of oak carved into an intricate spiral formation of vines and roses gave way into the ominous clouds of smoke and music. "Dead Petal." The name in thick old English writing, sat unevenly atop the western style saloon.

"Do you need anything?", Kris asked Scott.

He leaned over propping his arm up. He handed her a gold coin. "If you can, I need two tactical trauma kits, twenty doses of that shit you tried to kill me with earlier, pain killers… the good shit, and some ember wound seals."

"I can't take this. This is worth half my salary, like… for the year", she said trying to hand it back.

"Yeah. Well that's almost all my yearly salary. Just take it. You've patched me up more times than I can remember. It's the least I can do. We'll come by to grab it before we leave."

"See you then, sunshine."

"Later, Moonlight."

Marcos walked through the heavy batwing doors first, followed by Scott.

"Fletcher!", Marcos called out to the old man on the other side of the bar.

"What the hell are you old gravel crunchers doing? Heard you boys got into some pretty bad trouble at the southern gate."

Fletcher pulled a bottle up from under the bar and three glasses.

"Yeah, the southern gate was destroyed. They are rebuilding it right now, and trying to find the rest of the soldiers that were in the towers."

"Did anyone else make it?"

Marcos shook his head. Fletcher looked at Scott. "No, just us."

Fletcher was aged, in his 80's. Quite old for people of the Gun Walzer sector. An intricate mechanism with oxygen tanks and blood filtration system whirled and clanked from the cog-work. The leads and tubes ran down the bar and into Fletcher himself. Thick wire framed spectacles sat on his old face. He was pale with deep lines cutting into his thin face. He had a long, slim cigar sticking out of his mouth, snaking a thin tube of smoke into the air.

"Well, here's to them." He said pouring three generous glasses of the well-aged alcohol. He handed the glasses to the two boys. They held them up for the fallen as customary.

"I hope they died quickly." Fletcher said.

Scott replied. "As they should."

The three kicked their glasses back finishing the contents with ease, setting the glasses down on the table.

"So what's next for you boys?"

"We are leaving tonight", Marcus said looking at his watch. "In a little under ten hours."

"Where are you going?"

"South." Scott answered lighting a smoke.

"What?" He looked at both of them, confused.

"The fuck you mean south? There's nothing south. You know that most of all." Fletcher said pouring three more generous glasses.

"We're going to find those cocksuckers and kill them. Well... all but one anyway."

"Then we are going to find out what, where, when, why, and how the flying fuck they were able to do that to us in the first place. Then come back and live like kings."

"You know going out there, even the two of you is suicide", Fletcher replied.

After finishing his second glass, Scott laughed looking at the glass. "It wouldn't be the first time we lost any right to exercise any free will. I have a sneaking feeling it won't be the last during this little adventure either."

"You boys need anything just let me know, it's yours. Just bring your sorry asses home."

Marcus pulled out a gold coin and set it on the bar. "We can pay for it too."

"Your money's no good here. You can take that coin and shove it up your ass where it belongs."

"No...", Marcus started only to be interrupted.

"Don't make me come across this bar and whoop your ass", He stated sternly. The sarcasm could be seen in his eyes.

"Alright. Just need two bottles of your finest elixirs. And a barrel of ale, the good shit in the smoked barrels."

"Alright. Just promise me you won't tell my wife I had a drink and it's a deal."

Marcus laughed. "You old bastard. Deal."

Scott shook his hand and then Marcus's.

"Alright old man. We need to go take care of some things. Then we'll be back for dinner before we head out."

"We'll hold a table for you."

"Say hi to the wife for us." Marcus called back as they head out.

Outside the two can see the smoke still rising from the southern gate even this far inside their town. They could smell the burnt stone and smolder from here.

"Where to next?", Marcus asked.

"Guns", Scott replied.

"Guns", Marcus nodded.

The street is bustling as they walk down it. Patrols roved up and down both sides of the streets. Everyone carried a battle rifle of some kind. Even kids were armed and wearing their lightweight plate carriers. The houses and buildings didn't stand about three or four stories. The shops housed many custom workshops, tailors, cobblers, and the like. The entire town was oriented towards the art of fighting with a gun. Their technologies mirrored the many years prior but nothing still to this day compared to the same quality and devastation of the ancients. Not one machine gun could be found in the whole

Gun Walzer society. Their gunsmiths will not produce them as per their laws and tradition. A Gun Walzer should never utilize a machine gun, but must be able to shoot as fast as and more accurately than those particular weapons.

Spent Brass. In wielded steal letters above the stone building. Even throughout their area this was one of the oldest gun shops in the kingdom. Marcus and Scott walked in to browse. The owner gave a curious glance at the two fellows. Scott was slowly passing down the isle of gear and holsters and weapon sheaths. Marcus stood looking at the wall of rifles. The assortment was absolutely astonishing. Scott stood next to him, arms crossed, eyeing the many options.

"You ever shop here?", Marcus asked.

"When I can afford it." They both chuckled.

"You boys look like hell rolled over you." The man behind the counter stated bluntly.

Scott looked down and at Marcus. They were still covered in mud, clothing torn here and there. Their ponchos were scorched and shredded.

"You might say that", Marcus laughed.

The man's old grey eyes widened. "You were at the southern gate. What can I do you gentleman for. Anything particular you'd like to see?"

His tone had changed and he walked over to await their response eagerly.

"Well sir, we have a big list, and once we get a vehicle we will be able to pick it up. I have a question."

"Shoot."

Scott leaned in placing his dirty hand on the glass case. "What class are you?"

The man thought for a second. "Depends on how much coin you got, kid."

Scott grinned and reached into his pocket setting a gold coin on the glass. The old man looked down at it and then looked at him with a bright smile. "Welcome to *Spent Brass*, gentlemen."

"It's going to be an extensive list", Scott replied with a smile.

The owner pulled out a pen and notebook. "I've got all day."

Smiles on their faces as the two, mud covered, tattered Gun Walzers walked tall down the side towards their next destination. Odd looks shot across the street by bystanders as they observed the oddly cheery individuals strolling along. The two were headed for The War Stable.

The War Stable as it was known was the town's massive motor pool and offhand vehicle dealership. From custom built machines to rolling tanks, these mechanics were some of the best in the whole kingdom. Even visitors from other sectors have come down to pay the heavy price for their impressive ingenuity. Marcus and Scott stepped into the main hangar.

Filled with aircraft and tanks several styles of off road doomsday machines and big game hunting buggies. A site to behold. The two walked around aimlessly over to whatever caught their eye. Then both of them spotted the awesome machine sitting in the corner. Cables and tubes ran out of it. Tool boxes all around it parts scattered on tables and the cockpit opened up. A robot stood about 20 feet tall.

"Hey old man, ever fought against one of those?", Marcus asked his partner.

Scott laughed as he walked up. "Yes, actually. I have, you cocksucker. Back during the war to the south."

Marcus chuckled. "This thing is awesome."

"Yeah, until the pilot knows what the fuck he's doing. Then it's a bad fucking day. These assholes were something else. The Kingdom to the south didn't have people like us. So in order to combat us they used these old machines. What the fuck was the program that started these mother fuckers? It was the ancients that built them..." He thought for a few seconds. *"The Mad Project.* That's what the fuck they were called. Started a long time ago after the forest had spread across the earth like it did."

"And they still work?", Marcus asked as he climbed all over it looking at the damaged machine.

Scott lit a cigarette turning in the direction of fast approaching footsteps.

"Excuse me! Excuse me?"

The mouse-looking man called out to Marcus. He spoke with an annoyed tone and the sound of a stopped up nose.

"Sir, please get off of my machine."

Marcus popped his head out from somewhere in the back. "Oh yeah, no problem."

Marcus lost his footing falling flat on his face off the robot. Scott laughed. The small man rushed over to Marcus, a look of horror covering his face. But not to help the drunk bastard who had just fallen. The mechanic or technician or whatever he is was, concerned himself only with the fact that his machine could have been damaged by the Gun Walzer.

"What do you want?", the irritated man demanded.

"Whoa, calm down dude. We're just looking for some wheels, man."

"Well, you don't belong here. This place is off limits. You have any idea how hard it is to get components like these? The only reason why we have this is because of the wars. You break it you buy it and I know you can't afford."

"Look dude…" Marcus said, staggering to his feet. "We didn't break anything", he started. He took a heavy pull from his flask, finishing off the rest of his ale. "We need a vehicle, nerd."

Scott laughed.

"I'm not a nerd." The small man snorted. He reminded Marcus of a mouse.

"I'm a scholar from the Inner Kingdom and you will show me the respect I deserve."

Scott and Marcus looked at each other. "Calm down, kid. How would you like to earn a gold coin?"

The kid's tone didn't change. "For what could you Neanderthals want to purchase for such a price?"

"We need some old tech. Vehicle; four wheels all-terrain, manual drive with Anti-Chimera class armaments. Whatever your lightest and strongest armor is, and we need it in 6 hours. Can you do it?" Scott asked challenging the young scholar.

He pushed his glasses up the bridge of his nose. "It's possible, but that will require a war class frame, and those materials are constructed once ordered."

Marcus walked over to an old frame making obnoxious full body movements pointing to an old frame and then to a finished buggy. "Put the new shit into an old war frame."

The scholar thought for a few seconds nodding. "Six hours your vehicle will be ready."

Scott and Marcus left the scholar to his work and continued toward their home. Once at their building, which as built around a very old very large tree in almost a spiral of treehouses Marcus and Scott parted ways to get ready.

Marcus poked his head out as Scott walked up the rickety open wooden stairs. "When do you wanna meet down here to head out?" The young man asked.

Scott turned as he continued up the stairs. "I'm going to rest for at least 4 hours. Shower and then get ready. We'll leave here around 1600 and grab food then get our ride. Load up and head to the southern gate. Should be about time to meet up with these weirdos."

"Alright sounds good." Marcus called up.

Scott disappeared around the trunk of the tree further up the stairs. Marcus unlocked his heavy door and walked into his tree house cottage. Lights flickered on. He walked over to his small kitchen on the fall wall, opening his fridge. He grabbed a beer and opened it up taking a heavy pull. He stood there for a second lost in his own thoughts, leaning against the countertop.

"They could have killed us. Why didn't they?", he asked himself.

He lit up a smoke and walked over to his small round table. The bland metal legs and black table top with matching chairs fit well with the 1950s era style furniture that made up his simple room. A bathroom with no door. A small shower maybe two people could stand in. There were wooden floors that needing a good lacquer and polish. A thin screen with cables running into a large computer tower both acting as a TV stand and desk sat facing his single bed. The heavy metal four blade bullet fan whirled above almost quietly. He started taking off his clothes, starting with his boots.

Dried mud fell from them as he tossed them by his door. He got up, grabbing another beer from the fridge and turned on the shower.

Staring at himself in the mirror didn't distract him from taking a long pull as he looked into his own eyes.

"I should probably get some sleep…after this next drink." He giggled to himself.

Marcus took his clothes off, throwing them in a whicker hamper just outside the doorway leading into the bathroom. He threw open his fridge and grabbed a bottle of dark red liquor from the back. He pulled the cork and turned the bottle up. He pulled for a few seconds. Letting out a glorious sigh of relief, he squinted and cleared his through ended with a cough. The strong young man headed into the bathroom.

16:00. Scott rapped heavily three times on Marcus's door. He was standing tall. Clean shaven, dressed in black plated boots, dark green tactical pants held up around his waist by a thick black belt with a quick release buckle. His black shirt was tucked in. His ash gray jacket hid the amount of fire power he carried underneath. Slung on one shoulder was a heavy dark green worn bag packed almost to the point of breaking open at the seams. Again the tall man knocked on the door.

Inside he heard Marcus fall out of bed and shuffle to the door. Marcus opened the door half naked. Clearly he had passed out getting ready. His eyes thin with sleep and shock of brightness.

"Come on, you drunk bastard. It's time to go."

Scott walked in and sat down, lit a cigarette while setting his heavy bag on the table. Marcus shuffled around the room stumbling like a drunkard. He held his finger up running over to the fridge pulling a beer out for Scott then continued his mad shuffle to get ready.

Scott laughed, accepting it graciously. From a heavy billow of smoke, he inspected the room, and Marcus, with a raised brow grinning at the young man. Before he knew it, Marcus was ready to go. Looking a little scruffy, but dressed in a fresh set of clothing. Thick dark jeans, combat boots dark earth, a heavy leather belt his shirt tucked in. He grabbed his duel pistol shoulder holsters and put them on before pulling on his black and dark grey octagon printed jacket. He put on some aviators and grabb his black somewhat new bag in the corner.

"You finally ready?", Scott jokingly asked, standing up.

"Lead the way, big guy." Marcus says holding the door open for him.

As the two walk down the stairs Marcus asks Scott. "What bag is that?"

Scott continued walking as he answered his friend. "This old thing?" Scott joked. "It's an old bag of tricks, from the old days."

"What's in there?" Marcus raised a brow.

"It's my old kit from the war. I have a feeling I'm going to need this in the near future."

"Ahhhhhh…" Marcus spouted as he shook his finger slowly nodding in acceptance.

Scott stopped and pointed. "While you were wasting the day away, I got our ride and our supplies. However we need to hurry if we wanna eat before we head out."

Marcus came around the corner of the massive trunk where the stair well ended. He was completely stricken with awe. He turned and looked at Scott. Scott smiled and, with a heavy hand, patted his buddy on the back, ushering him toward the vehicle.

"Dude!" Marcus said. "Ahhh shiiiiittt…", he said as he walked around it attempting to take in the sharp, ancient design of the well-built doomsday machine. He continued around it, almost crawling to get a better look. Attempting to touch it, he would quickly pull away as if he didn't want to put his dirty fingers on their new vehicle.

The rally style armored race car resembled a plated skyline from days long forgotten. The rear end however had been turned into an extended cargo area. The frame has been reinforced with thick roll bars and stabilizer bars encasing the interior. The bulletproof windshield and rear window had steel bars to further protect the occupants. Four large tapering mufflers protruded out of the heavy plated bumper. The wheels resembled jet engine turbines housing thick brand new all-terrain tires. Metal plating was affixed and woven into the tire to further protect it. The vehicle was mean and devastating. The rear of the vehicle was very wide in spite of it missing its trunk cover almost resembling a fighter jet's intakes.

Marcus looked at Scott with an aggravated look once he saw the back of the vehicle. He just noticed what was missing and Scott could tell.

"Where the fuck is the weapon at?" Marcus demanded.

Scott held his hand up. "Calm down. They didn't have any way to mount it on this chassis. I told them it was fine. If we can't kill something with our weapons, than we are probably dead anyway. Besides all they had was machine type weapon systems."

"That would have been better than nothing." Marcus exclaimed almost pouting.

"You know the law. We don't use machine guns. Unless we have no choice. And not to mention they did something else for us." Scott says holding his hand up.

He quickly opened the driver side door and pulled a heavy lever. A loud clank and the hood wrenched upwards. He got out skirted around the steel brick of a machine and opens it up. Marcus peers down into the engine compartment.

"Oh my fuck", he spouted. "What is that?", he asked.

"They explained it as a turbine drive system, very similar to the propulsion systems in the mechs of old. This engine equates to 3500 horses. But normal drive is 1000. It has nine gears, and a very sophisticated computer to where we just switch the expected terrain in the options on the dash and the power output will send it to different locations. This thing literally could fly if it had wings and weighed a hell of a lot less."

"That's pretty cool. But I still wanted something just in case."

Scott patted Marcus on the back laughing. "We'll survive." He slammed the hood shut and jumped in. He started the engine. And the wine from the turbine began to whirl on. It sounded as if a jet was firing up. He pressed on the accelerator and pressed the clutch in. Marcus grabbed their bags and tossed them in the back. Scott slammed the heavy shifter into gear and the amazing machine was off.

"You know he could have at least put something in here for us." Marcus said as he was looking around the simple dash and interior of the vehicle. Wide bucket seats. Four point harnesses. The dash was bare for the most part save for several gages in front of Scott. A steering wheel fully adjustable with a heavy key in the column. On the dash at the far bottom right corner of the gage display sat the large ignition switch. Three non-slip petals. A small monitor showing a few touch screen options from music to engine status and suspension settings. AC and heat controls, and three buttons and a switch on the center console just before the leather wrapped shifter and gear box.

"What are these?" Marcus asked.

Scott looked down. "One is for the automatic height management system. The middle one is for the tires in case we get a flat. And last but not least, the one under the safety latch is the on switch for fuck everything in our way and everything trying to chase us."

Marcus laughed. "How is it on gas?"

"According to the little cocksucker who built it, as long as we stay in normal drive mode we have close to 1500 kilometers before we need to fill her up again. And the tank is only thirteen point five gallons. I have two five gallons in the back. Oh and it has a six gallon reserve tank."

"Why?" Marcus asked intrigued.

"In case we need to use this little guy." Scott answered pointing to the switch hidden by the red safety cover.

"Still wish we could've had a mounted gun." Marcus said, crossing his arms, looking out his window.

"Oh yeah. One more thing." Scott stated catching Marcus' attention. "Crank on that lever down there."

Marcus looked down and saw the window handle. He reached down and pushed down on it. The window slid down almost instantaneously. "Oh fuck." Marcus laughed continuing to play with the lever. The window shot up closing and shot down rather quickly. After a few times Marcus turned pointing his finger in the air. "You know, that guy was alright."

Once the two had parked the vehicle around back they headed into Fletcher's bar. He greeted the two Gun Walzers with a nod as they gave a wave in return. Taking their seats in the corner, the two were quickly approached by a rather young waitress. Tight jeans and a tucked in black shirt. Small apron with tray and note pad in hand she noticed the two rough individuals. Marcus waved with a genuine smile, she smiled back and nodded turning in her tracks to head for the bar. A few moments later she had their drinks in front of them.

"Dad says you guys are eating here tonight. Last meal he thinks. So we've prepared something special for you."

Marcus smiled looking at Scott and then back to the pretty young lady. "Well Helga, than we will have that." He sarcastically replied.

She giggled. "Your vehicle is being loaded already. Just sit back and enjoy your meals boys, it's on the house."

"Thank you, Helga." Scott replied.

And just as quickly as she appeared she was off to another table. The bar was particularly busy tonight. Odd for the middle of the week. The two were almost both lost in their own thoughts. Scott sat arms crossed slowly observing the entire room. Marcus was deep in thought but not so much to keep it from his partner.

"We lost a lot of guys up there with us yesterday." Marcus spouted off.

"Yeah, I've worked that wall with you for what now. Six months?"

Marcus nodded.

"And you know; I didn't even know their names. Not one of them. I've asked probably a hundred times and never could for the life of me remember." Scott said pondering to himself.

Marcus held up his glass. "To them. Hope they died quick."

Scott smiled. "As they should."

Before the two knew it, they were well on their way to being set right for the rest of the night. Almost drunk and with full bellies, the two men stood up and started to head out when a group of men blocked their exit.

"You the ones who survived the South Gate?"

"Who the fuck's asking?" Marcus shouted.

The bar got quiet.

"Our friends were up there. How the hell did you two morons survive and not them!" the man yells out. His group looked just as upset as him. Scott was already annoyed as he grabbed Marcus who was ready to go fisticuffs with these emotional individuals.

"No, no more hospital bills or damaged property. They are kids, you just need to walk away before we have to explain to the King right before we go on his little mission why the hell we were arrested."

Marcus turned from listening. Nodded his head and put his hands up. "Look guys, we got lucky. I'm sorry but there was nothing we could do."

"Of course there wasn't." the emotional man started. "Normal people like us just trying to make a living, and you two freaks end up surviving the only attack on that gate in ten years. Sounds like you ran."

Marcus' tan face turned red. It twisted into a snarl. Scott immediately shook his head letting a long bellow of smoke out of his nose.

"Fuck you", Marcus spouted completely calling every bit of attention to the scene. "You have no idea what happened out there. The fuckin towers blew up. They were in it. We got thrown off a wall. If it wasn't for him, we'd be dead and whoever the fuck attacked us would be in this town killing you while you slept."

Marcus was interrupted. "Likely story from two cowards who ran from the fight." He was now looking around the bar as he continued speaking. "Yeah, that's right. These two bitches were found unconscious several hundred meters from the gate."

Whispers murmured throughout the bar. Fletcher had his daughter behind the bar. His triple barrel shotgun ready on the bar top. Patrons whom felt too close for comfort picked up and moved to get out of the way or for a better few. Either way it was now becoming a spectacle.

"I ain't no coward!" Marcus roared reaching just under a table and flipping the heavy circular wood through the air. It spun several times before slamming into the ground. Splinters and heavy cracking of the table top almost echoed it was so quiet.

Marcus balled his fists tight and stood right in front of the accuser. The two stared each other down. In all of this almost no one noticed Scott. He was in between them in the blink of an eye. He turned and with his dead cold almost black eyes says...

"Go home kid. This isn't worth you ending up in the hospital over."

And for some reason. The man backed up. His group looked Scott up and down. He was leaning towards them almost in a haunting matter. His head bent slightly and leaning forward. His demeanor was frightening. Almost like a predator crushing its prey's will to live.

"Go home. Because..." He started bellowing smoke from his mouth as he continued to speak. "Do you really wanna have to explain to the King why you stopped us from going to find the ones responsible for this mess?"

The man was silent. "Yeah, so before you start some shit; know the fucking facts. Consider this a piece of advice. Fear men who survive an otherwise inescapable circumstance. It sucks, we've all lost someone along the way. It's been a while for us here. But remember them, and they shall never be forgotten by those who matter to them most. They died quick, that's more than any of us could ever ask for."

Scott grabbed hold of Marcus by the shoulder. "Let's go." He waved at Fletcher and Helga and walked Marcus around the dumbfounded group out the heavy doors to their vehicle.

Chapter 3

Union of Enemies

Scott gagged, catching Marcus attention. They were several miles from the still, smoldering gate. It was getting dark, the bright lights lit their way on the now dirt road winding through the valley toward their destination.

"You alright, old man?", Marcus asked.

Scott spit and gagged again. "Yeah, drank a little too much."

Marcus shot him a curious look. "No, you really didn't. In fact you've drank less and less every day for a while now."

Scott glared at him. "Don't worry about it, just worry about your own consumption. I'll survive."

Marcus put his hands up. "Whoa, I just mean we don't need you getting sober. It's bad enough when you are drowned. I couldn't imagine what it would take to kill you if you did become sober."

"It would be a good run, that's for sure.", Scott replied, staring at the road. He pressed down on the accelerator and shifted into third. The roar of the engine echoed off the hills surrounding them. They were reaching 250 kilometers with plenty still to go.

Before they knew it Scott and Marcus had arrived. The group was standing in the middle of their vehicles all in line talking and mapping out their route. The group had stopped to observe the two drunkards getting out of their vehicle. Scott leaned onto his door gagging once more puking a little. He simply spit and wiped his mouth.

"Fuck", he whispered just loud enough for Marcus to hear him.

The group on the other hand just watched.

"You see that?", Charles asked.

"Yes sir", his subordinate responded.

"That is a drowned Gun Walzer, late as per usual."

"Why do we have to take them with us Sir, if they are such a danger? They look to me if they can barely walk a straight line. How can they be considered an asset?"

"Sergeant Knight. Never again refer to them as an asset. Remember they can never be trusted and as soon as they start to turn sober, we must kill them before they kill everyone around them."

She looked back to Marcus and Scott walking up. They were odd to her. "Understood Sir."

Scott and Marcus greeted the group. From left to right, Marcus took measure. Charles Peterson, was of average height, slender and erect, fitting for an officer of the Dragonares. His black long coat hid the form fitted armored suit. Buttoned closed with heavy buckles and around his waist was a thick pistol belt holding a large pistol resembling the old Lugar P08. The only difference was that the barrel was much larger acting as a monolithic suppressor. He had dark hair highlighted with grey and blue eyes. His face looked young considering his age. Sergeant Jessica Knight to Charles's left was dressed similar-- sporting the exact same uniform and side arm. They both were wearing old officer caps with their ranks as crests. Their black uniforms and silver inlays at the seams made them look menacing and proper in their own regards. Sergeant Knight was a few inches shorter than the Colonel. Her blonde hair was tied tight into a very basic bun in the back. Her blue eyes almost shined in the dark.

"Well, hi, I'm Marcus Wormwood and this is Scott Cogwheel." Marcus broke the silence.

The oldest of the group, one of the two Boltiers, replied in her soothing voice. "It's a pleasure to meet you Marcus and Scott. I'm Phillis Knight, unrelated to the young sergeant over there. And this is…"

She looked and young Jimmy was over by their bikes. "Phillis?", he called.

"Yes, Jimmy", she answered without looking away from Marcus.

"What is that?", Jimmy asked in such wonder.

"It's a lightning bug, Jimmy."

"I've never seen one before, Phillis."

She almost sighed with disbelief. "Yes, Jimmy, we have them at home near the river."

"Oh, okay Phillis."

Marcus was smiling widely. Phillis continued. "And that is Jimmy Valentine. He is my underling. He is very, well, good hearted. But don't take his kindness for weakness my friends. He can hit anything with his bow."

Scott gagged again turning from the group to spit. He wiped his mouth grunting as he lights another smoke.

"Of course not ma'am", Marcus replied. "We know much about the great Boltiers. All our food pretty much comes from your territories."

She smiled. It was beautiful. Her bright green eyes and greying blonde hair almost don't make any sense. She was definitely older than everyone in the group. However, her body suggested she was the youngest. Her top was merely a wrapped sash around her small breasts. Her well defined mid-drift was something to be proud of. Her tight pants were held up by a thick leather belt leaving nothing to the imagination. Leather riding boots and a small black leather jacket. Her quiver hung from her belt to her left and on her right a large knife.

She turned to check on Jimmy near their bikes. Marcus and Scott both followed her with their eyes both noticing her perfect butt as she quickly moved away. Scott took a long drag and looking back meeting eyes with Charles whom was sizing Scott up. The displeasure on each other's face was evident to Jess who was starting to notice the tension in the air. And to everyone around them.

"Jimmy, what are you doing?", Phillis asked.

"I'm sorry Phillis but the little guy was so pretty I couldn't help it."

"Go over there and introduce yourself."

"Okay Phillis", he said, immediately walking over to the two Gun Walzers.

Jimmy has sandy blonde hair from what Marcus can tell. Brown eyes and very lean. He's wearing very similar clothes except his shirt is a white cotton with a V neck style cut, three buttons undone letting his strong chest breathe.

"Hi", he said holding out his hand. Marcus took it without hesitation. "My name's Jimmy. What's yours?"

"It's Marcus and this is Scott."

Jimmy held out his hand almost freezing as he looked into Scotts eyes. "Mr. Gun Walzer?"

Scott almost shook his glare away leaning down, almost giving his ear to the young man. "Sorry brother." He realized what Jimmy was doing. "Oh shit." Scott said taking the young man's hand. "Nice to meet you, Jimmy."

Jimmy didn't answer. He just nodded. Scott was taller than him. So was Marcus but not by much. Scott and Marcus could see the fear in his eyes. Then, without warning, the fear was gone from Jimmy's eyes and he smiled. "Yes, nice to meet you too."

Before they knew it, Phillis was next to Jimmy. "Did you finish tying down your gear, Jimmy?"

"Almost done, Phillis", he replied as he scurried over to his bike to finish.

"He's young", she said as she handed them two small wooden barrels.

"What is this?" Marcus asked.

"Something to heal your wounds. Fresh, from my gardens."

Scott pulled the cork out of the top of the very small barrels. Marcus did the same and they both took heavy pulls.

Both extremely satisfied, Scott leaned down a little. "Is this yours, did you make this? It tastes of a beautiful young lady, happy and innocent to the world."

She smiled, almost blushing. "I danced on those grapes almost thirty years ago when I was still young. How did you know?"

"It's been a long time", Scott replied taking another pull. "But this wine is something you never forget. Thank you." He said with a genuine smile on his face.

Marcus was awestricken as the two Old Guard Baronesses walk over. Phillis stood aside next to Marcus who was several inches taller than her. They stood before the two Gun Walzers. Elizabeth was in her white sharply designed knights' armor. It was a mix of the old plated designs and the more recent mechanized armor. Her helm resembled a motorcycle helmet with two long flat blades, more than likely sensors or antennas. A thin black line cut across the face of the almost seamless helmet displaying an optical sensor. Her armor only broke at the joints where the black under suit showed through.

Scott took her arm as she grasped his. Victoria, in similar armor except black with a red under suit, stuck her long spear into the ground holding out hers to Marcus. Marcus was too dumbfounded by her luscious, curly black hair and deep green eyes. She was very beautiful to him. In her armor, she was almost a foot taller than Marcus. Even Scott had to look up to make eye contact with Elizabeth. Her gold short hair and hazel eyes were mesmerizing. Elizabeth was holding her long pointed shield in her left arm. The massive sword was stuck in her heavy shield with the blade facing upwards along the inside. The handle with its odd gear crank jutted out towards the ground.

"Baroness Elizabeth of the Old Guard and Overseer of the Northern Towers", she exclaimed.

Scott let go of her arm and bowed ever so slightly. "A pleasure Baroness, Shield of the North Tower."

"You know of me?"

"I have heard of you yes, and it is a pleasure indeed to meet the woman who singlehandedly fended off the north during the War of Ascension."

She smiled and returned his bow. "That was ages ago Gun Walzer."

He smiled as they both stood facing each other. "As it should be, My Lady."

Marcus and Victoria, however, were now in competition in strength. She and the young Gun Walzer strained to beat the other in their handshake. He was starting to sweat and her arm was starting to tremble.

"I advise against attempting to best my Knight, young Gun Walzer." Elizabeth spouted smiling.

"Pleased to meet you, My Lady." Marcus grunted as the two continued.

Scott chuckled as does Elizabeth.

Phillis clapped her hands together. "Alright now that introductions are finished, let us continue with the plan."

Scott followed him Phillis over to the Dragonares vehicle which was more or less a tank. Its thick black armor and crude design were fitting for the two operators. Charles and Jess have a small thin computer monitor with imagery of the route they plan on leading out to the Southern Ruins. The group, save for Victoria and Marcus, were listening as Charles briefed their plan.

"You're very beautiful", Marcus voiced out loud.

Victoria immediately let his hand go. Flustered and blushing, the Amazonian woman quickly joined the group. Marcus lit a smoke and then headed over next to Scott.

"Alright, order of movement will be The Boltiers, myself and subordinate, the Drunkards, and rear security will be the Old Guard."

Scott walked off and headed over to their vehicle. He pulled out a large glass bottle of ale, unplugging the stopper. "We may be drunkards but on our worse day, we still beat the fuck out of your kind. Or did we forget our history?"

Charles grinned. "No, because history was written by the victors and as I recall. Your kind lost so much that you almost all but ceased to exist."

"What a shame, isn't it? That you have to work with the very people that stopped your little princess from becoming Queen. It's truly a wonder why her father didn't hang her and dismantle your little army of scavengers. Always reaping lost technology hoping to unlock its secrets and do what the ancients did all over again."

"And what's that, Gun Walzer?", Charles snarled.

"End the world all over again", Scott replied, grinning at the old Colonel.

Phillis stepped in before Charles could say anything.

"It's getting late gentleman. We need to hurry if we want to make it there before morning."

Scott held up his bottle to the gate. "To those that came before us, to those like us, and to those who want to be us. Fuck everyone else."

He drank all but the last swig. He lit a smoke and took a drag before pouring the rest onto the ground. "Onward to the Endless War young Gun Walzers. May you find not peace; only endless battle fields and enemies in your wake."

He turned and walked pass the group and got in his vehicle.

"Sir?", Jess asked.

"What Sergeant?" Charles replies annoyed.

"Why did he do that?"

Before he could answer, Phillis replied. "It's an old ritual for fallen soldiers. It is the Gun Walzers way of saying farewell to the dead."

The group walked to their vehicles. The Old Guard mounted their massive six wheeled truck. The Boltiers on their long swing arm motorcycles. And the Dragonares in their sleek and menacing looking tank. The engines roared and the turbines wined. The Boltiers led out than the Dragonares followed by the Gun Walzers and then the Old Guard.

Marcus broke the silence of their travels through the tall and thick forest. "Who is that?"

"Who?", Scott curiously replied.

"Charles. You kept glaring at him the whole time. The only person you paid any real attention to was Phillis."

"She's a fox, man."

"You old dog."

They both chuckled. "No, uh... I know who the fuck that cock sucker is. If he is with us then something is very important to the Dragonares we are going to so called stumble upon. That man cannot be trusted. He is a danger to us all. During the war he was known as the Fire Grapher. Mother fucker burned everything and everyone who faced him. The smoldering fields in our territory..."

"That was him." Marcus face turned into a snarl.

"If he shows any sign of betraying us. Kill him. I don't know about his little inexperienced counterpart. But he is definitely one to end before he has the chance to kill us. And I guarantee you he will make an attempt. His unit was designed to eradicate us back in the day."

Marcus eyes were wide.

Scott continued. "The so-called Dragonares were responsible for killing most of us during the war. But although we lost more in percentage they lost more in numbers than they were prepared for. No matter what technology they robbed from the graves of our ancestors it was barely enough to keep us at bay. The animosity amongst the Gun Walzers and the Dragonares will always be deep seeded and unavoidable. Never trust them. No matter what. I mean, hell, we can't even trust our own people."

Marcos changed the subject. "So what can you tell me about the Old Guard?"

"Don't think I didn't see you."

Marcus's wide eyed look at Scott, whom through his smoke, could see the devilish grin the old Gun Walzer had on his face.

"What, no. But that ass though", Marcus said in an exaggeratedly deep voice. Scott laughed.

"If you do happen to get into her tight ass armor you will be the first Gun Walzer in a long time to do it. You know how it is for them. They live a very valiant and strict life, although short, it is prideful and honorable. She is probably 18 or 19 years old and already betrothed to another Knight within their society. You will outlive her by decades, brother. In my opinion, best not to get too close. But, who am I to tell you what to do with your life."

Marcus was quiet, pondering as he took a swig from his flask.

"Which reminds me…", Scott continued.

"You going to be ready for your Bullet Waltz?"

Marcus doesn't answer.

"Hey fucker."

"Oh, yeah of course. I mean you taught me after all."

"Besides the point", Scott waved the complement off. "It's all you, nothing out there but you and your gat."

"How was it when you went through?", Marcus asked.

"I got my fuckin ass beat into the ground. And it was my old man who tested me. I lost but there was no beating him either way. I still was ranked because of how long I was able to fight. And I didn't miss, my groups weren't the most accurate but my speed was still to this day one of the fastest ever recorded."

The two carried on with their random conversations laughing and drinking as they maintained their interval between the convoy. The road next to the tracks was built on a raised ridge leading deeper into the forest. As they continued, the forest glowed bright green from the irradiated plant life clinging to the trees. Insects of all kinds, much bigger than they were centuries ago, flew about hunting along with the massive shapes of flying beasts they couldn't make out.

"We are stopping up ahead. Looks like a small station up here on the left", Jess said through the radio.

"Goddamn her voice is sexy as hell", Marcus exclaimed.

He grabbed the mic from the receiver and replied. "Roger."

The group pulled up, collapsing the convoy along the tracks. The station was small almost a tower reaching three maybe four floors. Vines had grown up one side. Bullet holes riddled the shot out windows. The door was long since missing. Marcus got out and walked around the vehicle sporting his brand new rifle. The Dragonares dismounted their tank and joined him standing in front of the building looking up at it. The top of the tower was blown out. Scott leaned on his door as Phillis and Jimmy walked up.

"How you guys holding up?", Phillis asked.

"Considering the only sleep we've gotten in who knows how long, was when we were knocked unconscious..." Scott lit a smoke. "Eh, not bad. To answer your question." They both began laughing.

Phillis finally replied through her laugher. "I read the report. When Jimmy and I were attacked they stopped and fell back into the tree line. It happened fast, but we didn't lose anyone."

"Hmmm", Scott sounded. He took a swig out of his flask and checked his watch. "Zero."

"We are making good time. But we need to just keep heading towards the ruins if we are going to catch these fuckers."

Phillis continued. "In fact I think you were the only ones who suffered any loss. The Dragonares reported no loss of life only enemy loss."

Scott laughed. "Let me guess. The bodies were burned so that there was no evidence or any idea who or what had attacked them."

"How did you know?", she asked.

"Because of him right there", Scott growled pointing at Charles. He spat before continuing. "The remains were so scorched that even the skeletal structure could not be identified."

"That's exactly what the report said."

"I guarantee that is exactly why he is here. To destroy any evidence or to keep us running in circles so we never truly find whoever hit us. I challenge to say that he knows exactly who and why."

"No", Phillis replied.

She turned and looked at him who is now watching Marcus and Jess head into the building.

"What can you tell me about the Old Guard then?", Scott asked.

"They lost a section of the wall. No casualties. Elizabeth and Victoria were doing their rounds when it hit the wall. But again as soon as they had attacked it was over as if their orders had changed in the midst of the fight."

"I wonder what they were looking for? And I wonder who she is. She wasn't human. She was something else. She reminded me of a dragon."

"You saw one?"

"Yeah, she blew our asses up. Destroyed both towers. And then, blew me up again. She can fight. And she was definitely looking for someone. As soon as she recognized us it seemed to me that her whole motivation changed."

"Or you were bewitched by the strong young lady?"

"The only one bewitching anyone around here is you." Scott said with a grin.

Marcus and Jess came out of the tower. Jess was breathing heavily. Marcus was excited.

"You two get a quickie in or what. What the fuck took you so long?", Scott yelled to Marcus.

Jimmy nudged Phillis. "What's a quickie Phillis?", he asked.

Scott and Phillis both burst into laughter until Charles interrupted.

"We don't need your heathen ways poisoning any of the youth from our great territories."

Scott put his hands up. "Calm down old man. It's a joke."

Charles walked back over to their tank with Jess.

"Sir", Jess said out of breath.

"Gain your composure, Sergeant", he replied.

"He is fast. I couldn't keep up. What are they? I mean, we learn about them in war college but the books do little to define their ability.

He cleared all three floors by himself and was heading down just as I was getting to the second floor."

"They are dogs Sergeant. Nothing more. The only thing they know is war. Even if they haven't been, they are bred for it. Born into it. That's why less and less of them exist and why so many died in the War of Ascension. They fought and died for no reason."

"Sir, I don't believe we could beat them in a full out war. Even with the numbers they still have. It would be a death sentence to our men."

"No Sergeant. That is where you're wrong."

Jess looked over at Marcus and the group talking and laughing. She finally caught her breath.

"Where are Elizabeth and Victoria?", Marcus asked.

"Where is Jimmy?", Phillis asked.

"Phillis!", Jimmy called playfully.

"Jimmy, get off of that beast right now!"

Scott lit another smoke. "Holy fuck." He said.

"Dude, do you know what that is?", Marcus asked.

Jimmy is hanging on the neck hugging the beast like a child holding on to their beloved pet. And the beast he was holding, the Chimera, was glorious. The head of a lion, muzzle like a wolf, horns black as night jutting out. Its long slender tail reached to taste the air, as all snakes do. Its massive hands were that of almost human with long sharp claws coming from the tips similar to a feline's.

"It's just a baby", Scott whispered to the group holding out his arm, quieting them.

"Jimmy, buddy. Say goodbye to your friend, and let 'em get back to his mother. It's time to go." Scott said stepping forward slowly.

"But we were playing." He spouted like a pouting child.

"I know buddy. But it's late and momma ain't going to be too happy when she sees you with her baby."

"Okay." He said, clearly upset. "Bye, Billy."

Scott chuckled. "He fuckin' named it."

Jimmy slid down the massive beast. He hugged the young Chimera. "Go home now, Billy. I'll see you again someday."

"I don't fuckin' believe this shit", Scott said. He looked back at Phillis who like a concerned mother was holding her hands to her face. Scott couldn't tell if it was horror or happiness behind her strong hands.

The Chimera took off into the forest disappearing. Jimmy walked up, almost giddy with joy.

"Is that your new friend there, Jimmy?", Scott asked as Jimmy passed by with a huge smile on his face.

"Yes, Mr. Scott. He was hungry so I gave him some fruit from our trees back home."

Scott just shook his head in disbelief. He put a hand on his shoulder and nodded. "Well alright there, bud. Glad you made a new friend. Don't go walking off like that next time."

"Okay", he said continuing on over to Phillis. "Phillis, did you see? He was big. We don't have animals like that back home. He was beautiful, wasn't he?"

"You scared me half to death, Jimmy."

"I'm sorry, Phillis."

Marcus observed her motherly scolding of young Jimmy. It was almost heartwarming if he hadn't been riding one of the most devastating abominations of the ancients known to their society.

"Alright let's get the fuck out of here before any more of Jimmy's friends show up for some more fruit", Scott chuckled to himself.

"Wait", Marcus said looking at Scott standing on the other side of the hood of their vehicle. "Where are Elizabeth and Victoria?"

"Ah fuck", Scott said. He reached in behind his seat pulling out his semi-automatic shotgun. He checked the bolt, ensuring a 10-gauge shell was in the chamber. Within a few seconds of Scott and Marcus readying to search for them, Victoria and Elizabeth emerged from the thick wood line. Victoria was dragging something behind her. The two stopped and looked at everyone that was staring back.

"We brought back a gracious kill for the morning's meal", Victoria spoke as she continued to drag the four-legged beast to their vehicle.

Marcus pointed his finger at them in acceptance with a smile on his face.

"You ready to continue?", Charles asked.

The group mounted up and headed out continuing south toward the Southern Ruins.

Chapter 4

Where the Train Stopped

As the convoy passed by a large break in the tall forest they came across the side of a gorgeous lake. The sun was clawing its way over the horizon in the distance illuminating little of the black, still water. A shimmer on the far side from what looked to be an ancient city of glass and steel long forgotten. Large, thin necks of massive reptiles from ancient times swam slowly about the lake in a family slew. The ancestors referred to them as dinosaurs. Now, they were simply a class of Chimera as they had been genetically produced in tubes and labs. Now at the top of the food chain, these magnificent creatures, once extinct, roamed the dense forest.

"I've never been out this far", Marcus spoke breaking the noise from the roaring engine.

"Oh yeah?", Scott replied blowing smoke.

"Yeah, never rode the train to any of the other kingdoms either. And the south was a battlefield and all unnecessary movements were forbidden until after the war."

"Yeah that makes sense. You were what; you're 24 now so you were 10 when the war started."

"Yeah. You joined back then, didn't you?"

"Yeah, I was 15 when I was sent to fight. I wasn't even a Gun Walzer back then. I fought for ten years. Almost 9 of them were where we are going. The last one was on the Smoldering Fields back home."

"You were there?", Marcus asked in almost shock.

"Yeah. There wasn't always a wall there. Once the Dragonares and Gun Walzers were one society. They started the War within our kingdom. And when we started fighting against them that's when old Charles up there set the battlefield on fire. We lost a lot that day. Almost crippled us."

"Oh my fuck", Marcus replied.

"I wouldn't trade anything in the world for it though. Regardless of what had happened. It was the worst and greatest moments of my life. But the cost was almost not worth the weight you carry in the end of becoming a true Gun Walzer."

"What started the south to attack us?"

Scott shrugged. "I have my theories."

"You think the Dragonares started it?"

"Yes. In the beginning the train just stopped coming. Then there was the declaration of war. The South said they caught spies stealing ancient technologies. We used to trade with them because they were able to find an abundance but at great cost. So you can see why it would set them off. Anyway..." Scott took a drag off his smoke.

"The first year was devastating. Our forces along with the Boltiers hit them hard making it into the second wall. The Old Guard protected the Kingdom along with the Dragonares being the multipurpose supplementary reaction force for land and air. Our elements destroyed much. Walls, entire towns, and cities. Factories and rebuilt ancient technologies. The South knew how to use them too. The M.A.D.D machines. The big ass mechanized robots; they were very effective against us. We had to change our tactics from frontal assaults to flanking maneuvers because the armor was too strong for our munitions."

"I couldn't imagine that many years", Marcus said lighting a smoke.

"Long story short, we learned how to defeat them. And we were reminded of why our society tends to leave the old technology alone. The strength of our ancestors is just as devastating as it was centuries ago. It's no wonder why the world had ended up as it did."

Scott laughed lightly. "It's funny, it was because of the old weapons that we were able to defeat the South. If we hadn't employed them, we may have lost the war."

"That bad, huh?"

Scott grinned. "It was against the law to own or possess such weapons. During the war, however, the Elder decided it was time to stop fucking around. He outfitted everyone one of us with weapons that we know and use to this very day. These weapons although simple compared to the Dragonares, are designed to defeat anything we decide to use them against."

Marcus, wide-eyed, stared at the ruins before them. The stone walls were easily a hundred meters tall. Blown in and riddled with bullet holes. Covered in moss with vines crawling up them, thick from the peak of spring time. The group slowly rolled through between the destroyed gate doors. Mechanized robot parts and bullet riddled chassis lay all around the gate, rusted and with light moss covering their hulls since their fall. Pilots' remains were mere bones in uniforms now inside of mechanical caskets.

There was static over the radio, then Phillis' voice. "We didn't even come back to bury the dead. We just left them where they fell." Everyone could hear the sorrow in her soft voice.

Scott picked up the hand mic. "We should have. Least we could've done for these brave soldiers whom stood against us. They died by the hand of worthy opponents. And for a moment were worthy opponents themselves."

"They started the war with executing our ambassadors and destroying the train route between our great kingdoms", Charles responded.

Marcus heard the mic cracking in Scotts' hand. "Leave them be. They deserve to be the ushers to all those who come to pass these fields", Elizabeth replied.

Again Phillis came over the net. The sorrow in her voice was even more noticeable than before. "Rest in peace weary souls."

They continued rolling through luscious land. Grass and plants all had overgrown spilling onto the paved roads. They were reaching the city. Unlike theirs, the Kingdom was made of steel and glass. The buildings were tall and magnificent. The glass sparkled along the ground and grass as it was blown out years ago. Holes from bullets and bombs, craters and rubble littered the streets.

The city center was decorated with a massive centerpiece. Fallen now, the stone guardian of a mechanized robot once stood for the Kingdoms technological might. The group decided to stop here and search the area. Scorch marks drew lines across the buildings as if a beam attempted to cut them down. Scott lit a smoke as does Marcus. They removed their jackets. They walked around to the back of their vehicle and pulled a black sleek metal box out into the open.

Phillis and Jimmy walked up with their simplistic but extremely powerful recurve bows. Their quivers to their right packed full of bolts. Phillis, dirt covered, pulled her goggles up onto the top of her head. Only clean part of her face happened to be under those large round lensed leather goggles. Jimmy pulled his bow back a few times before nodding to himself. The Old Guard Baronesses dismounted and in their own amazement look around them. Neither of the two knights had been to the Southern Kingdom before.

Marcus pulled out his plate carrier and respectable weapon rig. The Gun Walzers vest ash grey, form fitting and simplistic protect the chest and lunges. Two sharp shoulder plates attached by lightweight flexible plated straps protected from the shoulder to the mid upper arm. Pouches holding heavy 10 round magazines across the abdomen for his M1Trillion 13mm semi-automatic battle rifle. His battle belt was lined from the buckle around to the back with 3 smoke grenades and 3 fragmentary grenades in between them a holster for his 11mm 2111. The left side was lined with several single stack magazines for his side arm. A fitted sheath was diagonal on the back of the plate carrier for the large rifle. Marcus pulled the large charging handle jutting from the heavy bolt halfway back checking that a round was chambered.

Scott's vest was similar, except dark green. His rig was lined similar with magazine pouches along the abdomen. A small flat pouch on the chest. Two canted shoulder holsters built into the side protectors maintaining a slim profile. He picks up his battle belt. Two smoke grenades near the buckle on the left and 4 continuing to the right. A heavy blade in its magnetic leather sheath on the small of the back. And then continuing around to the left; 10, 6 round plunger speed loaders in their respectable molded leather pouches. Scott buckled the heavy battle belt around his waist. Pulling out his 10 gauge mag fed semi-automatic shotgun. Pulling his bolt back just as Marcus did, checking to ensure a shell was seated.

"The Gun Walzers are well disciplined in their trade, Baroness", Victoria stated as she observed Marcus checking the magazine and chamber of his pistol.

"They may be fools to the drink, however they are indeed, fine warriors", Elizabeth replied.

Marcus lit a smoke and took a pull from his flask. Scott sheathed his shotgun like a sword. The two without word started moving around the massive fountain searching and clearing. The group observed them for a moment before the Old Guard started cleaning and preparing the saber tooth for breakfast. The Dragonares moved their tank facing it south. Charles jumped out walking toward Phillis. Jimmy climbed up the fallen center piece crouching as a lookout.

"Phillis?", Charles asked as he approached her.

"Yes, Colonel," she teased.

"Call me Charles, please", he requested charmingly. "What do you know about those two? There wasn't much in any database about Scott. And Marcus is not yet a true Gun Walzer so his records have just started a few years ago."

"No more than you," she replied watching the two walk towards the base of a tall building that more than likely overlooks the city.

"I don't trust them. And neither should you," Charles scoffed.

Phillis didn't answer. She simply walked away to join the Baroness's while they skinned the large feline.

Scott and Marcus reached the top of a building an hour later. They could smell the meat cooking from the camp down below. Looking in all directions the city was a mix of stone castle structures, ancient skyscrapers, wooden and brick buildings. They were damaged heavily from the war. Bullet casings and mechanical parts rusted and tarnished from the long years. The air was fresh. The breeze was cool. The two light up cigarettes before sitting on the edge of the building. As they overlooked the city searching with their keen eyesight they noticed not what they had expected.

"Dude, what the fuck is that?," Marcus asked pointing at an odd ship of some sort taking flight from far south outside the city.

"Looks like an air ship", Scott replied.

"Out here?", Marcus inquired.

"Not any of ours from what I can see."

"What do we do?", he asks.

Scott answered shrugging a shoulder and with his palm up gesturing towards the ship with his cigarette. "We see where it goes. No way we would be able to catch it or even see it once back inside the forest. And unless we find imagery here. We won't know where these roads lead. Unless that cocksucker down there has one of his digital maps for this region."

"Should we warn the others?"

"Did you bring your radio?", Scott asked.

"No, did you?", Marcus answered starting to crack a smile.

They both burst into laughter. "Ah fuck it." Marcus continued.

The air ship continued until it shrunk from their sight. Headed south towards the mountains. Just before the two had turned to head down the city. Machine gun fire rattled off.

"Near the camp", Marcus spouted.

"Let's go", Scott said. They took off back into the building leaping every flight down to the next as they bolted in a hurry to the camp site.

The main gun swung around and fired. Jess missed. The massive beast leaped onto the side of a building hanging by its long muscular arm. The hairless ape with massive goat legs clung to the building roaring at the Baronesses violently. Its long snout lined with jagged chipped teeth shot saliva with its thunderous sound. Its horns curled and twisted forward.

"My lady!", Victoria yelled gripping her shield and spear readying in her lancing stance.

"It's a Minotaur Class Chimera!", Victoria yelled.

Elizabeth was quick to her side as they stood ready weapons in hand shields erect.

The two clanged their heavy weapons against their shields ringing out a menacing sound of war. The beast is now more than set on the two Knights. Charles hid behind the Gun Walzers' vehicle. Phillis, however, was ready with her bow drawn, ready to loose her bolt into the creature. Jimmy just like his mentor was ready himself. No fear. The innocence was a distant memory from his face. Only a look of pure resolve resided upon him like the sun beating upon his light skin.

"Where the hell are those two drunks?", Charles asked.

"They are coming, just keep quiet. It smells the food, probably hungry and found an easy meal." Phillis replied.

The beast leaped violently from the building for the two great knights. Elizabeth sidestepped sliding out of the way. The beast landed, cracking the ground and missing her entirely. Victoria spun and batted the beast in the lower abdomen lifting the creature from the ground. The Minotaur let out a horrific cry as it folded from the heavy blow. Elizabeth leaped well over the massive beast's height coming down to cleave its head. The beast once back on the ground, backhanded Victoria sending her crashing into the building adjacent to them. Elizabeth swung downward. Her blade rang out from smashing into the beasts horns as it turned towards her. Her shield was behind her from the motion of her swing. She took full force of the beast's skull as it rammed her into the ground.

Jimmy loosed his arrow straight and true. The beast had its arms up ready to pummel her to death. The bolt whistled and buried into the side of the beasts neck. A mighty roar and the beast ripped it from its neck. Turning its sights on Jimmy who did not waste a second. The second arrow burst the creatures eye simultaneously as Phillis blinded the other. Elizabeth rolled away back to her feet. Her blade behind her cutting into the cracked street. She swung across cleaving the beasts leg clean off at the knee. Its cry pierced their ears like cold ice picks.

Falling backwards the beast violently thrashed about holding its face, blood pumping by the gallon from its amputation. Victoria dragging a trail of smoke with her as she soared through the air, was now over the beast. She landed shoving her great spear through the beasts' chest into the street below. The beast slumped silently.

Marcus and Scott slide to a stop. "Ah fuck, we missed it", Scott said relaxing his stance sheathing his shotgun. He lit a smoke. "Go anchor that motherfucker down."

Marcus walked over to the beast just as Victoria wrenched her spear from its chest. Marcus stuck his barrel to the beast's head and with one hand with the long rifle fired. The shot rang out. The head exploded.

Marcus met Victoria's eyes with his. She was stunning to him. He held out his hand to help her off the beast. She looked down at his hand and back to him. She turned smiling ever so slightly and quickly jumped off the beast and headed to her vehicle.

"Where the hell were you two?", Charles barked at Scott.

"I understand your concern; however, it seems Phillis and Jimmy were more than enough to aid in projectile support of our two warriors. More than your tank or your sporadic gunfire." Scott laughed as he walks around Charles. "If I'm not mistaken you didn't hit anything. Pretty sure every one of your rounds hit concrete and metal. In fact,..." Scott turned and pointed the rounds out as they walked up the side of the building further down.

"...14, 15 and mother fuckin 16 8mm by 50mm standard issue Dragonare ammunition for elite soldier's small arms battle rifles." He finished pointing at Charles weapon before wrenching his head waiting for a response. Marcus thought he looked like a predator backing prey into a corner.

Scott ripped the smoke from his mouth taking in a deep breath bellowing with his irritated tone. "In fact, don't ever worry about us, I watched you, cowering down behind this fucking vehicle while a woman, three to be exact and a fucking child..." He paused holding out his hand nodding to the Baronesses and Jimmy. "No offense", he said apologetically.

Phillis shook her head simply as if it was enough said that she certainly wasn't. The knights both paid him no mind.

Scott continued "...Saved your miserable fucking life. Act like your life is worth more than that beast laying over there... and I'll show you how useless your little injections really are compared to the original, you synthetic worthless creature."

Scott spat and flicked his cigarette in Charles's direction before walking away. Marcus grabbed a radio from their vehicle before tagging along giving him space. The two vanished into the city.

Charles's hands were shaking slightly.

Jimmy walked up behind Phillis. "I don't think I like Mr. Scott when he is angry. He is scary."

"Yes Jimmy, he is."

Scott lit another cigarette as he continued walking away.

"Did you see my shot Phillis? I saved Elizabeth."

Elizabeth was walking up to him. She bowed to the young man. Confused, and Phillis could tell, Jimmy didn't really understand what to do. Phillis backhands him gently in the chest.

"Return the bow, Jimmy."

"Oh, yes", Jimmy fumbled to his knee, facing her. Elizabeth smiled.

"You have my thanks young warrior, I owe you my life."

"No Ma'am. We are a team. You would do the same for me", he replied sincerely. Phillis had a small, but pure smile on her face.

The two stood up. Elizabeth put her hand on his shoulder and kissed him on the forehead.

As she walked away Jimmy's face was beginning to turn beet red.

"Phillis, she kissed me", he exclaimed.

"That is good luck to receive such a gift from a Maiden of the Old Guard Jimmy. It means safe travels and good health."

"Should I kiss her back?"

Phillis laughed. "No Jimmy." She patted him on the back. "Let's help with breakfast."

"Okay, Phillis."

Charles sat in his turret setting his rifle in its rack. He monitored for the gun's sight of the main cannon glow dimly in front of him. Switches and buttons on a small console and a joystick with buttons and triggers to the right. Jess looked at him. Her station was very similar except a small steering wheel and set of pedals residing in a normal vehicle configuration was included in her station.

"Sir?"

"Those bastards are going to get us killed."

"Sir?", she asks curiously.

"Don't ever turn your back on those dogs, Sergeant."

"Yes sir."

Marcus and Scott continued walking through the cobble streets. Mechs, rusted and riddled with bullet holes, lay before them littering the sides of buildings and city streets. Vines overgrown and reaching towards the sky as they crawled up the sides of the tall structures. The two stop and have a smoke and drink. The intersection used to be a roundabout. The centerpiece had become rubble. Scott looks around and stands up, walking to an odd matting in the grass that had grown through the cobble roads.

"This is the route they had taken."

Marcus stood up to join him.

"Wanna go check it out?"

"Yeah. Let's go see what we can find out."

Several hours later, Phillis attempted to reach Marcus and Scott.

"Gun Walzer 1 or Gun Walzer 2…" She paused as the radio breaks with static.

"Yeah, yeah, we're here", Scott replied.

"It's almost dusk, where have you two been?", she demanded.

"Found the landing site. We're headed back now. They headed directly south. Give us a minute we'll tell you all about it when we get back", Marcus responded.

"Alright, be safe. Dusk is when the predators come out to hunt."

Marcus came over the radio snickering. "They are already out." Just before the radio transmission cut out Phillis could hear the two laughing from Marcus response. She shook her head.

The two Gun Walzers emerged from out of seemingly nowhere. Jimmy was looking at them as they nonchalantly stood over by the cooking meat to get some food.

They walked over and set their tin plates on the hood of their vehicle and started eating without a word. Jimmy watched them closely. As did the rest of the group except Phillis whom was stoking the fire. Once the two finished they wiped their plates clean and set them over by where they got them. Joining the rest of the group around the fire the night continued on.

"Care to explain where you two were all day?", Charles demanded.

Scott didn't pay attention in the slightest.

Marcus replied. "We found the extraction site for the group that we believe hit us. About nine sets of tracks. A craft of some kind, more than likely a zeppelin class carrier, small, built for insertion and extraction. No traces of camp though, nor food. They stuck to the craft."

"Which direction did they retreat to?", Charles continued interrogating.

"South, we observed them earlier leaving, but due to the excitement, we forgot."

"You forgot? Why haven't we left to chase them?", Charles asked excitedly.

Scott chimed in at this point. "Because they are airborne. We are on the ground, there is no way. One; we couldn't catch them and two; even if we did, what then? I don't know the lands past here. In fact, if I'm not mistaken there is another city to the south. The very ruins this kingdom once grave-robbed to obtain its vast collection of technologies and war frames. Isn't that right, Colonel?"

"Correct."

Scott continued as everybody watched the buzzed Gun Walzer. "Even so, we don't know the capabilities, we are honestly ill prepared to get into a fight in all reality. If we were to take any form of casualties we have nowhere to evacuate, nonetheless we don't fully understand the capabilities of our enemy nor the stronghold they are headed to. And from what I gather, and recall of my incident with one of them; a female no less…" He smiled. Phillis squinted at him reading him as best she could. "No offense to any of the females here of course; but she is strong; they're species is something we've never seen before."

"They're not human?", Charles asked.

"They are human-like. But something else. Her eyes intrigued me very much. Almost like that of a dragon's. If they still existed. Her skin too. Her hands. She was absolutely gorgeous. None so more than the moment she attempted to kill me. And then, when she realized we weren't the enemy, she decided to leave, as if the whole mission was based upon finding something or someone. I'd like to meet her on the battlefield once more." Scott held up his flask to the south in the hue of darkening colors of orange and purple. "I'd like to do more than just fight with her, that's for sure."

Marcus laughed. Charles didn't find it amusing. And Phillis could see the longing in his eyes. The look of a man who met his soulmate and wished to find her; even if it meant his end.

"Alright; it's time for this old man to hit the sack." Scott said, standing up lighting a smoke. He walked to their vehicle to grab his bed roll.

"What are we doing about guard shifts?"

Phillis put her hand on Marcus back. "Already taken care of. You'll be woken up when its time."

Scott appears behind Marcus suddenly. "Hey, faggot."

Marcus jumped. "What?"

"You going to go over there and talk to her?", he asked nodding toward Victoria.

Marcus took in a deep breath and spouted "Okay, I'll do it." Jumping up almost pumping himself up for a fight. He suddenly sat right back down.

"You know what? Fuck you."

Scott started laughing as he walked away with his hands in his pockets. "Goodnight fuckers", he said as he disappeared.

The rest of the group stayed up. Scott sat drinking by himself on a fallen mech. He poured a shot from his flask onto the dead machine. Looking out over a massive crater on the other side of the kingdom. The stars were bright as the moon loomed overhead. The ground was glistening from its glass-like state. Some structures' skeletons jutted from the outer ring of the giant indent. Scott peered into it as he did once many years ago.

"Rest well old friends. It was a pleasure to have fought against you all those years ago."

Chapter 5

A Long, Quiet Night

Marcus and Victoria were standing inside of a guard tower at the corner of the intersection overlooking all main routes leading to the centerpiece where the rest of the group lay sleeping in their vehicles. Scott, Phillis, and Jimmy were all sleeping within several feet of each other in their sleeping bags. The night was dark. Only the moonlight shed any light on this quiet city of ruin. The fire was merely embers now and slowly calming to ashes as the night went on.

Marcus couldn't hold his composure for too long as the height of his buzz was reaching its peak. Her dark, naturally curly hair was down. He kept making eye contact with her; her green eyes almost cut through the darkness and called to him. Her strong body was not left to any form of imagination due to her form fitting under suit. She was wearing only her sharply designed greaves. Her shield sat against the wall under the opening in the tower. Her long spear stayed at her side. He could see her muscular form under the octagonal patterned black one piece suit. Perfect breasts and a perky butt. She was absolutely the epitome of her race.

"So…" Marcus started.

"Yes?", Victoria quickly replied.

"Do you have anyone waiting for you when we get back?", he asked shyly.

She looked at him holding back a smirk.

He quickly looked back out. "You don't have to answer if you don't want to", he exclaimed.

She chuckled a little. As a maiden should, quietly holding her hand in front of her mouth. Marcus smiled. Her laugh almost brought chills across the back of his neck.

"I'm no one's to claim.", she started. Her voice was just perfect, the young Gun Walzer thought. "We, as Knights of the Old Guard, rarely find true love anywhere other than our duty. We are betrothed to another in order to keep our line strong."

"Please continue, Fair Maiden."

"From childhood we are chosen to train by our brothers and sisters in the honorable weapons of the oldest of ancient societies. Sword, spear, axe, hammer, shield and many other weapons depending on our choosing. We take great pride in our ways compared to the other territories. We've been protecting the King with our ways for centuries. Our weapons and armor have changed somewhat over the centuries and are designed to even be able to fight against your kind. But…", she paused a moment. "Our tactics and discipline have remained the same and effective even against the ancient weapons during the wars."

"Were you in the war?", Marcus asked.

"I was far too young", She replied.

"How old are you; if you don't mind me asking?"

She blushed. "Oh, sorry", Marcus quickly stated.

"No; I've just turned 18.", she answered.

"Oh my; you're so gorgeous", he said dreamily.

His eyes widened, as did hers. "I'm sorry if I've offended you, my lady."

The two exchanged smiles for a moment. Then he continued for his curiosity has taken hold through his drunkenness. "Why so young? I apologize; but I don't know very much about your race. We are only taught how to kill."

She nodded just before answering. "Like your race's constant state of inebriation our genetic flaw is our bodies. Although we are large and possess great strength our lives only last for around four decades."

Marcus shook his head. "Well, if I was destined to live until 40 I would make those 40 years the best years of my life."

She giggled as did he. "Sir Marcus, you are an interesting man."

He laughed. She was confused. "I'm no sir, my lady, but thank you."

"But just in this past day, despite what everyone knows of your kind, you have a good heart. Even Lady Elizabeth can see this, and she an eye for honorable warriors." Marcus eyes were wide from almost shock at her kind words. She continued. "Your resolve is just and you seek knowledge without judgment. That is the makings of a Knight in my eyes."

"My lady…", he started with a look of longing in his eyes. "That was the nicest thing anyone has ever said about me. Thank you."

She smiled at him. He returned it in kind. "We should take care of our charge", she said quietly looking out into the night. Marcus looked at her for a moment more taking in the moonlight beating upon her gorgeous body and face.

The night grew older and Jess and Jimmy took watch. This time they sat on the center piece together. Jimmy was looking at Jess with wonder. She was standing with her rifle at the low ready scanning with her night vision optics as if she was expecting the worst to happen.

"Miss Jess?", Jimmy asked.

She continued monitoring the area.

"Miss Jess?", he whispered loudly.

"What Jimmy?", she asked irritated.

"What is that thing on your face?", he asked innocently.

"It's night vision, Jimmy", she answered.

"Oh", he said. "What's it do?"

She looked at him. "It helps me see at night, Jimmy."

"Cool", he said starting to hum to himself as he looked around. "I don't need that, we can see really well at night. But that's good that you can too."

She held back a small smile.

"What type of weapon is that?", he continued.

"This or my side arm?", she asked.

"Marcus and Mr. Scott's weapons are really different from yours. Is there something special about your weapon that theirs can't do, Miss Jess?"

"Jess is fine Jimmy."

"Oh okay", he replied happily.

She walked over and sat down next to him. He looked at her as she pulled the thick goggles up onto her head. The green light dimmed out.

"This is…", she showed him her rifle. "A bullpup piston driven air cooled magazine fed rifle chambered in 8mm by 50mm. It is the elite foot soldier battle rifle. Comes with a 25 round magazine and is capable of penetrating half an inch of steel."

"Wow!", Jimmy said. "That's really cool."

He held up his bow pulling the wire back. "This is my bow. His name is Jimmy Jr."

"I hear your bows are very impressive weapons Jimmy."

"Oh yeah…", he said offering it to her. She took it slowly. He nodded to her to give it a try. She could barely draw it more than an inch.

"Why can't I draw it?", she grunted.

"Because it's a 500lb draw, Jess."

Her eyes were wide with shock. She handed it back.

"Not many people can draw them fully. Phillis can though, she is super strong. She has one of the strongest bows ever made. I can't even draw her bow."

"How can that be?", Jess asked.

Jimmy stated as a matter of fact. "She is one of our Heroes; during the war she saved many people. She talks about it from time to time. She even protected me when I was just a kid. I've been with her ever since."

"That's great Jimmy. Is she your mother?"

"No, my parents died in the war", Jimmy answered.

She was dumbfounded by his unscathed tone in the answer.

"Is Charles your father?", he asked.

Jess laughed a little. "No, Jimmy, he is my Commander."

"Ah, kinda like Phillis is in charge of me?"

"Yes Jimmy; I was hand-picked for this assignment out of the tower guards that night."

"You're very pretty", Jimmy exclaimed.

Jess was speechless. She didn't know what to say. She put her goggles back down and quickly stood up. Jimmy continued to humming to himself as she stepped away to take a lap around the camp.

"What's with this guy?", she asked herself. Smiling as she made her way around the area.

Jimmy was talking to his bow. "I think she likes me, Jimmy Jr." He continued humming to himself.

Their shift ended a little early as Scott and Elizabeth were up and already standing by Jimmy as Jess came back from her third round. Scott grunted as he lit up a smoke. Elizabeth looked at Jess as she approached.

"Anything to report, Sergeant?", Elizabeth asked.

Jess pulled her goggles up. "Negative, Baroness. It's quiet, other than the normal patterns of life from the forest."

"You are relieved. Get some sleep."

Scott patted Jimmy on the shoulder. Jess and Jimmy walked away. As she broke away from him, he stopped to watch her walk toward her tank.

He whispered loudly. Scott took a long drag from his smoke as he observed.

"Goodnight, Jess."

She stopped, looking at him. Scott could see her simple yet beautiful smile.

"Goodnight, Jimmy", she whispered back, mimicking him.

"Sweet dreams, don't let the bed bugs bite", he continued.

She chuckled. "Understood; you do the same Jimmy", she giggled. She turned and quickly headed toward her tank.

Jimmy sat down removing his boots as he snuggled into his sleeping bag. "She really does like me", he whispered to himself before falling fast to sleep.

Scott nodded. "Well done, buddy", he says to himself.

Elizabeth caught his words. "You are a very interesting man, Gun Walzer", she stated.

Scott laughed as he sat on the edge of the statues foundation.

"Nonsense", he replied.

The sky above them lit up as something burned through the atmosphere. The two watched as it flickered away breaking into several pieces before burning out.

"Old satellites from the ancients finally falling from the heavens", Elizabeth said quietly.

Scott took another drag.

"What a shame!", he started pulling from his flask. "The younglings missed a good show. Haven't seen a satellite fall in a good minute. Always gorgeous when you think about the reality of it all."

"How's that, Gun Walzer?"

"That no matter what lengths we've gone to; no matter what technological might we reach, we are doomed to never truly reach the heavens. Sometimes its manifest destiny for no matter how we attempt to change our fate; we are evolving into something else's prey. Like that satellite for instance; a prey to gravity and inability to sustain rotation around the planet. Or a failure in power life expectancy. Or just dumb luck that knocked it out of the sky. Regardless; it had to fall; because it was made by man, and thus doomed to fail."

"You are indeed, dangerous", Elizabeth stated as she watched him intriguingly.

"Not as dangerous as The Shield of The North Tower I'd say", he replied checking his shotgun.

"I've been meaning to ask, how did you recognize me?", she asked.

"My lady. There's not too many people who don't know of you", he took a long drag. Blowing out a heavy pipe of smoke he continued. "The Knight whom was said to cleave a battering ram clean in half. Single handedly stopping the tank from knocking down the only thing between the Anvil Cross Elites and the inner Kingdom. Quite the legend if you ask me", Scott said glancing at her.

"The Dragonares have come a long way from the reign of that crusading maniac", she replied.

"I kinda liked their old name though. The Anvil Cross Faction or Territories; whatever the fuck they were called. Little bastards", Scott laughed billowing smoke.

"You are very knowledgeable on the subject."

"My lady; your ability and strength are well known. Unlike most history books where only the victor writes what they desire, our books are written from every bit of known truth in order to maintain knowledge. Just like the reason why The Old Guard and Gun Walzers have never fought against each other nor worked together on the battlefield. The powers that be are afraid that your pride and our insanity will cause the worst war known to our Kingdoms history. Although…", he said smiling. "What beauty it would be to fight against your kind. How glorious would that battle be? Could you fathom it?" He almost growled in the thought of it.

"I see it is true what they say about your kind."

Scott regained his composure. "Is it now?", Scott growled.

"Do you know why all the territories are afraid of your kind Gun Walzer?"

"Do tell, my lady."

"Because you drink to keep yourselves under control. The only ones who literally torment their bodies and minds to keep from destroying everything around them."

"Is it torment? Or is it satisfaction?", Scott asked. "You see, Baroness…", he lit another smoke before continuing. "In our worst moment we are considered a threat to everything and everyone. Now imagine if you will. That we become sober…"

"Restraint or death", she replied.

Scott smiled pointing at her as he continued. "Fact; but why? Why are we, not allowed to be sober? It is possible but very, very rare at best. Only one every other generation becomes sober."

She answered. "It is because your drink keeps your mind true."

Scott laughed a little. "No, my lady…", he almost whispered. "It's because our mind sees the world never more true; than the moment we want to destroy it. The alcohol dulls our senses and maintains our composure. Without it; we are free. And that is something no one wants. It is said that before we lost much of our archives that the truth of our existence was in those books. A truth I was told after I first experienced war."

"What truth was that?"

"That like that satellite. We all will come burning to the ground to ashes and forgotten just the same."

"That cannot be", she replied.

"History isn't written so that we may not make the mistakes of our ancestors. It's written so that we may have an idea of what to do when we make those same mistakes."

She was baffled by him. He could see it. She didn't understand him.

"Gun Walzer; which side did you fight for in the war?"

"I fought for my own side. War is the only freedom we are allowed. But even after all these years; there is only one victor in the war. And that is the worthless people who set each one of us against each other. Those products of incest and stupidity that believe they have the right to rule over us."

Elizabeth stood drawing her sword and pointing it at the Gun Walzer. He didn't flinch. He merely took a drag off his cigarette. The cherry lit his face in orange. His eyes almost reflected no light, bottomless she thought.

"How dare you insult the King and his family?", she looked down on him.

"My lady...", he spoke coldly. "Regardless of your honor and duty. Royal Blood is maintained through incest. Can't have filthy commoners breed into the family line. Even your race understands that. Betrothed so that there isn't a mistake. Given away to another to ensure the great line continues. My Fair Maiden; like I said, our history books tell all truths."

"Do you hold no Loyalty to you King?"

Scott leaned toward her cocking his head slightly. "My loyalty toward a man that orders 8 individuals to traverse the southern regions of the Fossil Forest after an attack by highly skilled and unknown enemies. By which means to observe and or destroy if at all possible with weapons that could end up being absolutely obsolete against whatever lay waiting. For some gold and honor? Do I have loyalty to our King? No. I have no loyalty to your King who would send us to die for his glory. My only loyalty lies with this group here. And even then, only certain people deserve to claim such a thing from me."

She pulled her blade away.

"There is no King here. There is us; and that is it."

He stood and stretched letting out a sigh of relief.

"The King told me of your ways. I had no idea what he meant until now. You're an interesting man, Gun Walzer."

He laughed. "My Lady; as much as I would have enjoyed crossing sword and gun with you. We are for the moment allies. And hopefully for more than just a moment."

"What do you think lies in wait for us?", she asked.

"More questions than answers, Baroness. That I assure you."

As the shift came to an end Elizabeth went to wake Charles and Phillis. Both were getting ready as she approached. The two relieved Scott and Elizabeth from their charge. Scott merely packed up his sleeping back and sat in the front seat of his vehicle smoking and drinking. The silence was almost unbearable as the two stood watch. The morning was becoming cold as the sun clawed at the darkness.

"I'm curious", she started catching Charles's attention. "What does the Fire Grapher want with a mission such as this?"

He answered without missing a beat. "To protect our kingdom from any further possible attacks by this unknown enemy. I've been given orders from the Princess herself to destroy any remaining enemies we find along the way."

"Doesn't seem fitting of a Commander of your military accomplishment", she replied playfully.

He looked at her. "Fire Grapher." He said laughing to himself momentarily. "I haven't heard that in a long time."

"Not a name I would mention around the Gun Walzers."

"I did what I had to; those beasts would have killed every last one of us if I didn't set that field on fire. They would have wiped our entire society from existence if given the chance. And if I hadn't done what I did; they might have succeeded. So forgive my hatred of them. They are not like you or I or even the Old Guard. They cannot be trusted."

"Nor can a man whom set thousands of people on fire; burning a city and wall to the ground; what is that field called again?", she asked before answering herself. "The Smoldering Fields."

"Phillis...", he started clearly offended by her question of his moral standing. "I did what I had to do to ensure the survival of my race. The

Gun Walzers are the only ones who don't believe in order or morality. Even your society understands that they cannot be trusted. They will kill anyone for money, and fight a war just because it's a war regardless if it has anything to do with them. They will kill whoever gets in their way, women and children. They have no honor nor loyalty. They are a danger to us all; it was against my recommendation to even send those two along with us. Despite their Elder who spoke very highly of them."

Phillis interrupted him. "I'm glad they are here. We need them more than they need us."

"We don't know anything about them. Our records indicate nothing about Scott. Marcus has more of a record than Scott does. His war record just states that he had fought against the Anvil Cross, and the Southern Kingdom. Nothing else."

Phillis put her hand on his shoulder just as the day broke. "Why don't you just ask him?"

"You know more than you're telling. I will find out…", he stopped. His hands started to shake. The sun is rising over the horizon. He quickly pulled out a small syringe gun.

Phillis watched as he almost frantically pulled his sleeve up and injected himself.

"Some flaws are worse than others", she says as she walked over to Jimmy who was still asleep. Scott was standing lighting a smoke looking at Charles take in heavy breaths as he regained his composure.

Chapter 6

Further South Still

Phillis observed Scott as he bent down looking into the side mirror of his vehicle, shaving his face with a flat mirror finished blade. He slung it off and then continued. A cigarette hung out of the corner of his mouth as he squinted through the smoke.

"You Gun Walzers never cease to amaze. Last time I've seen anyone shave like that was my father when I was a little girl."

Scott peered over to her before looking back. "Yeah I don't know why; my old man taught me and I just never got with the times I guess."

"We are about to start breakfast", she stated.

"Already ahead of you", Scott pointed to the hood with his blade. A sizzling sound became evident as she saw the grill smoldering almost ready to cook on.

"Okay, I'll let everyone know", she walked away. Scott's eyes slid over staring at her butt.

Marcus nudged him. "You sly dog."

Scott chuckled. "I'd lick her asshole after a full day of fighting just to see what her sweat tastes like."

20 minutes later.

"You guys going to eat?", Marcus asked standing next to Scott who was cooking up something on a grill on the hood of their vehicle.

Charles and Jess turned and looked at the rest of the group standing their drinking coffee and carrying on with smiles and laughter while waiting for their food. Scott was drinking a beer from a glass bottle and taking drags from the cigarette in that same hand. All the while stabbing hefty slabs of meat and flipping them before throwing them onto the hungry patrons' plates.

"I think we will be fine", Charles replied.

Jimmy waved at Jess who waved back after ensuring Charles didn't see her.

Scott shook his head before yelling back. "Suit yourselves. One day you may be dying cold, tired, and hungry thinking back to this moment. Saying… 'Man I wish I had Scott's delicious meat in my mouth right now.' But no; you missed out a chance to taste my thick meat."

Marcus burst into laughter. Scott grinned as he set a slab on Marcus' plate. Phillis giggled. Victoria and Elizabeth held their laughter back as their mouths were full. Jimmy was looking at Marcus and Scott confused. He leaned over to Phillis.

"I don't know what's so funny. Scott's meat is delicious."

Phillis and Marcus looked at each other wide-eyed and burst into laughter.

"It sure is Jimmy", Phillis replied still laughing.

After breakfast Phillis and Scott stood with Elizabeth and Charles who held his touch screen pad in the middle of the group.

"You said the zeppelin headed straight south?", Charles asked Scott.

Scott looked closer at the screen. He pointed. "What is that? And why do the tracks continue south?"

"That would be a good place to start looking", Phillis replied.

"I agree with the elder", Elizabeth stated.

Phillis hung her head in shame at the remark.

"Forgive me Phillis, I meant no offense."

Phillis smiled slightly. "None taken."

Scott is attempting to hold back his laughter.

Charles answered Scott finally. "It is where this kingdom used to reap all the old technology from. It's an ancient city still yet to explore. The files recovered from the database here show that the most recent exploration team had discovered information about our genetic engineering flaws. Not to mention a fifth society."

Scott lit a smoke exhaling heavily. "That would make sense then. The creatures that attacked us were definitely something else. How much more do you know that you haven't told us, yet?"

Charles looked at Scott. "What would you like to know, Gun Walzer? That the war on this soil was merely about the information that they could have openly shared and spared their inevitable defeat? Or the fact that they were building weapons that were literally designed to kill us more effectively because of the data they had recovered from this city. Or would you like to know that we have started developing a cure for our very flaws in order to give Elizabeth here a longer life span. Or Phillis the peace of mind that her body won't randomly fail her one day if she pushes herself past her muscles capacity. Or maybe the antidote that could keep you vile beasts from killing everything around you when the booze finally runs dry. Is that what you want to hear?"

Scott laughed. "It's a joke. One big screen to hold over your eyes. The ancients failed when they designed us. There's no cure for our ailments. We are meant to live these lives as the price that we pay for the power we hold. We were never meant to live forever. What puts us up at the top of the food chain, compared to other animals or species on this planet, man-made or otherwise, is our ability to develop what we need to, to survive. Our minds. We think so therefore…"

"We are…", Phillis finished the line for him.

Scott continued. "If you take it all away; we are quite weak in all reality. So much that a micro-organism could wipe us off the face of this fucked planet. So we began to toy with ourselves. Tug on this pull at that." He violently made the gestures with his hands. "And then out comes us, sliding from test tubes and then set lose into the world. Perfect races built upon the exaggeration of any one great attribute. Those who collect and use knowledge", he pointed at Charles.

"Those who value life and duty and the need to protect", he pointed at Elizabeth.

"The basic instinct to coexist with the agricultural beauty and natural order of the world and its ecosystem", he pointed at Phillis.

"And then those who conduct war. The very foundation of our species existence. That burn the world to the ground in order to force it to spit out something in return to end us. And then repeat. Again and again and again."

"How could you think that way?", Charles replied. "As someone who has watched the worst of all sides during a war in all directions. This could save us. I say we start here. At least find some answers, maybe we can find what had happened to this fifth society. These creatures that attacked us were designed just like the rest of us. There has to be information regarding their whereabouts."

Scott shook his head. Phillis stepped forward placing a hand on Scotts shoulder. "He's right, you know."

"Then that's it, we check the information assuming we can even access it from those old ass computers. And then we leave. Don't need any more of the Ancient's mistakes waking up."

The group split up heading over to their vehicles and mounted up ready to go. The group started heading out and soon passed a loading station of rail cars and tracks that lead south. The gates were open with a train that had stopped halfway through. They saw a few rusty cars sitting off the tracks with vines growing around them. The tracks led further into the forest. Slowly, following the Dragonares' tank as it somewhat cleared a path for the rest of the convoy.

Elizabeth looked at Victoria peculiarly as she followed the Gun Walzers at the end of the group's convoy. Victoria had an interesting smile on her face. One that worried Elizabeth.

"Victoria?"

"Yes, my lady?", she replied.

"What is your measure of young Marcus?", he inquired.

"My lady?", he asked.

"You spent over an hour with him, what is your measure of the young man?"

"He is a worthy opponent", Victoria replied.

Elizabeth turned up her nose as she continued. "He is a fine young man; suitable features. We could do without his vulgar mouth. However, his heart is just and true."

"Yes, he is a fine young man", Victoria agreed.

"He is well over courting age as well", Elizabeth continued. Victoria's cheeks turned a shade of red.

"My lady?", she choked out.

"Strong and handsome, would make a fine husband and father", Elizabeth continued teasing the poor Knight.

"I'm not sure what you're implying, my lady", Victoria almost couldn't believe what she was saying.

"Do you fancy him?"

There it was. Cold and directly to the point. Victoria was stunned by the question. And try as she might, she attempted to say anything in her defense.

"But my lady; we cannot enter courtship. It is forbidden by all territories."

Elizabeth turned her head and watched the road satisfied with Victoria's answer. "Do well to remember that Knight. I understand how it must feel; but he is a Gun Walzer, after all."

Scott was squinting from the smoke as he held Marcus' smoke in his mouth and a beer between his legs. In the other hand, he held Marcus' beer. Marcus was on a knee pissing into a beer bottle with much difficulty, as Scott laughed at the same time, trying to keep the smokes in his mouth.

"Wow; that was a lot", Marcus chuckled holding it up for Scott to see.

He tossed it out the window and took his beer and smoke back.

"Okay so after you fucked up and said she was beautiful, then what happened?", Scott asked.

"She changed the subject man, I don't know what to tell you."

"Stop being a bitch and just say 'hey, I like your spear, lets fuck.'"

Marcus laughed. Scott does not. He stared at him intensely.

"We can't, man, you know the rules", Marcus stated disappointedly.

"Fuck the rules, dude. Those are in place to keep the species in check. How do you think the King has children that take after our different races?"

Scott held his finger to his head signifying to young Marcus to use his head.

"Ah", Marcus said.

"Besides..." Scott's tone changed to a monotone. "We don't know what is at the end of the road for us. Might as well enjoy what little life we have left. Never know when the black dog comes calling."

Marcus thought. "I just believe you know; love thy neighbor, eat the pussy."

Scott looked over at him. As they paused, smiles split their faces as they burst into laughter.

"As you should, my friend. As you should."

As the convoy hit a clearing, a massive herd of Mammoths slowly crossed the plains. They observed the group roll by. To their left was a thick forest that went on and on. Insects flew about under the tall, massive mutated pines. Stairways of mushrooms spiraled up them. The massive leaves provided hundreds of miles of shade under the vast forest floor.

"Fresh Mammoth steaks", Marcus blurted out over the net.

"If you're going to hunt; now's your chance", Jess replied.

"What's up?", Marcus inquired.

"The tracks stop ahead, looks to be a loading station. And just past that a passable paved route. We are scanning the area to ensure it leads to where we think it does", she replied again.

"Alright; we'll hold here and let the Old Guard pass us."

Scott and Marcus got out.

"Go bag us some dinner", Scott said.

The rest of the group stopped pulling off the raised platform that acted as a loading dock for the train cars. Stacks of railroad ties and track beams were laid out neatly in formation just outside the forest. Several trees lay where they had failed from the excavator machines that cut them and then started to turn them into usable wood ties. The machine that both cut and turned the massive trees into ties resembled a gigantic robotic crab. Its massive arms were designed to grasp the thick trunks of the heavy pines. A giant circular saw protruded from the left arm. Its mouth was like a turbine with razor sharp inward-facing teeth that would strip and slice away bark and limbs. Piles of ties had long since left from where they fell out the back of the machine ready to be stacked were swelled and cracked from the weather over this last decade. The facility was quite small considering the size of the robotic machinery that sat rusted and forgotten next to the end of the line.

"Jimmy. Search the wood line around those machines over there", Phillis pointed toward the aforementioned robotic crabs.

Jimmy set his helmet down and took off down the hill disappearing into the woods.

Phillis grabbed her bow and walked to the edge of the tracks facing south.

Charles and Jess both dismounted as well as Victoria and Elizabeth.

The group started walking into the dome like structure that, although small, seemed to have a viewing bay on the top of the building jutting out facing south.

A gunshot crashed, turning all their heads. They heard Marcus yelling and faint laughter.

"Dude, you fucking missed!", Scott yelled amid his laughter as he stood up attempting to propel his voice.

"I can't believe you fucking missed!", he continued his laughter watching the spectacle unfold.

"I know!", Marcus yelled running across the plain. The bull mammoth was gigantic. The ground was shaking as it chased him like a freight train across the massive field. Scott laughed as he casually walked over and grabbed his shotgun. He pulled the magazine out of the AK style receiver and then cleared the weapon. He pulled a different magazine out of his kit in the back seat. He inserted the magazine and charged the bolt.

"Hey dick!"

"What!", Marcus yelled back continuing to run across the field away from the massive beast.

"Bring his ass this way!", Scott yelled.

Marcus turned. The beast did likewise. The ground shook even more as the massive mammoth charged closer. Scott took aim and fired. The crash was loud and rang out, echoing through the valley. The herd stampeded into the forest as the massive beast slammed into the ground sliding to a stop. It bulldozed some of the tall grass carving a trail to where it lay dead. It was quick.

Marcus walked up the hill breathing heavily. "I thought I was going to die."

"Nah, you would have been alright", Scott said walking around the other side of the vehicle. He changed magazines with the muscle memory of a skilled weapon's handler. He charged the weapon, catching the heavy brass shell between his fingers. He set the weapon in his seat and then placed the shell into the magazine inserting it back into his kit.

Lighting a smoke, he leaned in and pulled out a backwards curved handled long bearded hatchet and a curved round nosed cleaver. He tossed the cleaver to Marcus who caught it without looking. He looked at what he caught and then shot Scott an odd look.

"Let's get to work. Skin, as much bone as possible and half the meat. Leave the rest of the forest", he said walking over to Marcus.

"How are we going to get it back?", Marcus asked.

Scott smiled mischievously at the young man.

"Should we go aid them, my lady?", Victoria asked Elizabeth.

"Despite their clumsy and moronic disposition; they are quiet capable and dangerous foes. I doubt a mere herd of Titan Mammoths would give them even a bead of sweat upon their brow."

"My Lady", Victoria replied looking in their direction.

Charles and Jess appeaedr from within the building meeting the Old Guard. Phillis was looking out from the platform on top of the dome.

"Did you find anything Sir Charles?", Elizabeth asked.

"Some documents, none of the computers are in any working condition. Pollen and dust covered everything in there. However, we did find out what they were doing. The workers here were a part of the Genetic Engineering Revival Project. They were building these tracks toward the city. According to the paperwork in there; they were supposed to be finished this year."

"What city are you referring to, Sir?", Victoria asked.

Charles looked at Jess and said nothing. She walked over to their tank without saying a word.

"You are familiar with the Treasure Laws and the Tomb Laws, correct?"

They both nodded as he continued.

"Those laws were not just made up for our kingdom. They were a treaty that was signed by all the kingdoms that currently exist that we know of across the world. However; these criminals did not follow such laws. They were attempting to revive dead technologies from one of the Ancient Ruins that is considered forbidden under the Tomb Laws. And this city from the information we do have is one of the most desired locations known to any of the Kingdoms. The secrets and information there is priceless. The answers to what went wrong and changed the world so, is hidden within those computers and libraries. The Laboratories, alone, hold the secrets to, many of these creatures that exist today. It is said that one of these dome cities holds the key to our very existence. A key that could unlock our very mortality."

Charles was starting to sound overly excited. The two women could see it. There was almost an obsession in his tone. The roar of the Gun Walzers' engine growled as they pulled up to a stop. The two Baronesses' eyes wide couldn't avert their view of the two men. Their vehicle was covered in blood. They stepped out of the vehicle and unstrapped the thick tarp of meat they had cut from the Mammoth. They lifted it up and carried it over to the group. Phillis landed next to Charles almost without making a sound. The Dragonare jumped in surprise from her landing, once he noticed her.

"I see you boys made out well", she said with her genuine smile.

"Oh yeah. We even have some bone. Didn't know if you wanted any of it, but we thought it would come to some use to you, Phillis", Marcus replied.

They set the tarp down on a large table that served as a planning bench for the workers, years back. They opened it up revealing a massive amount of meat.

"Could you have killed something smaller?", Charles scoffed.

"Yeah, but we don't eat human", Scott joked, pulling out his knife and spinning it between his fingers.

Marcus chuckled as they stood up. "Alright, whose turn is it to cook?", Marcus asked.

Phillis stepped forward cracking her fingers. "It's mine and Jimmy's. You brought us a feast. At least a few days. We will dry some of it out for some jerky. We will salt the rest for later."

Scott standing next to her, nodded as he lit a smoke. "Sounds good. So what's the deal with this shithole?", he asked looking at the small dome. He peered around eyeing the massive mechanized crabs.

"Holy fuck. Marcus, look at those big bastards. These assholes really knew how to build shit." He laughs walking towards to get a closer look.

"Oh man", Marcus spouted. The two stand there talking among themselves as Jimmy dropped out of a tree.

"There is nothing more than just pretty insects and beautiful animals roaming the forest, Phillis."

Charles was still in shock from Phillis and Jimmy's distance they had leaped from. He muttered to himself as Jess joined the rest of the group.

The Old Guard walked over to Phillis. Victoria lent her a hand. Elizabeth leaned against the table and watched Marcus and Scott joke and laugh at each other. Jimmy spotted a hugh bee flying around from gigantic flower to flower and decided to run after it.

Phillis yelled at him to come back and help her in such a loving way as a mother would to her child.

"Alright, we'll eat and then continue heading south to this Forbidden Ruin City. Charles, plan the route. Scott and Marcus, you're first on watch while we are here. Jess you join them."

Charles snapped back into the present. "Who are you to give me orders?", he barked.

"Sir, I mean you no offense. But for the moment I believe we needn't let our guard down. If you say that we are drawing closer to one of the Ruins; then it would be wise to assume we may face even more abominations as our journey continues."

Scott and Marcus didn't say a word. They grabbed their weapons and checked their chambers. They each grabbed a bottle of beer and headed into the building. Moments later, they both appeared on the platform dragging chairs with them.

The Fossil Forest

They sat down and cracked open their brews. They clanked glasses and held them up cheering to whatever they thought to themselves before finishing the bottles off. Scott looked over at Marcus. A smile cracked on his face.

"What, man?", Marcus laughed.

"You fuckin' missed, how the hell could you miss?", he laughed slapping Marcus on the shoulder with his heavy hand.

"I love animals. I don't know."

"He was the size of a building, man", Scott stated.

"I can't wait to eat Phillis' cooking though. I don't know if you know this. You being an older gentlemen…"

Scott laughed.

Marcus continued. "You ever eating anything from the Boltiers territories?"

"Oh yeah, it was some of the best food I ever had. She's older too so it will be amazing I'm sure."

He laughed again. "Unless it sucks. Then, it's going to suck."

They both laughed.

Jess stepped onto the platform. The two turn back noticing her. They both pull out bottles of beer from somewhere and offer it to the young lady.

"Pull up a chair there, young Sergeant", Scott gestured politely.

Jess politely declined their offer of booze and instead pulled up a chair next to them. She sat leaning into her long sniper rifle without saying a word watching the forest before them.

A loud roar off in the distance echoed through the land, stopping everyone in their tracks. Again, that roaring furnace of a sound. It was distant and out of sight, but whatever it was it is gigantic.

"What creature could make such a sound?", Jess asked. The Gun Walzers watched eagerly ready to draw their weapons if need be.

Jimmy was all smiles.

"It was probably a Dragon", he said.

"Jimmy, you know Dragons haven't been seen in decades", Phillis replied.

"I know, but if I were a Dragon, I'd want everyone to know I'm waiting for someone to find me and meet me. Why else would he roar randomly like that?"

The group was silent and somewhat worried. Everyone except the Gun Walzers.

And Jimmy.

Jimmy was excited.

Chapter 7

Ruins of the Gods

Marcos was drooling on himself when their vehicle slammed into the broken beginnings of an old highway.

"Ugh...", he said looking around groggy eyed. He wiped from the saliva from his chin. "I'm awake", he spouted squinting his eyes attempting to gain awareness of his surroundings.

Scott was hard-pressed kept his attention on the road, lit a smoke, and took a heavy swig from a half-empty bottle of warm ale.

Above flocks of massive griffins watched as the convoy rolled through the cleared highway toward the ancient ruins. Phillis and Jimmy rode casually behind the Gun Walzers. Jimmy was looking up and still consciously dodging pot holes and small debris on his bike.

"Phillis!", Jimmy called on the radio.

"Yes, Jimmy?"

"Look at all of those guys up there. They are huge. They look so pretty. I wish I could ride one."

Marcus looked at Scott and chuckled as he reached in the back to grab two cold ones. Lighting a smoke, he and rolled down his window.

"Where are we?", Marcus asked.

"I have no fucking clue man. Our navigators are in the rear. I'm just going off of what they say. Supposedly though...", Scott pulled the cigarette from his mouth and blew smoke. "This highway leads directly into the Ruins the Southern Kingdom was grave robbing. So we think anyway", he chuckled to himself.

The trees were well below them as the tall road reached into the sky. Vines had crawled their way from the forest floor below decorating the concrete path with green life. They headed steadily, as fast as they could with the restrictions of the tank in tow.

"Up ahead guys. There's our destination", Phillis said over the radio.

Charles replied. "Be ready for anything. This area is heavily populated with all manner of thriving species."

Almost as if he couldn't have been more right; Jimmy witnessed a flash of black pass through the flock of stalking griffins. The gigantic beast had snagged one out of the air.

"Guys!", he shouted in his helmet.

"Guys!", he said, finally through the radio.

"What is it Jimmy?", Phillis asked.

"Did you see that?"

"Holy fuck. Everyone, eyes right", Scott replied.

Scott slowed to a stop stepping out and leaning on the roof and door to observe.

"Why are we stopping?", Charles demanded.

No one answered. They all just observed. Even Jess was standing in her hatch to get a better look. Finally, Charles emerged. Jimmy and Phillis were parked on both sides of the Gun Walzers doomsday vehicle. And the Old Guard watched in wonderment standing on the side steps of their massive truck.

"You were right Jimmy", Marcus said pointing lazily with his hand as he leaned against the vehicle observing the beauty before them.

The Dragon was magnificent. The creature's massive wings resembled those of a bat. Its scaly skin was an array of dark green colors. Its belly, however, was light blue. The tail was long steering the creature toward the direction of its choosing. But the sight of the beast isn't the only shocking thing to the group. As the beast drew further away towards a small mountain in the distance, reflections of light flashed ever so slightly. Turning about like the propellers of a wind turbine. They were too far to see clearly.

"I don't believe what I'm seeing", Charles gasped.

Jess pulled out binoculars and looked with a concerned expression on her face.

"Sir, there is something on that mountain there. I cannot clearly make out the cause of that reflecting light, however, it appears to be working."

Charles took the binoculars from her. "Hmmmm", he mumbled.

"Sir?", she inquired.

"We will readdress this when we get to our next destination", he replied.

"Roger, sir", she said as popping back down into her hatch.

Elizabeth spoke out over the radio. "We needn't lollygag for too long. And our destination is upon us."

Without a word, the Gun Walzers got into their vehicles. Jimmy was smiling widely as continued after them. Phillis followed as did the Old Guard and the Dragonares. The light fixtures long since lost power flew by as Marcus looked out into the world. The group continued quickly down the paved overpasses that split into multi-lane highways. A storm off in the distance rumbled and rolled to the east as the road curved in that direction. Then they saw it.

The dome was heavily damaged as sections had fallen into its inner sanctuary. Giant stone statues of griffins towered on both sides of the gate guarding its entrance. Beams were tarnishing and rusting. The thick blast doors that made up the gates had been blown outward. Stone was hard-beaten by Mother Nature's weathering over the centuries. The massive opening to the main gates was somewhat dark. The group passed through them into a dark world of cylindrical skyscrapers and rounded structures spiraled like an array of mushrooms climbing up the base of a tree. The city was layered like a theatre. Each level that lowered to a manmade pond that was on the south side of the city; looked as a futuristic residential area with sky trains long since dead leading to their respective stops. Up each of the cities road ways climbing towards the top of the city; a massive building replicating an ancient Greek style design.

Its pillars cracked and some fallen laid upon its tall stairwells forgotten by all. The group began to navigate to a highway that led up over the city. Although some had broken away and fallen onto the buildings below, it was passable for the moment. However, The Old Guard and The Dragonares decided to stay on the lower city streets and work their way toward the higher levels.

Marcus lookeds out stricken with awe as he observed the few rays of light cutting through the destroyed dome ceiling above. Shedding light upon massive bonsai trees that have broken out of some of the skyscrapers reaching for the heavens. Their roots embedded throughout the tops of the buildings gripping hold like the tentacles of wiry octopi. Fire had scorched a third of the city toward the other side of the dome that opened into an overly thick jungle that is slowly clawing out from its smaller dome attached on the east side.

Abandoned vehicles littered the highways and city streets throughout the metropolis. They were small and very sleek. Their paint had faded and a thin layer of ash had settled upon much of this city. Some was washed away from rains and time.

"And this is what the epitome of scientific might looks like. This is the result of when predators bare what inevitably makes them prey", Scott mumbled to himself. Marcus heard it and nodded.

"Alright that looks like the Government Building at the top level. We'll meet there.,Charles called over the radio.

The group acknowledged continuing their movement through the abandoned and heavily damaged city. Ash and pollen rose as they drove past a few abandoned hovercrafts. Phillis drove up next to the Gun Walzer and looked at Scott. He peered over at her. He reached out and playfully tapped her on the thigh. She continued forward as Jimmy stayed in the rear.

The Old Guard and Dragonares made their way up the sharp turns that climbed up to the top level of the city. Burnt skeletons lay in the city streets. The bones were scorched from an intense heat. The remaining buildings were nothing more than husks stained black from the fire.

"This place is haunting", Jess called over the radio.

"Oh yeah, it is super scary. Look up at the buildings with trees. There's something flying around them", Jimmy replied.

Marcos peered out squinting into the distance. Griffins were soaring in from outside the dome landing in their nests in the ancient trees. Finally, the group was in view of each other and the two parties met at the massive art piece in front of the Government Building. They half-moon parked on the side facing the tall facility.

The group dismounted. It was mostly quiet out. They could hear the low hum of generators in the back ground somewhere in the city.

Lights flickered. Billboards lit up throughout the city. They could even hear some old announcements that were horrifically distorted. An alarm sounded in the distance and the power went out. The city was dark once more. The Old Guard and Baronesses looked up.

"It's a theatre, my Lady", Victoria stated.

Scott looked at her with a grin of absolute evil on his face. Marcus was watching him as he did. His mentor, even with all his faults, was a man that was once sought by many for his distorted views. Marcus watched as he looked up. Marcus gazed up and saw exactly what Victoria was referring to. The dome was fitted with lights everywhere. Like an ancient massive theatre. And they were all the puppets in the puppet show for the world to watch and its children to come and witness the fall of civilization.

"I wonder if you couldn't have been more accurate, Lady Victoria", Scott said lighting a smoke.

"I believe it to be true, Gun Walzer."

"As you should", Scott replied walking up to the beautiful statue in front of him.

He held out his hand, clawing at the thought before him. "The stage was set, for all the possibilities in human evolution, a chance to play the creator, and what did you do?", he asked the dead city. "You created your end, you created us, and what did it amount to? Nothing. The stage from which the last greatest show of human kind had taken place. And yet, it happened to be a fucking tragedy."

The group had gathered around as Scott was reading the inscription upon the memorial plate to himself. A small child. A girl with braided hair wearing a patient's robe stood before a grand Chimera. The beast stood over her bowing its head as she held out her hand to its face. The beast had a long slender wolf-like snout. It had horns split like antlers made of coral and the massive paws of a lion. Its seven tails were bushy and long tapering off to stout points. Its ears pined back showing a tameness toward the little girl. It looked as if it were a horned fox mixed with several other species.

Scott saw a small memorial marble stand. A tarnished bronze plate covered in a thin layer of ash and soot, it had caught his eyes. He walked over and wiped away the ash. He read it for a moment tossing his cigarette and lighting another. As he continued to read the monuments dedication his face began to change ever so slightly. Marcus watched as it went from carelessness to wonder as the Gun Walzer continued his quiet thirst. Scott took a heavy pull from his flask and then poured a small bit onto the plate.

He quietly walked away and took a seat on the bottom of the steps leading to the government building. He looked around taking in the city in all its glory. A genuine smile split his face as he continued to drink and take long drags from his smoke. Quietly and methodically he pondered to himself. Marcus was more than curious now. What did he read to put him in such a state of composure rarely seen?

The group walked over to the memorial and Jimmy read allowed for all to hear.

"In memory of Brooke Anderson,
2042-2049,
Through her, our future as homo sapiens will continue through the morning,
And through her sacrifice, our future has been secured.
This brave soul that stands before you is the epitome of what a Human Being is.

> A great tragedy in our attempt to save this young lady's' life has led to the means to save millions,
> Our memory of her will forever be observed for generations to come throughout the world.
> All those standing before her and her child, shall forever know, she was the key to our continued evolution and survival of this vastly changing world."

The group looked at the statue and then at each other. Confusion was painted across their faces for all but two of the group. Charles and Scott.

"So this is one of the secrets they hid from the masses all too well." Phillis spouted, breaking the silence.

"My Lady, our ancestors used a child to breed these creatures according to this monument."

Elizabeth did not acknowledge Victoria's remark. She was dumbfounded and it was written upon her face.

"Sometimes it is our manifest destiny to evolve so much that we yet again become prey."

It was all Scott said as he stood and checked his pistols and then his shotgun to ensure they were loaded. The group was dumbfounded by his statement. The group turn their heads to each other. Marcus walked over to Scott as the rest of the group decided what to do next. The sun was getting low. By the beams of light, it would be dark within a few hours.

"This place is a grave yard. I don't think we should search too far into these old ruins, man."

Scott looked at Marcus then looking over to the group. "Of course not my friend, we are merely going to ask questions until a ghost decides to answer us. Because that's the issue isn't it?"

Marcus didn't reply, he merely waited, because he knew it was rhetorical.

"We are always chasing our ghosts…" He held his hand up pointing with his cigarette clutched tightly between his fingers. "That's why as a species, we will never become greater than our past selves, because we are too busy chasing the fleeting moment of when we were better than our ancestor's ghosts. It's time we finally look past them…" He took a long drag looking off into the dark city stabbed through with rays of light. "…So we can finally see past ourselves."

He tossed his cigarette and walked over to the rest of the group. Marcus stood where he was pondering his mentors' oddly tainted conclusions. More importantly his hateful outlook, that so violently describes everything he sees in the most poetically philosophical manner.

Marcus took a swig and joined the rest of the group.

"You and Marcus patrol the streets. You find anything, don't waste too much time searching, because we will need eyes and ears. This city is massive and splitting up is the only way we don't lose too much time. We are still chasing this disgusting nuisance", Charles boldly barked.

"Phillis…", he continued. Her attention shifted to Charles.

"You and Jimmy search that lake down there and if you have time the gardens in that dome on the far side."

She nodded.

"Baroness Elizabeth, you and Victoria search this building here."

"And what would you have us do, if not to break every law of our Kingdom, your Kingdom, and go against our very faith. This city had fallen and become a holy ground for those lost to their own meddling in their blasphemous attempt to become God?"

Charles was taken back. It is written upon his face as he was struck with disbelief in her reply.

"We will not. These Ruins should not be disturbed. Leave these poor souls to rest in their purgatory."

Scott was smiling as he observed this spectacle before him.

"But these ruins hold the very answers to our survival, maybe even the key to unlocking the genetic code that will save us from their flaws. These, like it or not, are our mothers and fathers, aside from that, these ruins are our birth place before The Great Migration into the Kingdoms. We can't just pass up this opportunity to gain this priceless knowledge."

"We respectfully refuse…", she replied standing strong. "We will not betray our King and our Faith. We will wait here until you've finished your unethical work, Sir."

"So be it. I cannot ask you to betray our Kingdom, we won't be long and we will not disturb the dead. We will merely attempt to see if there are any records of the locations the surviving territories could have taken refuge. Would that be suitable, Lady Elizabeth?"

Scott's eyes were thin. Marcus heard the sudden change in tone as well. Charles's hands started to shake.

"Sergeant Knight and I will search for the archives and recover any information about where our enemy could be."

Elizabeth nodded. Victoria and the great Baroness left the group to their toiling and taken position next to their vehicle.

"I hate to agree with the old man…", Marcus started. "But he has a point. In these ruins are the answers. I'm tired of being worried that if I don't drink enough the next day I could be executed to save everyone else around me. If I become sober I'm a danger to everyone, including myself. Maybe, just maybe, we can find…" His fist was clenched in front of him now as he paused for a second. "…What went wrong when we were born and save ourselves. So we can be allowed to love another from a different territory, so we can live without being afraid of our own flaws."

Scott patted Marcus on the back. "I agree with him."

"So be it…", Elizabeth replied sternly. "We will not take part in it either way."

"My Lady?", Victoria said.

"My decision is final."

Elizabeth continued toward their vehicle. Victoria locked eyes with Marcus.

Scott tapped him on the back as he passed him headed to their vehicle. Marcus nodded and followed, looking once more at her gorgeous eyes before she, too, followed her mentor.

Marcus opened the passenger side door, then called to Jess and Charles. "Where will you two be?", he shouted.

"In here, and if we can locate the research facility we are going to search there as well. Is that all, or should I give you status reports every 10 minutes as well, young Trigger?", Charles replied.

"Motherfu-", Marcus said as his face twisted into a snarl. He drew in a heavy breath preparing to explode with anger.

Scott held his hand up attempting to calm the young man.

He turned and looked at Charles dead in the eyes. "Hourly radio checks, location, status, next known position. And especially if you get into contact."

Phillis and Jimmy put on their helmets and mount their bikes.

Charles continued to stare at Scott and Marcus as Jess continued up the stairs.

The power flickered on once again catching the groups' attention.

Everyone was looking around and towards the dome ceiling. The power stayed on this time. The city was alive once more. Street lamps, billboards flashing static and white noise, buildings lighting up, air-raid sirens whirling loudly, and humming from generators. Flocks of griffins took flight from the sudden power surge circling their nests.

"Three hours, and we meet back here. If you're late, whoever has made it back here will search building by building until we find the other group", Charles shouted.

Phillis and Jimmy nodded.

The Gun Walzers slammed their doors. Marcus punched the dash in front of him, leaving an impression of his fist deep into its metal. Scott grinned as he started the beastly machine.

"All in good time my friend."

"That dude is a fucking bitch", Marcus roared.

The Boltiers sped off as well as the Gun Walzers into the city.

Scott looked over at Marcus, "These mother fuckers couldn't drive a carrot up a chimera's ass with a frying pan, you ready?", Scott asked as Marcus laughed hysterically at his weird saying.

"Let's see what you got old man", Marcus replied.

Scott continued laughing and responded, "Let me show you what this young man vehicle can do with old man skills."

Scott dropped a gear and stepped heavily on the accelerator. And the two launched off and disappeared drifting around corners through the city streets. All that was \ heard was the roar of their loud engine and the screeching of their tires echoing through the ruins.

Phillis and Jimmy got to the pond at the edge of the dome to the south rather quickly. Dismounting their bikes, Jimmy ran to the edge of the pond excitedly.

"Phillis!", he said. "Phillis, look there is something in the water."

She crouched next to the young man. The pond was dark and very deep. Large generators and air purifiers jutted out the side of the dome just over the pond. A facility of concrete lined that very wall, thick coils and power lines snaked out of the facility into the depths of the water. A water plant just next to it hummed loudly. The pond ran off into several pools that served as the city's drinking water. Massive propellers could be heard from outside the dome. The large glass, long since clinging to its heavy frame, allowed them to see over the valley even from where they were standing. As Phillis looked closer at the glass she could see almost tinted panels spaced evenly between the panes of glass. Thin wiring running throughout the glass into each one of the panels to a small box at the bottom right corner. Every window had these solar panels. Huge blades passed in and out of view while the turbines worked caught her attention.

The pond was thick with algae. Several piers and platforms worked their way across the calm water. It was teeming with life. Brightly glowing species of fish, eels and jelly fish could be seen in its depths. Left untouched for so long it had thrived without any nurturing or hand from its ancient captors. The water felt warm as she brought her hand to her face to smell it.

Jimmy was petting a small jelly fish that was floating along the surface. He looked at her with a smile of pure wonder. "A child seeing an aquarium for the first time", she thought to herself.

"Alright little guy, you go back to your parents now, I'll try to come back and see you before we have to go."

He stood up and joined Phillis so very proud of his new little friend. Glowing fish surfaced getting ever closer to see what odd land based creatures were peering into their depths. Phillis standing now skirted the circular pond. The algae was gently clawing its way from the edge of the pond forming a thin moss onto the ancient artificial wooden walk ways.

"Its breathtaking, this place", she whispered.

The Boltiers continued their search of the area. The dome drew its power from the windmills, solar panel windows and the pond. Heavy coils lined the walls of the giant ecosystem. There was no telling how deep this aquarium was. But the few feet she could see into not only had coils and couplers drawing energy from this pool, but an intricate formation of coral. It was an artificial ocean, and one that literally was powering this city even still to this day. Lobsters scurried across the docks as the sound of the Gun Walzers roaring engine terrifyingly approached. The two drift buy as the rev limiter cried as Scott pushed the machine to the limits. Jimmy waved as Marcus waved back, they could hear his yelling slightly behind the roar of the powerful engine, and just like that the two were but thick black skid marks on the street.

Once the smoke cleared she turned to find Jimmy kneeled down staring at a lobster. He pointed at the creature about to touch it.

Phillis shook her head. "Those two can't take anything serious."

"Jimmy, don't mess with that."

"Why Phillis, he can't hurt me, he's just a little guy." And if irony wasn't there at the perfect moment every time. Jimmy cried out in sheer pain as he jumped to his feet slinging the rather large lobster into the water.

Phillis laughed as Jimmy was breathing heavily. "Phillis that little guy was strong, I hope he can swim, I didn't mean to throw him into the water."

She laughed even harder as she went over to check his finger. "He will be fine, now let's get out of here."

"Okay, but what was the red little armored creature. I've never seen anything like that."

"I don't really know, but whatever it was, he certainly got the better of you."

A power station hummed as they continued heading east in the great city on foot. Griffins were finally settling back into their trees. Occasionally one would swoop down into the pond and snag a small snack. Jimmy watched with wonder. The two decided to go back mounting their bikes to continue to the eastern most side into the massive green house.

"This is Arrow One, we are headed to the greenhouse on the eastern side."

Static as the radio breaks fills their helmets. "Find anything near the pond?" Charles asks.

"The pond is some sort of power source. The city is still drawing energy from the life forms that have flourished. I've never seen anything like it before. There are species in there that I've only ever heard of."

"Like what?" Charles continued his inquiry.

"Species from the ocean. I've never been so I'm not sure, but Jimmy was petting a pink gelatin mass with tentacles", she replied.

"What else?"

"A moss that felt alive, the water smells of salt. There are snakes with fins in it and fish that glow in the dark. I believe they are from the ocean, or they are just more of our ancestor's experiments."

"Good work", Charles replied. "We are attempting to access their computers currently with little to no success. Will report once we break through their clever security systems."

"Be careful, Mr. Charles, sir", Jimmy replied.

"You as well, young man."

Charles turned back to Jess whom was working with a small thin laptop with cables connected into a large computer tower. The towers sleek in design composed of an intricate of circuitry and sophisticated panels. They LED lights flickering from its hundreds if not thousands of processes clicked and buzzed. Large fans turned slowly above them. Cooling turbines from what Charles could gather. He paced around the many rows as Jess typed away frantically yet deliberately. She looks at her screen and then back at the massive monitor before her as code scrolled down the screen.

"Sir, these firewalls, these ancient systems are baffling. This is going to take some time. We are just not as advanced as they were. Our computers are not nearly as capable as theirs. I'm having a hard time attempting to decrypt all these locks. And some of the encryptions are completely corrupted."

Charles glared at this electronic library. He smiled almost peacefully.

"I have the utmost faith in you, Sergeant. We cannot leave here empty handed. This may be our only chance to unlock the failures of our creators and save our species."

She nodded and continued working.

"This looks good", Scott said.

The two drift to a stop.

Marcus and Scott stepped out of the vehicle. The two looked at each other for a moment and then back to what stood before them. The facility was burnt very badly. Stone and metal had melted into glass and solidified into smooth rivers that lay frozen where they cooled. Some heavily damaged robotic suits lay in the molten metal and rock. Some had been long since scavenged for parts. There were broken tanks around. Some had made it a just few meters before the crews were burned alive. Bullet holes and debris lay in every direction, tarnished and ash covered. Large, heavy fortifications were blown inside out more like cages locking away even worse weapons than the fallen machines before them.

"This is where it started", Marcus exclaimed. As he stood up from squatting, he tossed a casing to the ground.

Scott walked into the graveyard of weapons taking in as much as he could. In his mind's eye, he saw a vision of the battle unfold.

"We'll see what we can find. Maybe a few treasures still lay hidden within these walls. Be mindful, for being one of the centers of creation…" He takes in a heavy smell of the air. "The wild life here is scarce considering the nests throughout the city."

Marcus nodded as Scott continued into the facility.

Phillis and Jimmy stood before the grand garden. It was full of life. Large, brightly colored butterflies floated about. Large bees the size of a small child buzzed from flower to flower. The leaves were as tall as Jimmy. The flowers stood several feet taller than the two Boltiers.

"Phillis, look!", Jimmy spouted excitedly.

"Oh, how pretty Jimmy, lightning bugs."

There were hundreds lighting up the jungle before them.

"Phillis, why are these insects smaller than the ones at home?"

"Probably because they have been trapped in this dome for so long."

"We should let them out, than."

Phillis shook her head. "No Jimmy, I think they are quite happy with where they live now, we should leave them be. But let's go take a look and see if there are any more cute animals in there."

"Okay, Phillis", he replied.

The group had gathered back at the steps of the great hall as it were concluded by the Dragonares. The Old Guard had started cooking and put together a sizable fire. The city was still very well-lit from its returned power. The sirens were now silent. The evening was peaceful. Scott and Marcus were sitting on the steps. Marcus was intently observing Victoria. Phillis was talking with Charles as Jimmy was explaining to Jess what he found over by the pond. Jimmy's exaggerated hand motions and smiles left Jess smiling and giggling quietly as he told his tale.

"Scott?", Phillis called out.

He got up heeding her hand gesture to come over as well as Elizabeth.

Scott turned and pointed at Marcus. "Better go talk to her, before I whoop your ass up and down this shit hole."

And just as unnervingly serious as he was, he was over by Elizabeth, Charles, and Phillis.

"Did you find anything worth reporting?", Charles asked.

"Mostly unsalvageable weapons or what remained of the ancient's weapons. It appeared that the military facility is where this whole city began to meet its end. Whatever the fuck they had in those cages decided to get out. And it destroyed everything within its path. That's for damn sure. By the scorch marks and melting of concrete and steel, more than likely a dragon. There's also traces throughout everywhere we've seen so far, of Chimera tracks."

"What breed of the fearsome beast have you found it to be Gun Walzer?", Elizabeth asked.

Scott looked to the statue. "Like what that beast would leave behind...", he answered, pointing lazily. "I've never seen tracks like the ones in the pavement here. Hopefully it is extinct because it's big as fuck, my Lady. Around each paw print the ground was cracked from sheer weight. Not to mention that there is scorching in front of it where it had dug its claws into the ground. More than likely the particle beam weapons I've heard of. Supposedly there were weapons constructed to defeat these gorgeous creatures, it wouldn't be too farfetched to think that those creatures were designed to possess such weapons themselves. We couldn't find anything other than just traces of creatures, if they were here they were taken long ago when the inhabitants fled from their children", he chuckled to himself.

"And Phillis, anything else from the Gardens?"

She looked over at Jimmy just before she answered. "The plant life here is very old. Everything is much smaller compared to what we are familiar with. The vegetation and insects and animals are from a time long ago. Even in that pond, I have never before seen such creatures. The gelatin mass, the glowing fish, I've been around the forest all my life and never once witnessed a harmony like that. And the city is still drawing power from it somehow."

Elizabeth was stern. However, her curiosity had taken hold. "And you, sir, what did you find in those archives?"

"We were able to find some video logs from the archives, but they are still encrypted. Hopefully Jess can decode them so we can see what actually happened here. These were the latest of the dated entries in the vast amounts of logs and files compiled in those ancient computers."

Scott started sniffing the air, he looked around searching towards the south.

Without warning a loud banging and breaking of steel echoed throughout the dome. A ferocious roar rattled the buildings. Marcus readied his weapon. Scott was quick to his. The Old Guard gripped theirs tightly. Jess had activated the tank and traversed towards the south. Another loud crash. Beams and light fixtures came lose falling in the distance. Every Griffin had taken flight swarming towards the group. Paying them no mind the beasts flew from the dome as fast as they could.

A massive explosion through the ceiling of the dome rumbled through the whole city, debris and plumes of smoke shot in many directions. From the thick clouds two massive dark grey wings flapping slowly as the beast dropped into the dome. The smoke trailed it as it soared towards the west skirting the walls gliding effortlessly. It broke from its path flapping its massive wings once more stopping itself just above a tall skyscraper.

A massive plume of ash and dust picked up violently from the gale of the beasts mighty wings. A building, barely standing as it was, was knocked down by the force of the winds generated as the beast slowed itself. As it landed, the skyscraper nearly gave way, cracking and shattering glass. The tree atop it was smashed and thrown from the building.

"Holy fuck", Scott voiced as they watched the tree crash below.

The beast's underbelly, blue as the sky on a clear day. The dark grey on its back was the color of storm clouds. Its plated scales tightly protecting every inch of its slender gigantic body refracted no light. The beast's horns were short and jutted straight out from its head. Its snout was rounded and short bearing hundreds of razor sharp teeth.

THE FOSSIL FOREST

The dragon roared. The sound of a furnace burning out of control echoed throughout the city.

The power surged.

Lights out.

The sun was setting in the west pulling the few rays of light left.

The beast's eyes glowed bright yellow as it noticed the only visible prey before it.

"A dragon!", Jimmy shouted.

"It's a fuckin dragon", Scott laughed standing carelessly.

Marcus shouted to Jimmy. "I hope this is another one of your friends, Jimmy."

Jimmy all smiles shook his head. "No, but I hope he comes over here to say hi."

"My lady, we must seek shelter, we cannot defeat it", Victoria spoke quietly.

Elizabeth was stricken with awe. She didn't hear Victoria.

Phillis looked at Charles. "You need to get Jess out of there and we need to find somewhere to hide, right now."

Charles was frozen, in shock almost at the sight of this massive beast.

"Scott, bring out the big guns?", Marcus asked overly zealous.

"Dude, we ain't got shit that can stop that motherfucker. I challenge to say it's looking for something, probably us."

Phillis frantically looked around, the only realistic place to hide is the Great Hall behind them. Jimmy was waving attempting to get the dragon's attention. She grabbed him by the shirt and yanked him over.

"Get inside, Jimmy", she scolded.

"But Phillis, he doesn't look mean", he replied.

"Not up for discussion, Jimmy. Go, now. And get Jess too."

"Okay, Phillis", he said.

Marcus was halfway up the stairs as Victoria passed by him. Elizabeth was war gaming in her head as she took memory of all the buildings before her. Marcus watches as Phillis slapped Charles across the face snapping him back into reality. They, too, join Elizabeth that was now headed up towards the massive Great Hall. Scott was taking his time walking up the stairs. He stopped halfway and turned. He glared at the beast, or rather at something clinging to it.

"Do you see it?", Scott asked.

Marcus squinted. "Yeah. That is not part of that dragon at all. That is someone, not something."

"Well, should we greet em?", Scott joked.

"I don't think we have a choice", Marcus replied.

"Where's Jimmy?", Phillis asked.

Everyone looked on as he pulled Jess out of the turret. Suddenly the dragon landed. Its powerful gale blew Jess back inside the turret and Jimmy rolling off into the center piece. Marcus and Scott were knocked to the steps. The dust settled and Marcus and Scott were coughing.

"Holy fuck", Scott said blinking and shielding his face with one hand out lazily.

They could hear its breath rolling like a furnace as it faced them.

"Jimmy!", Phillis yelled drawing her bow.

Elizabeth jumped in blocking her.

"Move!", she said coldly. The look on her face was that of a fierce mother bear protecting her cubs.

"Lady Phillis, do not shoot. Look, Jimmy is fine. They are both fine.

"I think this is all you, dude", Marcus said backing away.

"What?" Scott asked, but he didn't need an answer.

"Not a bad way to go I think", he said as he walked down the steps focused on her.

Her feathering hair was thick and long, black at the roots and abruptly gold at the tips almost reaching the small of her back. Green snake like skin glistening from what little light remain. Thin blue scale spirals circled her shoulders. Rings of blue colored her arms coming to points at the backs of her hands. Thin blue scales like spear points ran from her cheek bones down her face. Several blue scales coming to sharp points clawed upwards from under her neck collar. She reminded him of a viper or, a dragon. Eyes of a burning orange and thin black pupils cut through him. She was the most beautiful creature he had ever seen.

Her body was petite. It reminded him of a fighter. Perky breast, tight core, strong yet feminine. Her military style blue pants snuggly hid her buttocks and legs but left nothing of her shape to imagination. Those form fitting military fatigues were held up under her tight abdomen with a thick leather belt. Her breasts were tightly bound by a black sash under her blue laced revealing t-shirt. Her black plated boots came to mid-calf. Her top fitted perfectly. Her jacket, fitted and hooded with thick fur puffing out of the hood and collar.

"Not a bad death indeed", Scott voiced aloud with a grin upon his scruffy face.

And to his further lusting love of this creature before him, he noticed her tail waving back and forth. Striped blue scales, dark green on the top and a light pink underneath. He was overjoyed. Marcus, however, was ready and waiting. She paid him no mind. Her target was Scott. Phillis and the others merely watched, that is all they could do with the grand beast looking down at Jimmy who was standing in front of Jess now.

"It's going to be alright. This is a good dragon, I can tell."

Jess couldn't believe him. She was pressing against him, her tense demeanor was starting to relax however. All she could do is trust him. And trust him is all she did.

Phillis watched as the dragon laid on the street like a feline. It merely snorted and blew Jimmy and Jess onto their backs, blocking them with its massive arms. Jimmy helps Jess up and turns towards the gorgeous dragon, locking gaze with the beasts glowing eyes.

"You're not here to hurt us, are you, big guy?", Jimmy asked holding out his arms.

The beast leaned down taking a deep breath of the young man. He snorted, and pressed its huge face against Jimmy. Jimmy hugged the beast like they were old friends.

Scott walked down the steps meeting her halfway. She drew a thick blade and swings. The Gun Walzer blocked it carelessly with his large blade. Leaning down getting closer to her face. She was wide eyed and taken back by this odd man before her.

"He looks like a predator cornering his prey", Victoria spouted just loud enough for everyone to here.

"What is she?", Marcus asked.

"She is a Chimera, unlike anything I have ever seen before", Charles answered.

"Is she the one who attacked you, Marcus?" Phillis asked still much focused on Jimmy whom is making friends with the dragon.

"Yes, you can't forget those eyes, she beat the living shit out of me." He laughed, "Hell, she beat the shit out of the big guy too."

The two exchanged blows against their blades like lightning flashes between storm clouds. She jumped dropping a grenade. Scott looked down, chuckling as he kicks it away. He continued down the stairs looking at his horribly chipped blade. He tossed it and pulled his pistol dropping it as well. He tossed two grenades his magazines and another blade to the ground. He pulled his second pistol out tossing it to the ground and then looked at her crouching ready to attack. Her tail impatiently swiping back and forth.

She gently leapt down and walked towards him dropping the only other weapon on her belt. The long slide pistol. She smiled as she got closer. The two clash. Punching and kicking swings and blocks. He was smiling. She was as well. Genuine and unknown, the rest of the group had realized that with Jimmy climbing all of the dragon like a kitten playing on its mother, they decided to start making camp. Jimmy introduced Phillis and Jess to the dragon, Charles merely observed with Elizabeth the two fighting on the other side of the centerpiece.

Marcus drank and sat with Victoria helping her prepare a meal for the rest of their group. The sun had set. Beams of moonlight cut through the broken city dome. Shadows danced around the ruins from the fire as the group prepared to eat. The Dragon Girl and the Gun Walzer continue their bout, heavy thuds of meat against meat, bone against meat, she was punching and kicking and attempting to pummel him. To no avail her attacks were useless. She was starting to realize it too.

Marcus looked over. "They are still at it, I don't know who she is but she is a beast. I'm happy."

"Should we go aid your master?", Victoria asked.

Phillis interrupts, "No, can't you all see?", she asked.

Everyone looked now. The two were dancing around under a beam of moonlight exchanging blows, attempting to bring the other one to the ground and then re-attacking. Heavy breaths, seductively she got close as he does before their arms and legs became into a blur, her always attacking, Scott on the defensive, almost playing with her. They showed no sign of even attempting to hurt one another, merely getting to know each other.

"It's almost like..." Phillis started with a subtle smile.

"They're dancing."

Chapter 8

The Answers Lie Ahead

Laughter filled the night breaking the silence. The two sounded like two lovers laughing at an inside joke. As they grew fatigued from their bout the two stood reading the each other. She looked him up and down, trying as she might to understand him. He sniffed the air as he took in her every scent, locking eyes with her. They charged almost flickering, she had ahold of his neck and he had his hand behind hers.

She was breathing heavily as he was came close to her face. Her snakelike skin glistened in the moonlight. It was as if something had changed between the two. The group stood by in silence observing.

"What's your name goddess?", he asked.

"You tell me yours first, human, now!", she spouted as if she completely decided otherwise about him.

"But, I asked you first", he joked.

"Why didn't you kill me?"

"How could I kill the most beautiful woman I have ever seen?"

She let go, stepping back.

"I'm Princess Suzanna, of the Draken race."

Jimmy was sleeping in the nook of the sleeping great dragon's arm. The night was calm. The rest of the group was sitting around the camp fire. All were staring as she sat next to Scott, she was inspecting the food as Scott devoured his.

"Charles, what is your assessment of the Dragon girl?" Phillis asked.

He glared at the dragon girl as she giggles at Scott choking on his food.

"We can't trust her. She was the one who attacked the Gun Walzers."

Elizabeth and Phillis only nodded but did not reply. Victoria was focused on Marcus who was eating his food very quickly. Jess too, was far more interested in one of the males. Jimmy was sound asleep snoring with the massive beast. She thought to herself, he really does look like a kitten being cradled by his mother as they both slept, breaths in sync.

Phillis observed for a moment, she looked back to Jimmy and the dragon. Turning back, she gave her motherly opinion and soothing voice of reason.

"She has had every chance to kill all of us. She has a dragon, not many even know how to defend against them. I believe she needs our help."

Marcus still eating just looked up replying. "Just ask her." He continued stuffing his face.

Elizabeth nodded. "I second that motion, what was her intention, and why did she decide to let the two Gun Walzers live, when she possessed the upper hand as she does now with such a beast at her disposal."

Charles interrupted, "With the dragon asleep and her having let her guard down, this is as good a chance as any to detain her and bring her back to the kingdom."

Phillis and Marcus burst into laughter. "There's only one person here who could bring that dragon down." She pointed at Scott. "And he is over there acting charming as could be trying to court that young dragon girl."

Everyone looked on. She was right, he was mesmerized by her and she was certainly intrigued by him. The group walked around the fire and all stand in front of her ready to introduce themselves. She stood up. Scott lit a smoke.

Phillis introduced them and they all shake hands. She greeted them all only showing distain for Jess and Charles. Jess walks away taking a plate of food over to Jimmy. The rest had taken a seat next to Scott and the Princess. Phillis was right next to her and then Charles. Marcus on Scott's side along with Victoria and Elizabeth.

"Who's that?", Susanna asked pointing at Jimmy.

"The young man who has taken a liking to your dragon is my underling, Jimmy."

"It's a pleasure to meet all of you", she replied.

"I know all of you have a lot of questions for me. If you would like, I'll start from the beginning. And then, I'll answer any questions you may have."

None of the group had objected to her statement.

"About a month ago, our kingdom was attacked by men dressed in similar clothing as Charles… I think his name was… whatever, they were more heavily armed. They took something from us that is very, very dangerous, and very important. We've been trying to find it, but they were using a type of craft that could hover and take off faster than even our greatest of aircraft and even our dragons. Needless to say, we lost them, they headed north. And while searching we found your Kingdom. We couldn't get close enough to see exactly whom was responsible due to large areas of your kingdom on the eastern and southern sides below smoke from your factories and oil fields."

"What else can you tell us about the attackers?", Phillis asked.

Susanna continued. "They used mechanized warriors from the ancients. They were different, better almost. And the pilots were very experienced. They didn't kill any of our people. They only took our future."

Scott looked at her. "What do you mean your future?"

She pulled a small cellular device out. The screen turned on and showed a picture of her and a young dragon with horns. A gorgeous young lady. Her sister. She quickly closed the screen out and put the phone away.

"She is my sister, my world. And she was taken from me. I aim to get her back at all costs. I need your help. I know you don't owe me anything, but a war is coming if we don't get her back. And it will be far worse than the hatred you brought down upon your own people."

"Betray our own kind for a girl that was kidnapped?" Charles asked, laughing to himself.

"Come to the castle, speak with my father, he will show you that I'm telling you the truth. We have video of when it happened."

Marcus stepped in. "You killed our people."

"No, the fuck I didn't", she replied to everyone's surprise. "Those towers blew up as we were getting ready to knock your door down. Someone else attacked your people and killed them. You think if we wanted to attack you it would be your gates, please. We have dragons, we could easily fuck your whole world up if we wanted, but, we are a peaceful people who just want our princess back."

Scott pondered a moment as the rest of the group present stood in a circle and talked it over. Phillis quieted everyone and walked over in front of her. She was standing now facing Phillis, they are about equal in height.

"We have much to discuss before we could honestly give you our answer, young lady", said Phillis again.

Scott stood up. "I'm going for a walk, let me know whenever you've all decided. In my opinion we should go with her, even if it is a trap at least we will be out of this shithole, when we do die." He chuckles to himself.

As he lit another cigarette and walked away, Susanna stopped him by grabbing his arm. "I'll go with you so your friends can make their decision."

"Okay", he replies.

He looked down. She did as well realizing she had locked arms with him. She pushed him away.

"Alright, let's go", she said and stormed off.

He shrugged grinning and followed.

With a heavy yawn, Jimmy sat up looking around rubbing the sleep from his eyes. He found a plate of food next to him. He looked around to find Jess just making it back to the group around the fire. The young man looked over to the dragon sleeping like a giant cat. Head straight up, eyes closed, but behind those big eyes, dreams keeping the creature almost conscious.

"What a wonderful woman, what do you think sleepy head?" Jimmy asked looking up at his purring friend.

"Sleep well, big guy", he said just before starting to eat.

"Now that Jess has arrived we can begin...", Phillis started. "Simple question, do we believe her or not?"

Jess raised her hand. "Believe what, Elder Phillis?"

Phillis's left eye twitched. "That the reason she infiltrated the Kingdom was to retrieve her sister that was taken by unknown forces from the Dragonare territories."

Jess thought about it for a moment. "Elder, there are not operations being conducted by our forces that I know of. Especially kidnapping a princess from a species we haven't even attempted communications with. If there is, this will be the first I've heard of it. Our territory may have a horrible history among the many territories in our great Kingdom, but starting a war with a species we know nothing of is highly unlikely."

Charles stepped in to add his weight in words. "I agree with Sergeant Knight. We may have done many terrible things in the past I, myself included. However, this is not how we operate. But, there could be benefits to humoring her request."

Scott and Susanna had found a library they decided to walk into. Books upon books were lining the walls on the spiral structure. Computers lining the bottom floor. Chairs and rubbish littered the floor. He was watching her, she was absolutely beautiful to him. He couldn't help, but keep his eyes trained on her, taking in all of her figure. Her tight strong, yet petite body. Her slick and smooth skin called to him, and she caught him looking. Her demeanor changed somewhat, more seductive as she turns towards him leaning on a long table. He stood next to her, leaning against it as well. He flicked his cigarette out the two large blown-in doors.

"So, what kind of gat do you carry?", he asked pointing down to her hip.

"Oh, my pistol?" she drew it twirling it around her index while winking at him. She flipped it around handing it, pistol grip first, to him.

He ejected the magazine, racking the slide, and caught the extracted shell. He placed the shell back into the thick magazine. Tacking aim he dry the-fired the weapon. He was certainly enjoying himself and definitely approved of the weapon. It was written all over his face, and she could see it.

"It's my Military Police 10mm, it's actually a few hundred years old from the ancient Smith and Wesson gun makers. My mother got it for me a few years back from one of her campaigns on a different continent. The Kingdom we live in has been outfitted for recreating many of the old worlds' technologies and comforts, we are pretty far advanced compared to you silly beasts."

He chuckled. "Oh yeah? Either way, this thing is bad ass princess", he said.

He loaded the weapon changing the slide over the top in a way that she was even somewhat impressed by. He spun the weapon around catching the long slide handing her the weapon. She took it and holstered the weapon. He pulled his out and handed her two. One, his under barrel auto revolver and his 2111. She was excited. She, with some difficulty, pulled the slide back on the 2111 to ensure the weapon was chambered. She took one look down the sights that glowed green in the dark. She handed it back and started inspecting his odd revolver. Its rounded grip was large in her small hands. The revolver was very heavy. The harmer large and the cylinder uncut. The weapon was very worn and used, but smooth beyond all belief.

"The revolver is a .454 cassul, very old bullet, even well before the fall of mankind. She has a twin but I left her in my bag at camp. The 2111 is…"

"Do not insult my intelligence I know what it is. Not bad for a remake, haven't changed the design at all from its predecessor."

He smiled. "You know your weapons."

"Of course I do, dummy, I'm more than just a princess, you know?"

Her tail was shaking, almost vibrating with excitement. She was now walking around in front of him picking it up into her aim. He was staring.

"What?" she said sticking her tongue out winking at him.

"Nothing", he said.

She tossed his pistols back to him.

Her smiles kept his gaze trained as he holstered his weapons fluidly, without thought.

"So yes, moving onward." He says as her gaze cut through him.

"Wait, where are you going?", she asked as he walks around the library.

"Ah, here it is", he said after searching through the many old shelves of almost forgotten treasures.

"Here what is, you know you're not making any sense. Are you retarded?", she asked in a condescending tone.

"Quite the opposite, princess", he said as he pulled a black book from the shelf.

"This", he said turning and showing the cover to her.

She read the title allowed. "*Mobile Assault and Defense Project*, sub-project to *The Forced Evolutionary Genetics Program*."

He cracked it open, pulling a light from his pocket. Then he clicked the button located on the battery cap once and placed it onto the shelf behind him and opened the book. The spine cracked and popped, dust and pieces of paper fell from it.

"Ah, fuck. Oh well, whatever." he spouted continuing to read.

"What is this?", she asked.

"Long forgotten answers to many kinds of long forgotten questions."

"That tells me nothing", she replied.

He chuckled. "It's probably the one book that holds all the answers to what I want to know about why we failed so miserably. Why I have to drink to maintain sanity, why all of us have serious problems that inevitably will kill us. And this is it, maybe from it we can find a way to save ourselves from the failures of our ancestors."

She placed a hand on his arm. "Maybe, you were never meant to know."

His eyes slid over meeting hers. "Maybe, but I'm not going to miss my chance to find out, especially with such treasures still intact... somehow, this place has to be a couple hundred years old." He paused for a second, then continued reading.

Scott's radio in his back pocket started beeping. He pulled the simple device out. The Princess looked at it attempting to hold back a burst of laughter.

"What?", he asked cranking a knob on the top.

"That is hilarious, is that how you communicate?" she let it go, her laughter filled the library.

He shook his head.

"What's up bud?" he asked.

Static. "Come back man, they finally made a decision."

"You know, either way, we were going", Scott replied.

"I know man... you've been-" Scott turned the radio off and stuck it back into his pocket.

"You didn't let him finish", she said.

"Come on, let's go." He said taking her hand and tossing the book, quickly making their way out of the library.

"What about your book?" she asked.

"It's worthless, talking about the mobile destroyers from the old days, those machines quit running a long time ago. They are just cities that look like giant dead spiders."

The Princess was standing next to Scott.

The group to include Jimmy was all standing in a half moon around her.

Phillis stepped forward. "We will go and meet with the King, when do we leave?"

She smiled.

"In the morning."

The night was calm. No wind due to the dome and thick forest all around. However, they could hear the hollow subtly calling to the dead city from outside the city. Scott was sitting by the embers smoking and drinking. Everyone was sleeping. Jimmy on the arm of the Dragon. Susana on the grand beasts head. The Old Guard in their luxurious tent. The Boltiers in the sleeping bags. Marcus on the hood of their vehicle, and the Dragonares taking turns scanning in their tank.

Marcus randomly woke up thrashing about. Scott leaning his rifle against his shoulder sitting just off the edge of the great centerpiece. Marcus slid off the hood lazily and stumbled over to his mentor.

"You good, bud?" Scott asked.

Marcus sat and grunted taking a swig from his flask. He lit a smoke and joined in on the watch.

"I've been thinking", Marcus said aloud.

Scott grinned. "Do tell, my friend."

"Charles acts like an asshole, because there are so many intelligent people around him able to make decisions faster than he can. He isn't used to having soldiers who can think so he doesn't know what to do. He seems like a good guy, under all that discipline and rank, he seems like a normal guy. I know you have your own opinion of him, because of the war, but maybe he's a good guy after all, you know?"

Scott's eyes slid over, gazing into the darkness of the city. "Possibly, but he could just be an asshole."

They both laughed.

"Why did you play with her so long?" Marcus asked.

"Who?"

"Her."

Scott let out a hefty cloud of smoke. "I wanted to get to know her. She is passionate, an explosive waiting to burn down a city. She is the most beautiful thing I've ever laid eyes on. I don't understand her, she is a paradox to me. Like a devil seeing a goddess for the first time. Like the wind meeting fire for the first time. She hides a lot of pain behind her eyes. Yet… somehow she shows a strength I've never witnessed save for the battlefield."

Marcus took a drag.

"That…" Scott continues. "and… I really wanna know what she tastes like."

Marcus laughed, and replied with his mentors' favorite line. "As you should."

"As I should", Scott smiled.

Marcus could hear the longing in his voice.

"You handsome devil, you, you really like her don't you?"

Scott sighed. "Yes, I do so very much. If she'll have me, now that is the question."

"So, what are we doing now?" Marcus asked.

"How do you mean?" Scott replied.

"What is our mission here, now, because it has changed. It's not about bringing her in. I believe her story. I think she is telling the truth."

"We…", Scott let out another thick cloud of smoke. "Are probably starting the next greatest war of the century, my friend… I just hope I'm there to see you suffer the weight in its worth for the price you will pay to become a true Gun Walzer. For you to know what it's like to be the worst you could ever become for but moment."

"One day, you old bastard."

The two chuckled and carried on into the morning.

Chapter 9

They Wouldn't Do That

"Where is Scott?", Susanna asked.

Phillis looked around. "I think they said something about going back to the armory they found yesterday."

"When will he be back?", she demanded.

"There's a lot of unexplored areas. It might be a little while, but they did leave early."

She was impatient and didn't care for Phillis's answers. "I'm going to go look for him."

"Whoa, hold on young lady", Phillis started. "Stay and talk to me, they will be fine and probably already on their way back."

Susana was still showing signs of being annoyed. "Okay", she replied.

"How old are you, dear?", Phillis asked.

"27 calendar years."

"You are only a year younger than he is."

She crossed her arms. "Really?", she asked leaning against Phillis's bike.

"Yes, you fancy him, don't you?"

"What?", she asked becoming flustered. "No, no, no, he just intrigues me is all."

Phillis laughed. "If that's what you call it."

The dragon perked up, looking towards the entrance where the group had initially entered the city. Jimmy was jarred awake.

"Good morning everyone", Jimmy said yawning and sliding off the beast to stretch himself.

Susanna and Phillis both searched for the origin of a slight creaking and rumble. The feint smell of carbon dioxide filled the air. The squeaking of a heavy track pad needed oil and road testing. Elizabeth, Charles, Jess, Victoria all stood by with Phillis and Susanna. Looking off into the distance, the sound of engines grew louder. And they were traveling fast now. Whatever it was, it was headed straight for them, up the route that the Old Guard and the Dragonares had taken.

"Expecting company?", Susanna asked.

"Not from the kingdom. Could they be looking for you perhaps, Princess?", Phillis replied.

"No, my Kingdom knows exactly why I'm here."

Everyone looks around. "The Gun Walzers!", Charles yelled.

Victoria instantly denied it. "Impossible! They will be right back. This is not their treachery."

"If it isn't, they sure fooled all of you."

"You don't know that for sure, Charles", Phillis interjected.

"They are nowhere to be found whenever we face real problems. You ever notice that?", he asked walking towards his tank.

Elizabeth stood in his way.

"Out of my way, Knight!", he yelled.

"I smell treachery." Elizabeth said drawing her long sword and pointing it at Charles.

Jess picked her weapon up. Jimmy was standing on the dragon's head now, looking out. shielding his eyes from the sun.

"They look an awful lot like the broken tanks here guys. I don't think they're our friends. We should probably leave!", he shouted. The dragon sat down.

"They are not our men and this isn't our doing", Charles replied waving his hands in the air carelessly.

Jess, still training her weapon on Elizabeth, answered. "Baroness, he isn't lying. We haven't reported anything to higher of our findings or current location since our communications with Headquarters stopped."

Victoria had her spear ready to thrust forward into Jess. Jimmy, coming from out of nowhere, appeared in between Victoria and Jess. He slowly moved into Jess's view with his hands up.

"This isn't going to solve anything. We need to be getting ready to go and defend ourselves from those scary guys down there."

Jess started to let her guard down. Suddenly realizing it, she picked her weapon back up pointed at Elizabeth's head. "You need to get out of the way, Jimmy!", she roared.

"No", he said, now holding his arms out, standing between Jess and Elizabeth. "I'll get out of the way when you all can start acting like adults again."

Suddenly, the group was distracted. They lowered their weapons as the whistling sound grew louder. Charles and Jess got down. The Old Guard picked their shields up. Jimmy turned blankly and looked at the sky. Phillis yelled to him.

"Get down, Jimmy!"

The corner of a building down the street a little way exploded. The Dragon, without hesitation grabbed Susanna and took flight. The group jumped to their feet, searching for the culprit. The machine possessed camouflage that mirrored the woods and lush life of the forest floor. The massive tank was much larger than Charles and Jess's, very sleek and simple. Its heavy tracks tore up the paved roads and crushed cars as it clunked and chugged up the street towards them.

Susanna was looking down from the Dragon as she soared over head to get a better look at the forces in the city. The tank had several outer pods and two large barrels. Two remote weapon systems sat on top with Gatling style machine guns jutting out from them. As she passed over, one of the guns sprung alive and started firing a volley of machine gun fire. The two broke away flying as fast as the beast could go strafing as the rounds chased them.

"Winston, kill them!" Susanna said patting the side of the beast's neck.

The two banked. The beast roared horrifically as it flew lower for the attack. The sound of a massive furnace echoed throughout the city as the beasts charged its fire. The group, watching this spectacle before them, quickly ran into the government building to observe from a safer place. Gun fire from the other automated weapon started firing at the entrance, chewing up the concrete.

"What are we going to do?", Jess asked.

"I don't know who they are but that tank is definitely something from the ancient technologies. Who could have built such a thing?", Charles asked.

Gun fire rattled off the stone walls in slow bursts.

Jimmy was looking out a window very careful not to expose any of himself from the second floor.

"They are soldiers. All their uniforms match, but they don't have any territory colors on their shoulders", Jimmy yelled down.

A horrifying sound of wind thrashing and thunder rolling spouted from the beast's mouth as the city streets were set ablaze. The vehicles behind the tank were melted to the ground. The foot soldiers walking in between them didn't even have enough time to scream before they became piles of ash. Winston and Susanna soared around the top of the dome for another attack. A tank emerged from the fire with missiles firing from both rectangular pods in the back. The hissing from the rocket engines burned and soared propelling the warheads through the air. Winston quickly banked and flapped his great wings. The gusts of wind knocked a building down and a few missiles from the sky.

"Phillis, I'm going to help Winston and Susanna!"

Phillis stepped out firing an arrow into the track of the tank as it continued to roll towards them. "Be careful, Jimmy", she yelled.

Jimmy leapt from the entrance just as Phillis stepped out to fire another arrow. The bolt struck through the heavy bullet proof glass from the large control center of the tank. The crew inside frantically looked at each other and then back at the arrow sticking inside their supposedly impenetrable glass. One of the drivers hit a button, activating a heavy metal shield that slide up from the turret. The gunner, sitting in an elevated chair with screens and joysticks, panels and switches all around took aim.

Phillis turned back to Jess and Charles. "They are getting closer. See if you two can slow them down."

"With what, all we have is pistols and rifles, our heavy guns are on the tank", he replied sarcastically.

"Where are those two foolish, Neanderthals?", Victoria asked.

"They will be here soon, just wait a little longer!", Phillis answered.

She stepped out sending another arrow straight and true, into the thick glass stopping the shudders from closing. Jess popped out just behind her firing a volley of heavy fire at troops dismounting from the sides and back of the massive tank fortress. Phillis stepped back in pulling Jess with her.

"Get down!", Phillis yelled.

The heavy barrel fired, kicking up dust and ash. Debris was thrashed up from the concussion, the round ripped through the corner of the government building, exploding as it whirled and screamed into a small building behind it. Phillis looked out observing Susanna and her dragon skirting the side of the dome being chased by now falling missiles. Small explosions littered the city as the missiles sputtered out and fell.

Phillis popped back out firing another arrow into the window of the tank. It almost went all the way through. The driver let out a scream flinching wildly before realizing he was still in fact, alive. Phillis again stepped up out firing another arrow sticking a sprinting soldier to the tank. The body hung lifelessly as the rest of the soldiers became even more frantic with their movements to cover. Jess stepped out just behind her firing bursts as the men continued moving across the street. She pulled back in and ran upstairs to the second floor. Firing another burst of accurate fire killing a few of them. The soldiers noticed her and fired into the window. She was already moving to the third floor onto a large balcony. She poked her head out taking in the small battle field.

Another tank had moved from the entrance of the city in order to engage Susanna and Winston as they attacked the soldiers seeking cover in buildings just inside the dome. The beast set a building on fire with a thick superheated beam. The tank, sister to the one near the rest of the group, fired off more rockets and missiles. Winston pressed off another building and took flight once more.

Jess tossed a grenade on top of several soldiers crouched behind a vehicle. The grenade exploded just above them pelting the soldiers with shrapnel, killing a few, knocking some out, and wounding the rest. She followed her attack up with more machinegun fire killing the rest of the disoriented and badly wounded men. She moved back inside the building once more. The machine guns continued to fire as the tank let another round firing off into the building. The building was extremely fortified. The round exploded against its thick walls only scorching the outside and cracking the side slightly.

A squad of the unknown soldiers cleared from the streets into a road way leading towards the rear of the building. Phillis had observed this and immediately barked orders to Elizabeth and Victoria to guard the rear entrance.

Jimmy stealthily made his way outside onto a tall building overlooking much of the area around the shelf the government building resided on. He pulled a small cylinder from a pouch on his belt. Locking it into the front of an arrow he took aim, drawing his bow string as far back as he could. Susanna and Winston were flying away from a missile that has proved to be relentless in pursuit. It was only gaining on them.

"Come on, they need my help!", Jimmy said aloud as he let it fly. The dust and ash blew away from him as the bow thwacked forward.

The arrow soared through the air, straight and true. The bolt screamed and whistled as it disappeared into the distance.

"Come on", he said again.

The missile exploded. The arrow had hit its mark. Jimmy jumped for joy. "I got it!", he exclaimed.

"Nice shot, Jimmy", Marcus said.

Scott was standing next to him on top of a building watching the whole ordeal. They could see the tank firing on the government building as well as the fires burning near the entrance. Scott picked up a long slender tube with one pistol grip and two hard sights.

"Shoot that mother fucker", Scott said.

"Who?", Marcus asked.

"Are you serious?", Scott barked. "The mother fuckin' tank, dude."

"Ah." Marcus says. He took aim and pulled the trigger.

Nothing happened. Just a metallic click. Scott pulled his fingers out of his ears and looked at Marcus who pulled it off his shoulder.

"What the hell?", Scott asked.

Just before Marcus could set it down, the missile fired off. Marcus and Scott were wide-eyed slowly turning their heads towards where the wild explosive was flying. It was sputtering and putting along. Losing flight, then kicking back up and firing off. It spiraled and flipped completely over shooting the tank. It gave one more spurt of propulsion shooting off to the left. The explosion blew out the side of the dome, knocking down building after building setting fire to everything around it. Debris shot in all directions. Part of the dome was completely removed, sent off into the sky. The blast sent dust throughout the whole city and debris in every direction. A mushroom cloud slowly rose into the sky.

"What the fuck was that?" Marcus asked Scott.

"Fuck if I know, it had a dot and three oddly shaped petals on it, like a shitty flower."

"Oh, my fuck!", Marcus spouted as they stood there in awe at the damage that weapon had caused.

"Got any more of 'em?", Marcus asked with a huge smile on his face.

"That was the only one I could find. Did you find anything?" Scott asked.

"Nothing. Everything was all melted and burnt to a crisp", Marcus replied.

Scott lit a smoke. "Well, my friend, let's go fuck someone in the face with a rifle."

Scott and Marcus leapt off the two-story building. Marcus fell into a pipe jutting out of the side of the building. A loud clang rung out and his voicing of discomfort, he smashed into a pile rubbish. Moments later he came crawling out, grunting to his feet. Scott laughed as he opened his door. The two got into the vehicle, popped caps off their bottles of beer, clanking the bottles together, then finishing off the whole bottle each. Scott started the engine and threw it into gear.

"By bullet and blade my friend, the Black Dog will find us worth our weight in lead."

"As he should", Marcus replied.

"As he should", Scott growled.

Soldiers on top one of the buildings near the massive opening in the dome were frantically setting up communications. Winston the Dragon landed by latching onto the building. They looked up in horror as the beast inhaled. Susanna looked down on them without remorse. "Kill them!", she said coldly. Winston fired down through the building. The building blew out floor by floor. The beast leapt back taking flight slowly as the building crumbled and burned. A dust cloud was finally starting to clear from the rest of the city. The valley winds were blowing through the massive opening in the city dome.

Jimmy made his way from building to building several blocks from the government building. Susanna and Winston fly by overhead. He yelled out. Both her, and the dragon looked at the young man waving his arms at them. She patted the beasts head, and without word the beasts' swings around to grab up young Jimmy.

He ran and leaped as high as he could. Winston caught the young man perfectly with his large hands.

"Wooooo!", Jimmy yelled at in excitement as the city flies beneath him.

"We are coming!", Jimmy called out.

The three quickly approached the tank overhead. The tank was now adjacent to the entrance of the building, its turret pointed into the entrance. Suddenly Phillis and the group heard someone yelling. Jimmy was cheering as two bolts slammed into the barrel blocking the heavy cannon from firing. The tank fired. The top of the turret exploded, the barrels peeling open like a banana. Soldiers started spilling out of the back of the vehicle in utter fear. Some were smoldering, some were on fire.

Screams and cries came from the men as they ran from the burning tank. Susanna and Winston carried Jimmy back. Stopping dead with a massive flap of Winston's wings throwing strong gusts of wind down the street and blowing out the tanks fire, he set Jimmy down gently. He looked over the side of the building. Soldiers were fleeing down the street. He let the tension out of his bow and put his arrow back into his quiver.

"Where the hell are those traitors at?", Charles yelled tossing a grenade down the hallway of the back entrance into the government building. The grenade exploded and collapsed the ceiling onto the soldiers that have made it in so far.

Marcus and Scott slid down the street slamming into the center piece. The two got out of their vehicles totting their main weapons with them as they walked past the smoldering tank. The group had come to the mouth of the horribly shot up entrance. They all watched casually the two strolled down the street. Scott slightly swaying back and forth and Marcus with a serious look on his face.

Jimmy waved at Phillis from on top of the building. "Hi Phillis!", he shouted waving at her.

She returned the wave.

A soldier hopped up out of cover taking aim. Marcus shot the man in the face without even looking down his sights. The two looked at each other and then back down the street. The two continued walking cigarettes hanging out of their mouths.

"Bout time those lowly dogs showed their faces, just in time to clean up the mess as per usual", Charles barked.

Marcus sprinted off sliding to a stop into a vehicle one soldier was kneeling behind. The soldier stood up attempting to fire. Marcus shot him up through his chin. His helmet flew into the air as the body slumped to the ground, blood splattering from the massive whole in his head. Another soldier across the street watched in horror as his friend was killed. Marcus lazily took aim killing the soldier with his pistol. The soldier slumped backwards. A grenade flew into his peripheral. Without a second thought, he swatted the explosive back. It skipped down the street detonating next to a car.

A soldier yelled out. "Mass your fires, flank them!"

Immediately the machine gun fire picked up down the street. Marcus rolled further behind the car to the other side of its wheels. The bullets slowly chewed through the weak material of the vehicle. He swapped his magazine out for a full one and checked his long rifle. He sprinted firing so fast it killed all the three men firing automatic weapons at him before they could blink. A dust trail leading to his cover was all they saw. The firing picked up again. Marcus sprinted with blinding speed firing his horrifically accurate rifle with one hand, killing two more men. A grenade fell behind that piece of cover perfectly. The explosion killed another two that were cowering next to the previously deceased.

Marcus continued pushing down the street. Soldiers busted out of a building behind him. He paid them no mind. He continued his movement down the street ferociously firing with deadly accuracy and unmatched speed. Smoke grenades fell behind Marcus completely obscuring the view from the soldiers attempting to chase him. The soldiers all stopped and got back behind cover. From the thick cloud of smoke something was dragging the smoke with it.

They all turned looking back towards the government building. Then back towards the smoke. Scott stomped one of the men into the rubble crushing the soldiers' helmet, killing him instantly. Another soldier turned pulling the trigger wildly. Scott caught the rifle effortlessly. Ripping it from the soldier's hands, letting it go spinning like a boomerang, it smashes into an unsuspecting soldier behind cover across the street. He struck the soldier that was still kneeling in shock before him upside his head. A loud crunch and the soldier slid, rolling to a stop into the middle of the street. He, too, was killed instantly by Scotts attack.

Scott was already within arm's reach of the other soldiers. They didn't stand a chance, the Gunrbinger didn't even waste his bullets. He cut them apart with his horribly chipped blade. The inside of their thighs, armpits, necks, he didn't kill any of them quickly. He just let them bleed out. And just as he had manifested the Gun Walzer faded into the smoke. His laughter could be heard as screams came from the city crying out in absolute agony just before they died.

Scott walked out of the smoke methodically down the street. Marcus flew over him upside down. Marcus fired with his pistol and his rifle killing a man running down the alley way and one behind rubble. "Fall back!" A soldier shouted. Machine gun fire picked up from an intersection as Marcus landed in the middle of the street. He leaped into the air spinning. He fired in all directions, headshots dispatched all of the remaining soldiers, quieting the frantic fire.

Scott was surrounded as he stood lighting his cigarette. The poor fools! They thought they had him dead to rights. However, they weren't prepared for what he was about to do. Scott flickered. Smoke trails follow where his barrels were pointed when they fired. He shot all except for one in their chests. Their bodies tumbled away. Before the soldier right in front of him could pull the trigger, Scott had kicked him under his jaw straight into the air. Scott holstered his revolver and reloaded his 2111 and fired. The blast blew the head off the soldier right before he hit the ground. Scott holstered that pistol before continuing down the street.

"Could you see his movements?", Elizabeth asked.

"Barely, his Ghost Touch is the fastest I've ever seen", Phillis answered.

"Phillis, what is Ghost Touch?", Jimmy asked.

"It's their form of martial arts named simply for their innate ability to utilize their guns and physical attacks with such speed and accuracy. It's as if they were never there."

The group averted their attention from her back to the Gun Walzers clearing the rest of the street out. Victoria let out a sigh of relief. Jess was amazed. Charles was impressed. Jimmy watched in almost horror. Elizabeth had a look of approval on her face.

"I wager, they are not allies with these cowardly soldiers", Victoria joked.

Another unfortunate group of soldiers thinking they had the drop on Marcus this time presented themselves around a corner of a building, ready to fire a rocket munition. Marcus turned, the soldiers fired, he blurred his weapon batting it into the warhead knocking it up into the air. It spiraled out of control, exploding into the face of a building behind him. He sprinted towards the shocked and stunned soldiers. Head butting one, his neck exploded from the impact. He had another by the neck, choke slamming the man into the street. His lifeless body bounced into the air, Marcus fired his heavy rifle killing the third without ever looking at the poor man.

Several observing this, dropping their weapons they started running away. Scott was standing in the middle of the street as Marcus was standing next to him now. The men were running for dear life, some stumbling through the rubbish of the streets. Marcus takes aim with both hands with his rifle, he fires killing one, two, three, and just before the last Scotts arm burred and comically chopped Marcus rifle. His shot was then thrown off from Scott's interruption. The bullet ripped through the soldiers' lower back paralyzing him.

"Go get him!", Scott said.

Scott turned to find a soldier running at him yelling. Marcus paid no attention. The soldier had a belt of grenades across his chest and two in his hands, the spoons flying off. Scott grinned. He crouched into a ready sprinting stance, he then blurred before coming to a sliding stop. The soldier was soaring through the air from Scott's blinding palm strike to the stomach. The grenades were let go. As the soldier flew from Scott, his arms blurred once more as he drew his pistols firing rapidly empting both weapons. The soldier was cut apart. His limbs were separated from the hail bullets. His face was torn apart and brain mater splattered across the pavement. The body bounced into a bloody mess as his limbs landed with wet thuds.

Scott laughed to himself reloading his pistols with unequaled muscle memory. The two grenades exploded on both sides of the street. The group watched as the two finally walk up, Marcus dragging the soldier by his leg up the street. Susanna landed with Winston tearing down another portion of a building. She dismounted. Marcus tossed the unfortunate soldier against the steps of government building. Blood slowly pouring from the large hole through his abdomen.

Susanna and Phillis walked over to Scott who was sitting on the edge of the memorial. Marcus drew his pistol and put it in the soldier's mouth. The soldier struggled as he might but could not break the grip of Marcus from his hair.

"Is everyone alright?", Scott asked.

Susanna nodded. Phillis replied. "Yes-"

Phillis was interrupted by Charles.

"Where were you two? Gallivanting around this old city while we were under attack? I have half a mind to kill you right here and now-"

Charles stopped dead as Scott's eyes met his. Charles was speechless as he saw in his eyes something evil at that moment. Scott stood up calmly and walked over to Marcus and the others.

"Alright kid..." Scott started. "You got two options..." He knelt and put a cigarette out in the frightened man's face. He let out a muffled cry. Scott lights another cigarette.

"One, we kill you slowly by removing your skin, muscle fibers, then cauterize the wounds and start over on the next limb. Or you answer every question, and we kill you quickly without mutilating your body."

The group all looked at each other trying to keep the horror from showing on their faces from what they just heard.

Scott tapped Marcus on the shoulder, Marcus pulled the weapon out of the man's mouth. The soldier gasped for air as Marcus stood up. He frantically held his wound now. But shock was starting to settle in.

"Let me just pull his arms off", Marcus said impatiently, "He's going to die anyway, all I wanna do is get one arm rip in, that's all, I'm not asking for much."

Scott laughed sinisterly, dark, not one any of the group had heard before. He knelt smacking the horrified soldier several times. "Look at me, look, before I cut your eyes out, pay attention, you have but one chance, lad." He smacked him across the face again. The soldier's nose was bleeding. Scott drew his revolver.

The soldier was shaking. Victoria, Jimmy, Jess, even Elizabeth had walked away. They didn't want any part of this horrible method the Gun Walzers were so known for in acquiring information.

"How… did… you… find…ussssss?" With every word, he poked him in the face with his revolver leaving circular marks.

The soldier opened an eye. His face was starting to bruise, his other eye swollen, he was starting to go into shock. Tears were rolling out of the soldier's eye. Blood started pouring from his wounds. His veins started popping out of his head. The blood stopped as his wound seemed to be sealing up. The soldier started laughing hysterically. He showed what he was holding. A small injector of some kind.

The soldier began to stand up. Scott sighed and looked at Marcus. He immediately stomped the soldier into the steps. Then putting a knee in his chest, he struck the soldier's face two more times. The soldier was unaffected by the powerful blows. He only grinned showing broken teeth and blood against the broken backdrop of pulverized steps. Scott drew his pistol and fired, the round splattered the soldier's head and his body twitched violently. Scott backed away shaking his head.

"That was Madness he used", Marcus murmured.

Scott turned talking out loud walking past the group. "Kinda convenient that they would show up now, considering we just met the princess. Not when we got here no, but once we met her. So, logically, we are being tracked, realistically we are being sold out, so remedy one…" He had made it over to his vehicle and pulled something out and loaded it into his shotgun. He fired into the Dragonares tank, the tank explodes.

"What are you doing?", Charles yelled picking his weapon up.

Scott flickered and knocked away Charles's rifle. His weapon skipped across the concrete. Simultaneously, he tripped Charles onto his back. Scott's strong hand was choking the man as he pressed his revolver into Charles's eye. "Remedy two…", Scott growled.

Phillis stepped behind him. In a flash, Scott had drawn his other pistol aiming at her using his knee now to pin Charles by the neck to the ground. Jimmy drew his bow and aimed at Scott. Marcus was ready to draw but did not move. He only observed. Her hands were up and she did not move. Even though Scott was only looking at Charles.

"I know what you're doing. I understand, but this isn't you, this isn't how we are. Those men even if they came from their territory, they still tried to kill them too. So everyone calm down. Put your weapons down. There's been enough killing for today."

Scott stood up by pushing off Charles's face with his pistol. He then holstered both. Charles quickly scooted away getting to his feet holding the left side of his face.

Scott turned and pointed at him with a knife hand. "You're lucky, her reasoning outweighed my own, you, owe her your life."

Scott was a different person, even to Marcus. His eyes were so very intense it brought chills to everyone's skin. As he passed by Phillis he spoke in a low growl. "That was nothing but reflex. I apologize for taking aim at you."

"I understand. I apologize too for thinking I could stop you, but thank you for not killing him."

Scott continued to his vehicle cracking a bottle open and downing the whole thing before finding another.

Victoria looked at Elizabeth. "My lady, why would they attack us? How can our Kingdom allow this to happen? The King himself sent us on this mission personally."

"I do not possess the answer. However, I vow to find out whom was responsible."

Scott caught everyone's attention as he voiced his theory.

"It was part of the plan from the beginning. We are more than likely being used to get to her castle, but if they stole her in the first place why would they send us out...?" Scott stared momentarily before continuing. "Your castle is even in the same location", Scott said to Susanna.

"But they wouldn't attack their own people like this", Jess spouted.

Scott laughed hysterically. "They wouldn't do that? Of course, they would. They, the powers that be, have done it many times. Send the death squads. Send the men. Go expire this person and that person. They will do the most horrible things to you and your family without a second thought just to get whatever they need to gain. Don't ever forget that. The Kingdom we live in, contrary to popular belief, is certainly just as bad as the very people who created us. Because in the end, they are their children too."

The group was quiet as they took in the Gun Walzers jaded views of their home.

Susanna spoke to everyone. "We leave for my home, in ten minutes."

Chapter 10

Inheritors of the Earth

Scott was leaning against the railing of the airship the group was flying on. Winston was to their starboard side gliding slowly along, flapping only when needed. Jimmy was having the time of his life riding on the back of the beast's neck. Susanna was cleaning her weapon watching Scott. Her tail cat-like, hooked back and forth as it hung off the table she was sitting on. Charles walked over and leaned out looking off into the ocean of clouds.

The sound of propellers filled the air from the old-school sail boat, retrofitted with many outboard rustic propellers and a canvas overhead to provide shade. Another dragon dressed in a mix of tactical gear and knight-like greaves and gauntlets. They steered the massive helm on the upper deck as they carried onward above the clouds.

"You know what this means right?", Charles asked.

"Yeah, we're fucked", Scott laughed, taking a long pull from his flask.

"I understand you and I have a lot of bad history together due to the war. Regardless whether we're enemies…. we are now enemies of the Kingdom. We can never set foot back there again."

Scott glared at him for a moment. He turned leaning over the railing and staring off into the horizon. "Fuck 'em! They tried to kill us. And over what?", Scott replied angrily.

"I couldn't imagine their reasoning. They could have waited until we had left or maybe they thought we were about to betray the Kingdom. It could be any matter of things or maybe that ruin held some mystery in it. Something that some unknown scientist doesn't want anyone to find out", Charles continued.

Scott looked at him. "You're high enough ranking. Tell me exactly what you know about this whole situation. I know you've had to of heard something through your chains. That's how you Dragonares operate, isn't it? Back doors, black mail, information being worth more than a life?", Scott picked sarcastically at Charles.

"You Gun Walzers really are vile creatures. And to answer your question, that is not how we operate."

Scott interrupted him, "No, that's not the question. It was rhetorical. I want to know what you know."

Charles sighed. "Apparently, our people knew about a floating kingdom for a few months now. We picked it up with one of our prototype radar systems. Sent some people to investigate and they found it. Someone high up, possibly even the Princess, our Queen made the decision to move on these beasts. For what reason? Possibly one of the Godless Projects."

Scott laughed. "That's actually a pretty bad ass name. Either way, doesn't matter in the end. They are now our enemies. Unless your Queen, the King's sister decided to go behind her brother's back and send those so-called soldiers to attack us…I doubt he wouldn't know about it. But then again, it was his wife who betrayed him in the beginning. Because of his expired ex-wife that cocksucker has more spies than he does followers."

"Probable. However, we are dealing with something well over our ability to affect. This whole ordeal could bring on another war", Charles replied.

Scott took a pull from his flask. He lit a smoke next with much difficulty due to the wind.

"All I wanna know, is are you going to bury a knife in my back when I turn around?", Scott said standing up facing Charles.

"Not if you don't become sober and try killing everyone around you", Charles replied.

The two shook hands.

"I can respect that", Scott replied with an evil grin split across his face.

"Where are you going?" Charles asks as Scott walks towards Susanna.

Scott turned. "Where the fuck do you think?"

Marcus watched as Scott sat next to Susanna and started up a conversation. She laughed quietly as he pulled out his pistol and started spinning it around. He handed it to her and started looking at her parts scattered around her. Her tail was slightly vibrating. Her long pointed ears perked up. Her long-leafed hair was lightly blowing in the wind.

"Marcus?", Victoria asked shocking him back to what they were doing.

Victoria was on top of their vehicle that was parked and chained down to the long deck of the ship. She handed him a tank of gas, then leaped down herself.

"They said we were going to their home land. According to our scholars, nothing but ruins lie to the south. Where do you think our journey ends?"

"I have no clue, but for some reason, if Scott says we will be fine, then I believe him."

Moments later Victoria and Marcus approached Scott and Susanna.

"How far away is this place?", Scott asked.

"God, do you ever shut up?", she asked looking at Scott with a sarcastic grin.

He glared at her wide-eyed. Marcus and Victoria almost stopped as they observed the two.

"You wanna get your ass beat? I'm not above hitting a woman?", Scott held up his fists.

"Psh, yeah right! I'd love to see you try", she replied.

Scott hopped off the table, standing in front of her. "Come on, round three, you and me."

"Oh please! I don't wanna hurt you in front of your friends", she said putting her weapon together. Winking at him with her tongue out, then quickly laughing, her face went back to its sexy seriousness.

She stood up and walked towards him. He let his guard down as she got closer. "You're cute when you're mad you know that?" She placed her finger on his chest drawing small sensual circles.

"You haven't seen me mad yet", he growled leaning in closer. Marcus and Victoria could see he was leaning in for a kiss.

"That sly bastard", Marcus thought.

"Princess!", the helmsman called.

"What do you want?", she scoffed.

"We're about to dock and received word that your father wants to see you and your guests immediately."

"Yeah, yeah, hurry up and dock this piece of crap!"

"Yes, my lady", the helmsman replied.

The castle was magnificent! Small waterfalls flowed out the side of the lowest of the giant walls. A second level was protected by an inner wall. The stone was crème colored with some covered in moss and others in vines. The castle had three main levels. The center possessed a large tower overlooking the entire Kingdom. The lowest level was the largest with pools and docks for air ships, gardens for food, and grazing pastures for livestock. On one end, there was a small village on a grassy hill. The next level up was more city-like with vendors and shops, markets and libraries, machining shops, manufacturers of all kinds. All the structures had a light crème color to them, the plants and forestry growing all over the kingdom left untouched gave it a wondrous look of ancient beauty.

The top part of the cake-level style Kingdom held the castle with its massive tower in the center and several sky bridges leading into other parts of the multi-towered castle. Its court yard contained a large garden with crystal clear waters teeming with life. A large tree growing from the top tower provided shade for the top two levels of the kingdom. Its long thick branches reached out far. Nests of dragons reside in some of its branches. Many mystical creatures roamed around the plains. Pegasus and Unicorns, Phoenix, Griffins, even a Chimera was running with her young into a forest on the far side of the lowest level of the Kingdom.

The group stood in awe. The Kingdom was anchored to surface by massive cables. It sat floating just in between two mountains. The bottom was covered in vines and roots from the massive tree that provided shade for the entire floating country. The black rock the entire kingdom sits upon was like a top, tapering to a crooked point at the very bottom of the island. Several structures and an intricate network of wooden houses and stairs leading all throughout the cave systems of the core of the floating country.

"This is your kingdom?", Marcus asked in absolute astonishment.

The Princess answered sarcastically. "Duh, where else would you live, on the surface?"

Marcus and Scott laughed. The rest of the group was still observing the sight. The second level of the Kingdom had giant windmills lining all around its tall walls. Their giant wings of the propellers reflecting light from the solar receptors that act as blades. A long walkway jutted out from the middle of the main tower spilling crystal clear water down into the pools of the lowest level. Its pillars supporting it leading straight down the Kingdom. Vehicles driving around, farm equipment running over fields, there was an entire thriving ecosystem working and living upon this magnificent floating island.

The air ship was flying on banks around to the other side of the Kingdom, revealing a heavily equipped military facility. Ranges and motor pools, full of mechanized robotic dolls, four legged tanks, sleek multi-directional flight capability air craft carriers, and ranks upon ranks of soldiers going through their training. The square towers sported anti-aircraft munitions from missile launchers to three and six barreled machine guns all remotely operated. Sophisticated sighting systems attached to the remote weapon systems allowing the users to remain safe in the towers while being able to attack any threat imaginable. Not to mention the exact style of weapon systems jutting from the bottoms of each of the towers to attack anything attempting to assault the island from the ground.

"It's a floating fortress", Charles exclaimed as he observed the impressive armaments. He looked at the Princess. "Why do you, the Princess of your lands fly around in this rickety craft?"

"None of your damn business!", she replied. Scott laughed. She continued. "Because it's quiet, and this particular model is capable of carrying all of your crap."

Jimmy leaned over to Phillis. "She doesn't talk like a Princess. She is mean", he whispered.

Phillis giggled. "It's because she doesn't usually talk to people like us, and doesn't know how. But she has a good heart Jimmy, and she is strong, she is going to have to be if she wishes to have any kind of relationship with that man."

"I still think she could be a little nicer", Jimmy replied.

The ship landed on a large balcony, the propellers still spinning, a ramp sprung out from the side slamming into the stone floor. She dismounted and the group followed.

"What about our effects, your highness?", Victoria asked.

"They will be taken care of. My father is waiting for us in the gardens", Susanna replied.

In the tower, the group spiraled down the red carpeted stairs, carved wood railing and gazed at the hundreds of pictures lining the walls. Finally, the group hit the bottom landing and out a large double doored opening out into a cobble pathway leading towards the main castle tower.

The gardens at the bottom of the castle were surrounded by several clear pools of water. Moss covered trees grew from these beautiful waters. Fish of all kinds swam about along with jellyfish and sharks. Cobbled and wood bridges arched their way through the pools leading to the steps of the Kingdom. Her father, the great King of this floating fortress was standing at the top of the steps conversing with several elders.

She hurried up the stairs and leapt into his arms.

"Sweetie, where have you been? I saw the explosion from here, reports of you being attacked have reached my ears. Are you hurt?"

He sat her down holding her shoulders looking her up and down for injuries.

"I'm fine… and those pilots need to mind their own damn business", she replied.

The King was very tall. His scales sparkled pure white in the light. His eyes were blue like sapphires. His snout was slightly longer with features belonging more to a snake than a dragon. His horns spiraled upwards from the side of his head just above his long pointed ears. His wings draped over his body like a cape. He as very muscular standing at least eight feet tall. His body was human in form. His long, thin tail coming to an arrow head point of black bone like his black sharp claws jutting from his fingertips.

The group all stood at the bottom of the great steps watching the King and his daughter reunited. He realized their presence and walked down the steps to them. The group all bowed except for Charles and Scott who only nodded. The King gestured for them to stand. Scott couldn't stop looking at the tall black horns on his head.

"Is there something wrong, young Gun Walzer?", the King asked Scott.

"No. Your Highness, in fact, I think your horns are quite awesome actually."

The King let out a hissing laugh.

"Welcome to my Kingdom. Come with me", he said.

He walked down around the circular steps with the group following. He led them through an archway of vines and trees tangled together forming a long archway. Blue and black flowers lined the lush ceiling as they were led to another series of pools. Massive lily pads and fresh water life were thriving in the beautiful scenery. Another arching bridge lead the group to a gazebo. Blue roof shingles curved upwards at the corners of the open area. Circular cushioned stone seat surrounded a large stone fire pit. The King sat with his daughter as the group took their seats on the other side of the fire pit.

The garden of trees growing from the gorgeous pools completely darkened out all the light. Only the blue burning lamps hanging from the corner of the gazebo shed any light around the group. Lightning bugs blinked off in the distance. Small splashes of water could be heard from fish eating any insects that dared to land on the water. It was peaceful, almost too peaceful Marcus thought.

"I asked for your company here today for one reason. I need your help."

The group all looked at each other and then back to the King as he continued.

"My daughter has told me much about all of you. And from the reports and our intelligence you are all the best of the best from your respectful territories. Honorable people. Now, she has explained to you why I need your help, however this is my reasoning behind it."

The group leaned forward as the King continued. "We don't want a war."

"And how is us helping going to stop one?", Charles asked.

The King pointed with his finger as he makes his point. "Colonel, I have every right to move my island north of there and obliterate that entire Kingdom until I find my youngest daughter. I will kill every man, woman, and child if I have to. However, that is not the way of my people or how I intend to live the rest of my life with that massacre on my hands. But, if a small team of people from their kingdom, who were sent out into the forest to die, infiltrates and retrieves my daughter and brings her back to me. A lot less of a reason to conduct war, don't you think?"

"Betray our Kingdom to return a kidnapped child, that either way could possibly ignite another war. That sounds unrealistic in stopping anything, in my opinion", Charles replied still pondering how he knew his name.

"You all know your lands, and could easily retrieve her from her captors without killing or injuring people you care for, because if I have to, there will be no lengths I will go to get my baby girl back. But, this isn't a task that will be left unrewarded, if you so choose to accept my offer. You bring her back to me. You will never be betrayed by this Kingdom. That will be in your repayment and will be your home that will ask nothing more of you for as long as you live. And… I will cure your genetic faults. I will keep your body from burning out before its time, Phillis and Jimmy. I will extend your life to the fullest capacity, Baroness Elizabeth and Victoria. I will cure your addictions that will kill you, Charles and Jessica. I will sate your bloodlust and hatred for all human beings, so you may be sober, Marcus. You have my word as King. This I promise you. Succeed or fail, you'll be rewarded for even attempting such a task."

"Your highness, this isn't a decision we can make lightly. That is our home", Phillis replied.

The King stood up and walked over kneeling before the group. All of them stood as the King looked on them all. "They betrayed you all. I know this as we intercepted the transmissions from your territories from your so-called King. This was merely meant to test our fighting capability in the event you ever found us. And you were being tracked the entire way, so that if you betrayed them, they would kill you all. If you don't believe me, you already experienced it in the ruins. That is why Susanna was sent to find you and bring you here."

Scott lit a cigarette. "You all know what I'm going to say. I'm in. We were attacked by someone in our Kingdom whom pulls the strings. We can't go back now even if we wanted to. This sounds like a chance to actually live for once, something worth dying for. I'll help you burn that kingdom to the ground."

The group wasn't surprised at his words. Phillis took the King's hand pulling him up.

"Jimmy and I will as well."

Marcus nodded as the King looked at him.

Elizabeth knelt as well as Victoria.

Jess replied. "I will help you as well. I will not call myself a subject of such a Kingdom that would kidnap children."

Charles sighed shrugging his shoulders. "What the hell!"

The King grabbed all of them with his long strong arms pulling them in for a hug.

"Thank you all! Anything you need will be yours. You name it. Weapons, vehicles, equipment… it is all at your disposal to accomplish this task. I will never be able to repay you. But I will do everything I can to ensure the rest of your lives are spent in bliss."

Victoria and Elizabeth stood.

A voice from the bridge called to the King.

"Sire. Your guests' rooms have been prepared as you have requested." Her young voice echoed through the dark garden.

"Excellent, they will be along shortly."

"Yes, Sire." And then her footsteps faded into the darkness.

"Susanna, take our guests to Dr. Hamel before they are shown to their rooms. Also, to you all, tonight there will be a banquet held in your honor. As customary of our people to celebrate its warriors before you leave for your mission."

"How long do we have to prepare?", Marcus asked.

"I would ask not more than a day. I know your journey has been long and treacherous. However, she has been held for some time. I fear if we wait any longer, she will die in there. And I will destroy that entire Kingdom."

"How do you know she is still alive?", Marcus asked.

"Dr. Hamel will explain everything to you, young Gun Walzer", the King said placing his large hand on Marcus's shoulder.

Susanna stood next to her father. "Please follow me."

The group followed. The King stayed in the garden trying to hold his tears of joy back.

The group is led back across the stone and wood bridges illuminated by blue torches. Out the front of the tall castle entrance, then back the way they had come. Passing the tower, they group ended up outside the inner walls. Marcus looked behind him as the archways of the entrance to that portion of the cast had overgrown walls of vines spilling from them. Marcus looked back as a vehicle was pulled out of stables lining the outside. The bus-like off-road doomsday ride, bright orange sported large mud tires. Its top was open exposing the passengers seating area. Small steps that folded out were dropped by the driver.

A skinny kid appeared wearing a crooked bus driver's hat, a button-up shirt, and combat pants tucked into black military boots.

"My, Lady, your chariot awaits you and your guests."

"Take us to Dr. Hamel's place."

"As you wish my lady", he replied running comically down the aisle to his seat. He threw it in gear as the group took seats throughout the luxurious vehicle.

The large machine spat dirt and they sped off down a cobbled trail. It seemed about 20 minutes or so before they popped out of a thick forest. Just on the other side of a small rocky hill, an old windmill attached to a large mansion of a cottage was spinning. A dome was on the back side with a large telescope jutting from it aiming at the sky.

The group got out of the tall doomsday bus.

"This place looks ancient. Who the hell lives here?", Marcus asked.

Susanna said nothing. She was already on the porch waiting. Scott was standing next to her watching her as she was just waiting patiently. She noticed him looking at her.

"What do you want?", she barked at him.

"Nothing", he replied sinisterly.

The door opened by itself. Scott drew his pistol without thought. Susanna laughed.

"Calm down, nothing is going to pop out and attack you, geez", she said walking in.

The group followed her inside. She walked over to a stairwell closet door and opened it and headed down. The house was massive, well-furnished with many things from centuries ago. The door slammed behind them. A small droid was standing in the corner observing the group as they turned unexpectedly.

They continued down the stairs.

After several minutes, the group came to a landing. The room was pure white with glass sliding doors, florescent lights, and cameras completely changed the setting the group found themselves in. The doors opened and the group followed Susanna in. The doors closed behind them. The room's lights changed to black lights and the group is hit with heavy blasts of air. The doors in front of them unlocked with a heavy hissing nose and slid open.

"What was that?", Jimmy asked.

"Pressurized sterilization chamber. This is a clean room, and due to the Doctor's health, he rarely leaves this basement."

The hallway was dimly lit in yellow as the group passed by incubation chambers of yellow liquid. Murky forms of humanoid entities floating inside sleeping in their amniotic fluids. Some chambers were frozen. Condensation flowing from the chambers like thick mist as the machines hissed and blew pressurized air from tanks in the back. The group came to a large well-lit circular room.

The catwalk led all around the massive warehouse basement. Machines, weapons, ancient technologies in perfect conditions. Large ballast doors were in the far back. An elevated platform with an entire wall sporting one large thin screen with multiple images and camera feeds display. Keyboards lay here and there on desks that curved in a half-moon shape with one rolling chair by itself. A continuous screen bent around atop the moon shaped desk.

An old man in a long white coat hunched over, standing alone, his arms behind his back as he watched a small portion of the large screen displaying an array of mathematical equations. An old flip chalk board

THE FOSSIL FOREST

with unknown equations scribbled across its green back ground, sat behind him. A small robot with four spider-like legs sat next to the Doctor with a screen showing his vitals. Leads and cables run from the small droid under the old man's coat.

"Ah, Princess, what brings you into my laboratory on this fine day?", his cracked yet energetic voice floated to their ears.

"Dr. Hamel. I brought the team from the Kingdom in the north", she replied walking up to the old man giving him a small gentle hug. He didn't avert his eyes from the screen holding out an arm returning the hug.

"Good", he said turning towards them. His spectacles adjusted by themselves. Small optical lenses spun out in order to focus on the group before him.

"I see, two from each of the territories, good. And their decision from the Kings offer?", he asked.

"They have agreed to help", she replied standing next to him.

The old man before them had messy grey hair. A scruffy face, deep lines cutting into his face from the years passed. He wore a cream-colored sweater under his lab coat, a pair of slacks, and rather comfortable looking slippers.

"They would be fools to not agree to such terms that guarantee their futures."

"Who do we have here?", The old man turned and walked closer to the group. The little android followed him closely. "Ah, Phillis, The Breathless Arrow, and Jimmy, her youngling. Both formidable archers from the Boltiers region." They both nodded smiling as he stepping back and looking up as much as he could.

"And my goodness, Lady Elizabeth, the Shield of the North Tower, the greatest swordswoman in all her land. And of course, young Victoria, a Knight of the highest regards. It is an honor to make your acquaintance, my fair Maidens." The two Baronesses bowed their heads.

"The Fire Grapher, Colonel Charles Anderson, and Sergeant Knight, Jessica. Two of the finest Dragonare Elites! Or should I say one of the greatest generals of the Anvil Cross Regime, Charles?" The two did not nod, they merely observed as the old Doctor continued down to Scott.

"Scott Cogwheel, The Smoldering Ghost. That's what your men used to call you if I'm not mistaken. Or was it the Chimera Slayer? You had many names over your time upon the battlefield, didn't you? That was before they forcibly retired you from your position before disbanding that psychotic battalion of murderous soldiers. The Sober Soldier experiments. Unfortunately, your collar ranks and Battalion call sign mirrored a very horrible ancestor. But fitting nonetheless. It was an interesting attempt to fully utilize you Gun Walzers. The King wasn't expecting such results in the end however. In fact, that project worked too well." The old man chuckled to himself.

The group looked at each other.

"How could you possibly know any of that?", Scott asked.

"Dear boy, I've watched many of the remaining humans on this planet for almost a century now. And your kind that survived have always intrigued me. And when your Elder decided to build that efficient unit of sober soldiers, I couldn't help but observe. The last time a unit existed like yours, it was at the height of humanity's scientific might. Around the time they sent the voyages into space to another planet."

Phillis, Charles, and Elizabeth all looked at Scott in disbelief.

"Lady Elizabeth, he can't be him. The Chimera Slayer was said to have been killed by the beast." Victoria whispered.

Jess spoke aloud, not meaning to. "Impossible, how could this drunkard be the one of the most dangerous Gun Walzers to have ever existed?"

"You know the answers to all my questions, don't you?", Scott asked.

"Who?",Susanna asked looking at Scott with even more intrigue.

"My Lady, your friend here has an interesting and long history of death in his background. His element once were considered the most dangerous Gun Walzers to ever exist. They were disbanded due to fear by their own so-called leadership. These men were responsible for the longest recorded fight in history conducted by one element. Hundreds of thousands died at their hands. In little under a decade these beasts destroyed entire generations of unfortunate souls."

"Will you answer my questions, Doctor Hamel?", Scott asked once more.

"And one day, I will. But at this moment…" The old man stuck Marcus in the arm with a small syringe gun.

"What the fuck?", Marcus jumped back drawing his pistol in a blur.

"Calm down young man, I merely want to see how far you and your kind have made it genetically considering you all should have never existed up to this point."

The group looked at each other with confusion written all over their faces.

The old man walked over to his desk pulling the small vial from the gun. He inserted a syringe and extracted some blood from it. He dropped a few droplets of blood into another vial on a stand. He swirled it around looking at it in the light. It turned blue. Then pulling another syringe from his coat pocket, he pushed a few droplets onto two slides and placed them under a microscope.

After peering into the scope, the old man leaned away smiling. "Magnificent, absolutely astonishing! It goes to show that even when melded with, nature always prevails."

The old man started walking down his elevated platform towards an archway. The flooring was glass as well as the rounded ceiling. Reflections of light bending from the water above and below danced around the long hallway. "Follow me, younglings."

The group obeyed. Walking down the glass tube towards another room, the group couldn't take their eyes from the ocean around them. Ancient whales and sharks and large schools of fish, starfish and jelly fish and gigantic squids moving about in perfect harmony. Jimmy couldn't be happier constantly stopping with Jess to gawk at the gorgeous ancient beasts they have never seen.

A large school of dolphins spiral around the tube following the group as they walked behind the old Doctor. His little machine walking by his side. Susanna walked next to him as they passed into the next underground facility built into the bed rock.

More glass walls with habitats among habitats of Chimeras and Dinosaurs of all kinds. It's an arc. This entire facility was an ancient arc of genetic might. Species of insects long extinct, wolves, foxes, elk, buffalo.

"I'm assuming these are all clones", Charles spouted breaking the silence of wonder.

"And you would be right", the Doctor replied. Finally, the group passed into another large room. A library spiraled upwards, housing hundreds of thousands of books and hard drives filled with priceless information. The group stopped at the center of the large circular floor. A desk with a small keyboard on it and a large curved thin screen hanging from the ceiling. A large circular leather couch of Victorian style wood and dark ascents, inviting the group to sit.

The old Doctor gestured for them to take seats as he stood off to the side with Susanna.

"Doris?", he called.

"Yes, Doctor." A beautiful voice answered.

"My dear, could you bring up the video from the night of our Princess's kidnapping?"

The screen clicked on playing a video. "Of course, Doctor. Would you like the edited version pertaining only to the incident?"

"If you would, my Dear", the Doctor replied.

The video continued playing. Outside a large circular balcony. Thin curtains slowly swaying from the cool night's breeze. Suddenly, the wind picked up and a large carrier spun around dropping a ramp as it hovered just over the balcony. Its large embedded propellers whirling constantly adjusting to keep the sleek stealth carrier level. Several men sprint from the loading ramp into the room and then in a blur are back inside the carrier. The ramp quickly retracts closing and the craft fires off out of view of the camera. Suddenly the room explodes and the camera goes black.

"How do you know she was even taken?", Charles asked.

"Glad you asked, you see, how dear King had given his youngest daughter a necklace that also contains a small but very powerful tracking device."

"Doris, show them her trail just before it was no longer traceable."

"Yes, Doctor."

A three-dimensional projector flickered on. The center of the table became a recreated map of the land to scale with near perfect imagery of the land. The lights dimmed. The group watched as the blinking light moved across the top of the Fossil Forest's tree line. It banked Far East and then turned back. The blinking light disappeared just as the craft passes over the castle walls of the group's kingdom.

"You see, we think she is in this building here. Unfortunately, due to the lead lined walls and jamming devices, we were unable to fully penetrate its walls to map out the facility. But we know that it is the most logical location she is being held. More than likely experimented on, we need to retrieve her before she is inevitably expired. And a massacre is brought upon the rest of this Kingdom due to the crimes of few", Doctor Hamel explained.

The image was now of a large rectangular building in a large field far from the Dragonares industrial parks and housing complexes. A stairwell was the only internal imagery the projector could produce.

"We have the ability to get you there without detection, provide you with weapons and equipment even extraction. All we need is your strengths and unemotional attachment to correctly retrieve our dear Princess and divert the King from destroying that entire Kingdom. Everything you need is at your disposal, you have but to ask my younglings."

Marcus stood up, peering hard into the structure. "Jess, or Charles, have you ever seen this facility before?"

Jess leaned forward. "That looks like one of the Elite Special Weapons facilities. Only the highest ranking of Commanders are allowed in this area. Patrols constantly revolve about a kilometer around it. There are many reaction forces about 10 minutes from supporting that facility. I have no idea what is housed inside, but if she is held there…" Jess pointed to the building. "Then we can expect heavy retaliation from the forces assigned to that sector. This will not be easily accomplished without receiving contact from heavy ground and air forces."

Marcus pointed. "You get us on top of it, we will get her out, no question about it."

Charles stood walking around it. "It is probable, however, only a dismounted element could accomplish such a mission, setting up vehicles on the outer walls here…" He pointed towards the forest. "And here…" He pointed to another spot further out. "As a contingency for ground extraction, have the pick-up site here…" He indicated a clearing atop a hill further to the east. "We could, as long as we are able to make the trek on foot to these positions. We could escape before the forces could cut our escape routes off."

The group nodded.

"Sounds like we can do this. So, let's start getting ready", Marcus stood up excitedly.

"Marcus and I will work the weapons piece", Scott stated.

"We will work supplies then", Phillis answered.

"I will work the air portion of the plan with a suitable crew and placement of the extraction points", Charles exclaimed.

"And we will acquire suitable modes of travel", Elizabeth said.

"Alright…" Phillis said clapping her hands together. "Let's prepare."

The Doctor spoke out loud. "Doris, please inform the King to gather the Motor Stable Overseer, the Relic Collectors, and the Admiral of the Docks. Have them meet with our guests immediately in the great hall to go over the plan to rescue our dear princess."

"As you wish, Doctor."

The group was led out of the room by Susanna.

"Scott?", Doctor Hamel called.

"Yes, Doctor?", he replies turning, as does the group to hear what the old Doctor had to say.

"I have but one question before you go?"

Scott gestured for him to continue.

"What is the purpose of a Gun Walzer?"

Scott smiled. "To meet the Black Dog upon the battlefield."

The old Doctor laughed, coughing slightly. "No, my young unranked Grand Master, you are the storm that washes away all before you. So that the Inheritors of the Earth may thrive upon this world without our disease. But I think you already knew that."

"As I should", Scott growled.

Chapter 11

Tell Me A Secret

Evening was starting to settle in as the sun was slowly falling behind the horizon. The group was taken into a large marble spiraling stairwell reaching up the circular tower. A glass elevator reached upwards from the center of the tower. Suspended walkways at each of the glass sliding doors led into the landings where the steps stopped for each floor. The walls were dark blue with golden vines and flowers bordering the bottom and tops of the gorgeous décor. Pictures of ancient artwork from around the world hung at each landing. Small tables with vases full of exotic flowers were at every landing.

A servant girl stepped into the elevator waiting patiently for the group to join her in the large clear cylinder. They all fit into the roomy cylinder without issues. The group was then taken up to the top floor. The doors slid open quietly. The servant girl walked out elegantly. She stopped at a large, tall red door with heavy black hinges and a door handle.

The group was given their own rooms around the circular inner balcony. Each walked in amazed by how gorgeous the furnishings are. Each room contained a large bed draped with thin curtains around its well carved tall bed posts. A long dresser black with gold leafs decorating the corners and handles. A tall oval mirror stands in the center. Another mirror in the corner. The carpet was soft and blue with black spirals of varying sizes all over the room. A giant, spacious bathroom, its bath could fit about ten or so people in it. There were showerheads all around a glass spacious shower with three or four seats jutting from the marble walls. A long mirror covering the entire wall, a blocked off toilet on one corner and elevated sinks with tall curved facets and beautifully designed handles.

Tall doorways led out into a wide, round balcony over-looking the entire Kingdom. Their clothing had been washed and laid out onto their beds. Their gear was hanging on thick silver metal racks with weapons slung almost positioned very similar to a samurai's armor stand. They were left to themselves in the luxurious suites.

Food for them had been wheeled into their rooms on carts. Fruits and vegetables along with sandwiches and small cakes and desserts. Marcus and Scott's carts, however, had many different buckets of wines and brews buried in ice in theirs. Scott took a bucket with him to shower.

Half an hour later, Scott's door opened. Marcus walked in calling for him. "Scott? Where you at, old man?", Marcus sarcastically called.

Scott was sitting on the massive balcony in a large chair with several buckets of water and quite a few empty bottles set to the side. The stone fire pit in front of him was lit burning slowly as the sun was starting to set. His hair was combed to the side, but still somewhat unkempt in its normal good looking way. He had shaven and a cigarette hung from the corner of his mouth.

"Pull up a seat man. Try one of these bad boys. They're good as fuck", he said tossing a bottle to Marcus behind him.

Catching it, Marcus slid a seat over and sat with Scott looking off towards the setting sun.

"Dude, this place is amazing. I feel like a king here. I honestly feel very relaxed for once."

Scott smiled. "Yeah, good man."

"Like we haven't had a real chance to really sit back and enjoy anything. It seems since that night it's been go, go, go. And our guys, they need this as much as we do. I passed by Jimmy in the hallway, him and Jess just got back from walking the gardens. They said there are plants on this island that have been extinct for centuries."

Scott lit another smoke just after he put his other out. "Yeah, the creatures here too. Hell, the dragons! I watched one shit as it was flying up into the tree. It almost took someone down there out. It was fuckin' hilarious."

"Oh my fuck!", Marcus said as they both laughed.

"So how are you doing with all this?", Marcus asked Scott.

"How do you mean, brother?"

"What was it like?"

Scott took a long drag.

"What was what like?"

Marcus lit a cigarette. "Being sober."

Scott laughed. "It was wonderful. Never have I ever been so strong, so fast, so in tune with my weapons. We were unstoppable. Almost impossible feats were nothing but everyday occurrences for us. It was horrible, but the greatest moments of our life."

"What happened to the rest of your element, you never talk about them?", Marcus continued.

"Like me, they were stripped of rank and sent to guard towers or train young and upcoming Gun Walzers. The greatest one of us went to run the Bullet Waltz fields for the Elder. I miss all of them at times..." Scott takes a drink and another drag from his smoke. "It was rough, long days and even longer nights, couldn't carry enough ammo to sustain a gun fight, had to constantly call in resupplies as we all continued pushing forward by means of hand to hand. Got to the point we started carrying multiple main fighting weapons so when we broke them we could draw the next and so on and so forth."

Scott stood as the sun set. Stars were starting to gleam in the distance.

"Never have I seen such strength, violence, hatred, capability of men to conduct war. It was like watching a storm pass over the land erasing every sign of life in one fell swoop."

"Did you really kill a Chimera?", Marcus asked.

Scott laughed. "I had no choice, if I didn't, then we would have more than likely died ourselves. I regret it every day, but if not me than who, you know?"

Scott turned to looking at Marcus. "If not us, than who?"

Marcus shook his head, unable to answer.

"Fuck it, it was a good run. But those cocksuckers that pulled the strings, they couldn't have seized a better opportunity to wield us. A war in the south, send the SS Battalion, they will surely win the war for you. We fought against our own people, the Boltiers and Old Guard had to pull their warriors out because it made no difference to us who we killed. It was everyone in our path", Scott laughed. "But it's over now. So we will let it be where it should stay, in the past. Dead on those battlefields. Where it belongs."

Marcus put his smoke out. "What did he mean?"

"Who?"

"Doctor Hamel…before we left. He said we were the storm that washes over the earth so that the true inheritors could survive. What did he mean?"

"Who knows?", Scott said.

"Come on, don't bullshit me."

Scott glared at Marcus. He walked over sitting back down.

"What do human beings produce that keeps the world in harmony with the rest of the inhabitants from the smallest organism to the vastness of the forests?"

Marcus pondered for a moment.

"Nothing", Scott answered. "We give nothing to the world except for hate, war, and an illusion of self-righteous notion that we think so therefore we deserve to maintain our existence on this planet. We are fairly weak creatures. Up until people like you and I existed. However, animals have fur and claws and teeth designed to hunt and defend themselves. Some of them can survive in the harshest of environments and are immune to certain venoms and toxins. You take away our infrastructure, clothing, weapons, what then? Our bodies can be brought down by a single organism. Because in the end, we were never meant to exist. Insects eating others that destroy a certain percentage of uncontrollable plant, bees carry pollen, bats carry seeds… Every creature exists in order to maintain that fine balance that keeps this world turning. Without them, we could never survive. Mother saw that we were the problem back in the day, and she decided it was time, the forest spread uncontrollably and consumed much of our so called great cities. Then some smart ass mother fucker decided we could beat it, the pollen and disease, they started playing God and then we popped out. Somewhere along the way I believe one of the founding fathers of the genetics program decided they were never meant to exist and helped it along."

"You've looked at the world in such a way, it makes the rest of us look like morons compared to you", Marcus stated with a smile.

"Regardless, my friend. That is what he was referring to. The real secret to our existence was not to be able to survive the harsh world that was taking a swing at the human species… We were designed by the greatest of minds to combat the disease that was killing our dear Mother. Humans, we are the cure. We are the cancer that was changed on a molecular level in a petri dish and placed back into Mother's body to attack the cancer that was killing her."

"Impossible", Marcus replied pausing for a moment. "It's starting to make sense."

"It's merely just a theory. But I'm certain. A man much smarter than I told me on the day I became a Gun Walzer, 'Your soul is only worth the weight in death that follows you onto the endless battlefield. And that one day I would know exactly what he was talking about.' He was right. We only feel when we are on the battlefield. We only understand suffering and hate. And that makes us worth much more than the rest of these worthless humans because we feel we don't deserve that we are the only ones who do. It's because we hate so much that we deserve the purest of love. Everyone hates the Gun Walzers because they could never understand what it means to know that a blades whisper is never sweeter, and a bullet never lies."

Marcus was completely blown away by Scott's words. You could see it all of his face from the dancing light of the fire. "I would expect nothing less from you, you old devil."

"We did this all to ourselves my friend. But the fact that these creatures here offered us sanctuary when our own people threw us out, goes to show you that even after all this time, the powers that be will always be the enemy, always trying to turn the people against each other, always trying to keep their filthy fucking hands clean by forcing others to dirty theirs. They have been playing this game long before us. I just wanna know why now. Why these creatures? And why the fuck did we get the chance to be free for once in our miserable fucking lives?"

Marcus lit another smoke. "Maybe it was just our time."

Scott laughed for a second. "You know… When I watched that beautiful creature's life finally fade from its eyes. I realized at that point that I just killed our Goddess a little more. And it hurt much more than all those souls I tread upon. I never forgave myself for that. I honestly wished that she would have killed me instead."

"Tell me something", Marcus started. "Do you really regret all of it?"

"Yes, every goddamn day, but regardless my friend. I would do it all over again if I had to. With all them, with all of you, and this next thing we are about to do. I think I'm going to take great pleasure in what we are about to suffer."

Marcus looked at his friend. "Why did you never tell me who you were? Why did you keep it a secret?"

Scott laughed. "Because it was supposed to be forgotten, we were never to speak of it again as if it never happened. But that's also the joke of that name, The Smoldering Ghost." Scott let out a hysterical laugh. "Something was there, you know you saw it, come out of the smoke and take with it so many lives and just like that ominous smoke, it faded away as if it was never there at all."

"How did all of you not kill each other when you were sober?", Marcus asked.

"We found that common hatred that kept us going, we hated something more than each other and that was all it took to wield us. And we used it like a gun."

"Did you ever lose control?"

"Some did and we had to expire them. A lot of our own people were killed by us. We had no choice, but there were no emotions in it. Just the reason for our existence at the end of the day. To eradicate, to war, that's all we were ever bred for my friend. To live and die by the bullet and blade."

Marcus was silent.

Scott laughed. "As we should."

Chapter 12

Jimmy's Moment

Jimmy stood in front of a huge mirror attempting, in vain, to tie his bowtie. He sported a black suit with two long tails on his coat with dark blue pants. His coat was buttoned wrong. His hair was slightly messy still and he was beginning to become frustrated.

Laughter down the hallway fast approaching ended right at his door. He quickly threw open the door. To Marcus and Scotts surprise, the poor boy was a mess. The two burst into laughter at his expense. Jimmy, very nervously but demanding all at the same time spoke. "I need your help guys, I can't tie this thing at all."

Marcus and Scott came through the door patting Jimmy on the back.

"Don't worry brother, I got you", Marcus laughing.

Scott sat in a large chair fit for a king and observed the two at the mirror.

Marcus was dressed in a similar coat; however, his trim was a dark shade of blue. His matching vest had pointed wing tips. Scott's suit had a long swallow tail style. All black with green trim and vest to match. His black tie was not a formal bowtie.

"Jimmy, oh Jimmy." Marcus chuckled. "Let's get you ready."

"Oh please, Marcus, I'm so nervous, I've never worn such nice clothes before."

"Why are you nervous, hmmm?", Marcus teased as he fixed Jimmy's tie.

"I have to look my best tonight", The boy exclaimed.

"Why is that? You handsome devil, you." Marcus asked as he buttoned Jimmy's coat properly.

"I want to look my best for Jess. I think I'll ask her to dance. I wonder if she has a boyfriend." Jimmy blurted out nervously.

Marcus and Scott laughed. "You should definitely ask her to dance, buddy", Marcus replied fixing his hair.

"What if she says no?", Jimmy asked.

"Tell this handsome man, no?", Marcus let out a ridiculous laugh.

"Yes", Jimmy responded seriously. "I'm worried that she won't want to dance with me or Charles won't let her."

"You leave Charles to us. He won't be able to keep her from you. And as far as a boyfriend. No. It's safe to say she doesn't, but you can ask her. She won't tell you no, Jimmy."

"How do you know?", Jimmy asked.

"Because no woman in the world could say no to you Jimmy. She will definitely dance with you." Marcus was now behind him sweeping his hands across his shoulders knocking off lint.

"Hell! I would dance with you", Marcus joked. Jimmy gave him a strange look.

"But I don't want to dance with you. I only want to dance with her. I really like her."

Scott let out a hysterical laugh as did Marcus.

"No, Jimmy." Marcus managed to get out through his laughter.

"It was a compliment to you. Kinda like a joke, but you mean it in a good way", Marcus explained.

"So you think she will say yes, then?"

"Yes, Jimmy. I'd bet my weight in gold on you. You are going to be just fine tonight. You have nothing to worry about", Marcus replied.

"Promise?"

"Promise, buddy", Marcus said.

The three handsome men were standing at the bottom of the great spiral staircase just below another massive set of stairs leading into the great hall. They were waiting for the rest of the group to come down. Many people passed behind them into the great hall where music laughter and merriment could be heard every time the massive wooden doors opened.

Scott was smoking a cigarette standing next to Marcus and Jimmy on his right. Marcus was talking to Jimmy trying to calm him down as he was still nervous. A door opened and out of the ground room Charles appeared. He walked down the steps towards them. He looked sharp. His face was shaved, his hair freshly cut and parted in the middle, slicked back into place.

"Look at this old dog", Scott spouted.

He was almost gliding down the stairs towards them. His dark grey matching bottoms and coat, tailless, 6 large black buttons holding it closed. A red bowtie and black shirt protruded from the grey background.

"I find it impressive that they had tailed fine dress attire for the evening in such short notice. Not to mention they had many accommodations designed specifically for each of us in our rooms already."

"Indeed", Scott replied.

"You look very handsome, sir", Jimmy confidently spouted, forgetting his nervousness for a moment.

Charles replied. "Thank you, young man. You look very handsome yourself."

Marcus looked and Scott who returned the confused look.

"Find anything interesting today during your travels around the Castle?", Scott asked.

"The facilities here are astonishing, regardless of their ancient and ruin outer structures, the interior is far superior to anything I've ever seen", Charles started.

"The species is of some kind of dragon-reptile mix of other species and of course, the humanoid genomes that gave much to the physical form. They are our brothers and sisters, but superior in the way that they do not suffer from the same genetic defects as we do. They only evolve and get stronger as their generations continue to exist. Did you find anything during your visit through the city?", Charles finished.

Scott answered. "The people here call themselves Drakens. Real original if you ask me." He chuckled to himself. "Either way, their weapons and aircraft, vehicles and equipment are mainly renewed versions of some of the greatest designs from the ancients. Not to mention this castle is floating by some form of mechanical magnets that push off the planets core. This was originally designed to be a weaponized piece of land that could relocate and take over entire countries, but it was instead used to flee from these people's creators who wanted to kill off all the normal humans left on the world. It has been an interesting day nonetheless."

Charles was nodding. Jimmy could care less. Marcus was waiting for the girls. Scott pulled out an old dented silver flask and takes a pull. He offered it to Marcus. He drank some and then he offered it to Charles.

Charles took a pull and with a heavy sigh and slight cough he handed it back to Scott.

"What is that? It burns like fuel?", Charles asked in a hoarse voice.

"It'll put hair on those old nuts. That's for sure", Scott joked.

Suddenly their laughter was quieted by a door up the stairs opened and shut. The four stood tall next to each other. Jimmy was starting to get nervous again. Scott nudges Marcus and hands him back the flask pointing to Jimmy.

"Oh, Jimmy, here take a swig of this. It will definitely take the edge off."

Jimmy took the flask and looked down. He looked back at all of them who were nodded with huge smiles on their faces.

"Phillis doesn't let me drink. She says I'm a handful."

Marcus looked back at Scott and they both start laughing.

"It will be fine for tonight. Hurry up before Phillis gets down here", Marcus said.

Jimmy held up the flask to all of them. "To my new friends…and to a night we'll never forget."

Jimmy hesitated for a moment. He inhaled deeply then took a huge pull from the flask. His face twisted into pure bitterness.

The guys let out a small cheer. Marcus patted him on the back. Scott grabbed the flask and took another swig before putting it away. Then the girls caught their attention.

"I see you all are getting along just fine. And here we were worried you'd all be fighting", Phillis joked as she ran her hand down the marble railing. Her red, strapless dress sparkled slightly, a long slit in the bottoms revealing her strong legs as she almost floated down the stairs. She got to the bottom of the stairs and did a spin. All the men were amazed. Her dress had no backing, revealing her muscular back and light blue tattoos of arrows forming wings. Her hair done up in a complex, but short pony tail held in place by two long needles with ends shaped like feathers.

Behind her were Victoria, Elizabeth and Jess.

Jimmy was baffled by her beauty as soon as he laid eyes on Jess. Her hair was curled and let down with flowers in it. Her dress was a light blue that sparkled. Her heels only a few inches open toed matching the dress's elegance. The sides of it were laced in red. The gown was split like sharp flower petals layered offset formatting 6 points. It was held up by two thin red straps. The low V-cut front revealed her tight abdomen and cleavage held tight by red lace.

"Oh my goodness", Jimmy whispered just loud enough for Marcus to catch it.

"You lucky dog, you", Marcus said nudging him.

He was dumbfounded by the woman he had his eyes locked with. Victoria, not only made his jaw drop but Marcus dropped a bottle he was holding. In a blur, Jimmy caught it.

"Whoa, you dropped this Marcus", Jimmy said handing it back to him.

In a dreamy voice, Marcus replied "Thanks buddy."

Victoria was dressed as grand as she was tall. She was like the pitch-black sparkling of deep blue in the light. The front pushing her breasts up bound in heavy blue lace that crossed over each other down to her navel. The blue straps drooped lazily around her shoulders. The bottom was multiple layers of leaf shaped fabric black and blue. Her heels made her another three inches taller. Black lacing wound around her calves tied somewhere under the dress. Her hair was held up in a gorgeous mess of curls and thick locks tied with a long blue ribbon.

"Well, goddamn", Marcus spouted in his deep, velvety voice.

And lastly, Lady Elizabeth's dress. It was almost identical to Victoria's, except it is pure white. The lacing was thick and black. She, however, was wearing long gloves coming up to her strong biceps. Her hair let down gorgeous and curly.

Scott lit another smoke.

Charles stepped to the stairs holding out his hand ready to receive Phillis. She held out hers elegantly. The look on her face was seductive one so far none before had seen.

"You, look ravishing miss. May I have the privilege of being your date tonight?", Charles asked smooth as silk.

"You may", she replied with an almost sinister tone.

Scott watched as the two walk by him. Marcus and Jimmy could have cared less. He was the only one who noticed. He shook his head turning back to some relief in watching Marcus now at the stairs holding his arm out for Victory.

Marcus leaned over. "My lady", he said in a deep, velvety voice.

She giggled taking his arm without a word. As they walked past, Jimmy stared on the two passers-by. Scott chuckled to himself as he watched the pair walk arm in arm. Marcus was considerably shorter than Victoria by a full foot. They stopped turning slightly so Marcus could watch what they all have been waiting for.

Marcos yelled out uncontrollably. "Sweep her off her feet bro!" Victoria quieted the drunkard with a finger on his lips.

Jimmy nervously walked up, wiping his sweaty palms on the back of his jacket frantically. He regained his composure as he got to the steps looking up into her big beautiful eyes. The two seemed to have stood there for much longer than a moment, almost drifting nearer.

"Miss Jess?", the young man asked quietly.

"Yes, Mr. Jimmy?", she replies softly, nervously.

"You…you look amazing tonight. But you always look amazing. In fact, I like your uniform a lot better because you can fight in it."

Scott started coughing randomly to break Jimmy's nervous rambling compliment.

He took a deep breath. "Will you be my date tonight?", he blurted out.

She nodded. They exchanged a smile as she took his hand and walked down the last few steps. She gripped his strong arm tightly as they joined Marcus and Victoria.

"Good for you buddy", Scott and Marcus said out loud.

Everyone was leaving. Scott turned to watch them all leave him, standing there. Even Elizabeth passed by looking back with a smile he'd never seen before.

"Come now Gun Walzer. Let's go show these Dragons how warriors drink."

Scott looked out the main hall terrace into the night sky.

It was clearer than he'd ever seen it.

"As we should."

Chapter 13

Feast Upon The Night

The grand hall was lined with hundreds of tables. The tall curtains tied to the sides of the large walkways out onto gorgeous balconies were slowly swaying from the warm night's breeze. Thousands of torches lit the entire ball room with a light that danced with shadows. Chandeliers overhead hung high decorated with jewels and long shards of light, blue glowing light.

Large, red tables were set with silver and crystal glassware. Clay plates and cups, napkins and centerpiece flowers sat on every table. The dancefloor was just as grand as the rest of the room. Its multicolored floor was marble, black with sparkling flakes spiraling out as if it was made by them and set in such a pattern.

A set of steps with blue and gold embroidered carpet fitted to it. The King's and Queen's Chairs and long table draped in a similar blue cloth sat observing the whole ball room. On both flanks of the King and Queen's chairs was another chair. Each one was fit for a princess, blue cushioned and gold encased.

Hundreds of people sat drinking wine. Soft music played from the orchestra in the dome facing the dance floor. The group was standing waiting with the rest of the audience, the subjects of the kingdom for their King and Princess. Marcus and Scott laughed with each other as they joked about everything they could. Victoria stood next to Marcus quietly and properly. Children came up and to talk to Jimmy who was more than willing to entertain their questions and curiosity. Jess did as well, like two lovers without children, but were more than ready for them.

The blast of horns signaled the entrance of the King and his Daughter. The whole kingdom fell silent and stood. The children giggled and ran to their parents' tables. It was a wonderful sight to behold. The group sat along the King's side of the table. The Queen's side, however, only lay set but not occupied as one of the princesses was still captive.

The King entered. Cheers and clapping filled the hallway as he and his daughter walked to the center of the dance floor. Scott was dumbfounded, Marcus nudged him while nodding his head. He couldn't take her eyes off her. She wore atop her head a black, sharply pointed crown that almost sucked in the light from above. Observing her dress, he now realized why his suit was trimmed in green.

She wore a five tailed strapless dress, three points in the back and two in the front. The black corset tight just under her perfect breasts, the tight dress continued around them tightly. A pendent sat in her cleavage from the chain around her neck. Her tail was waving back and forth slowly. Her long dress boots came to just under her knees, thick laced, the noes sharp, and the heels only a few inches with a continuous soul. Two black pearl bracelets worn around her wrists, she is absolutely stunning.

The King had his white wings over him as usual. The only visible dress he wore was his heavy plated boots and the end of a long sheath on his right side. The king raised his heavy hand to calm the crowd. His blue clothing had gold trim, a functional uniform. Susanna stepped back as her father spoke to the crowd.

"I know it's been a long time since we've been able to celebrate anything in this Kingdom. The war with the demons in the east… the humans in the north have taken our very princess. However, we have hope in our midst. As you all know those brave men and women behind me were welcomed here on my behalf, and I thank you all for showing them respect regardless of where they hail from. They are our guests of honor tonight."

The crowd watched and listened quietly. Some wore their emotions on their faces, but none of animosity towards the foreigners. The King continued.

"They have heard my request. They have thought on their choice and they have accepted to help us stop another war and bring back my baby girl. These people before you possess the highest character and honor I've ever seen and will be welcomed back to our Kingdom if they so choose as our people."

A subject hurried across the floor handing a giant mug to the King and the Princess.

The king turned towards the group. "If my wife were here, she too would be just as grateful. We wish you safe travels on your journey and that you all return to us as you left. You all are honorable people, and this is your home now, so hurry the hell back."

The group and the audience all laughed. The King bowed as did Susanna and the rest of the entire room. The group quickly bowed in return. Everyone then raised their glasses.

"Drink, and be marry, for this night, is for you." The King roared before downing his entire pint.

The King sat down, as did the rest of the group save for Scott whom was waiting for Susanna to sit. As she passed by him she got close, almost smelling him, making eye contact, then acting shy and pushing him away. She sat. Scott was still inhaling her scent of lavender as he turned joining the rest of the group.

Marcus leaned over calling his attention. Scott leaned next to Marcus. "The princess wants that old Gun Walzer dick." Scott chuckled and replied.

"If she'll have me."

Marcus laughed and sat back up as Scott. Both waiting for the feast to be brought out. Music continued to play and conversations fill the hall. The food was then served even to the guests on all the tables.

Marcus asked out loud. "What is this delicious smell? I've never smelled anything like it before."

Large slabs of meat were set in front of them, potatoes, and spinach and asparagus. Scott stares at it with absolute intent behind his eyes. He spun a blade around his right hand. He put a juicy cut of the meat in his mouth.

"Ah", Scott said after enjoying the bite. "I think it's what our ancestors use to eat. I think it was called bison or beef. It's an ugly four legged creature with hair and horns. Kinda like a Mammoth, runs around and eats grass all day, tries not to be killed by… everything that wants to eat it."

Susanna and Marcus both laughed. The king even let out a chuckle.

Scott looked over at Susanna. "Am I right?"

She held a hand in front of her mouth nodding. He happened to ask her just as she took a bite herself.

The King answered. "Of course boy, you think we would eat creatures similar to us. We can't eat humans. We can't eat any of the blasted reptiles. Hell! I think one of the men tried eating a dinosaur not too long ago. Ended up in the hospital for weeks. The poor bastard."

Marcus looked at Victoria who was being proper. Marcus had his mouth full but didn't care. "It's so good, have you ever had anything like this before."

She giggled and shook her head. Marcus covered his mouth realizing what he had just done. Scott held up his glass. Susanna did the same. They were hungry not so much for food by the way they look at each other. Jimmy and Jess giggled among themselves. Phillis and Charles were talking and eating slowly. Elizabeth was being talked to by a small dragon boy. The Gun Walzers and Susanna finished their food before everyone.

The King looked over at Scott. "Tell me, Gun Walzer, are your people drunkards like they say?"

Scott replied. "Due to a defect in our genetic make-up, we require to be slightly drunk in order to maintain our mind. If we become sober, we unravel and become psychotic within a few minutes. Only once, maybe twice a generation, one of us can become sober and not lose our minds in the process. They usually are the best of us and become the elder of our territory."

"Interesting! This might seem rather melancholy to hear on a night like this, but I've read much about your people and our ancestors whom created us. Are you prepared to hear what I have to tell you?"

Scott took a drink. "By all means, great King."

The King nooded. "Your people were designed by the ancestors to do one thing. To kill off every human being left on earth to allow us to thrive. You, the Gun Walzers, are the apocalypse of the human species.

That's why your kind kill themselves when sober, that's why your kind hate as much as you do, and somehow alcohol was the answer to save your particular strain of genetic might."

Scott sat back pondering for a moment. He raised his glass. "As we should." He laughed and finished off his glass of wine.

"Not surprised I see?", the King attempted to read the man.

"It makes sense to me, being nothing more than an old soldier whom only longs for battle. It makes sense. Unlike many before me, I've never wanted to end my own life, just others. I care for animals more than people, I seem to be enjoying myself too much since my being here in your kingdom."

The King laughed. "It's because my boy, you were designed to pave the way by tooth and nail for our survival. Your kind is the very reason why the world is the way it is. You and your people, you are the catalyst for our great Mothers survival. It was the Gun Walzers that destroyed the ancient cities and freed our people, it was your kind that freed the Chimeras, it was your kind who saved the world. What did they call your people when the first were produced…?" The king leaned on his fist thinking deeply.

Susanna answered. "Gunslingers."

"Yes, that is correct. As simple as it may be, your kind washed across the world ending millions of lives, lost thousands yourself and there weren't many of you to begin with. But your kind were rather hard to kill, being able to dodge bullets, outrun vehicles, destroy great weapons with your bare hands. I hear it is the same to this day and age." The King boasted.

"More or less", Scott attempted to not enjoy the compliments.

"Well I have something special for you two Gun Walzers then." The King gestured a servant girl over. He whispered something in her ear and she smiled and quickly hurried away.

Scott nudged Marcus.

She was gone for a moment. When she returned, she had in her hand a tray with three black glass bottles. She served the king first and then sets one each in front of Marcus and Scott.

"For as much as you two drink, I can hardly tell that you are even drunk or buzzed for that matter, your tolerance must be very high, even compared to my own. So, challenge, I can drink both of you under the table", the King exclaimed.

Scott and Marcus laughed. "Challenge accepted!", Marcus replied.

They all pulled the corks from their bottles and clanked their glasses together.

"To you all, who owe us nothing and have given us hope which is worth more than I could ever repay you. I hope that you return as you left. And if not, that you find what you've been looking for in your end."

"None more suited than that…", Marcus replied, "We can only wish for your daughter's safe return, with or without us."

Then Scott. "To those that came before us, to those that want to be us, and to those just like us. Fuck everyone else."

They all laughed.

Bottoms up, all three gasped at the taste and powerful contents of the bottles.

The King spouted through his raspy voice. "This is the strongest wine we make in our Kingdom. Due of the Morning Moon."

Scott nodded and took another pull. "This is the best I've ever had."

The bottles were all finished. The King slammed his bottle down. He looked over to the girl, "Bring us another my dear!"

The rest of the group carried on. The music slowed and the King stood, holding out his hand to Susanna. "My dear. May I have this dance?"

She took his hand and the two proceeded onto the floor. The entire crowd had stepped aside to watch quietly as the King spun his daughter around and slowly waltzed across the floor with elegance.

The group watched as the two danced like a father and daughter would. Scott was memorized as he couldn't take his eyes off her. She kept making eye contact with him as well. The King and Princess carried on with their own conversations and small chuckles and giggles back and forth to each other.

The song was over and the two bowed to each other. Another had started and the two continued. Jimmy looked over to Jess.

"May I have this dance, my lady?", the young man asked.

She said nothing and took his hand pulling him towards the dance floor. The group was impressed as the two moved in sync with one with the other.

Phillis and Charles were soon to follow. As they passed by Jimmy and Jess, Phillis gave Jess a look of approval. Charles nodded to Jimmy whom was smiling as wide as could be. It was amazing to watch the three couples spinning about in such a classic waltz.

Marcus stood up bowing in front of Victoria holding out his hand. She quickly wiped the corners of her mouth and set the napkin down. Turning towards him, she placed her hand in his.

"My lady?", he asked making eye contact lustfully.

"Yes, Sir Marcus?", she shyly asked.

"May I have this dance…?" He was cut off.

"Yes." However, instead of him leading her onto the floor, she dragged him out there.

The two glided across the dancefloor, him spinning her and catching her into a dip. She came back up and the two continued closely like lovers across the floor. The audience clapped at their skill.

"It's a good night", Scott said to himself lighting a smoke and sitting back in his large chair.

Scott looked over at Elizabeth overhearing her judgement. "I know Marcus is shorter than her. That's not even close to the small of her back. And why is she so close? She is basically shoving her bosom into his face. That is not how a baroness presents herself."

Scott laughed to himself as he too observed her displeased ranting first hand.

"As they should", Scott said aloud.

The sound of a heavy chair next to Elizabeth slid away. The tall Dramon was a well decorated Knight, more than likely the leader of the King's Guard. His golden scales shined as they catch the light around him. His face was very human, but he was almost equal in size to Elizabeth. She was wide eyed as he bowed in front of her.

"My lady, I am Gabriel of the Kings Guard. May I ask the name of the most beautiful creature here?"

With a look of surprise, she answered. "I'm Baroness Elizabeth of the Old Guard."

"May I have this dance, Baroness?"

Scott nodded and smiled at the two.

Elizabeth looked him up and down taking his measure. He was taller than her at a total of seven feet. His spins were spiky in all directions upon his head. Very muscular. Eyes blue as sapphires on top of the background of green. His face and neck were a light cream color. His slick black uniform sported many medals across his left breast. A large claymore at his side sporting an odd hand crank on the hilt much like her weapon.

"Yes, you may great Knight", she replied.

Scott was looking over his bottle at the dance floor, following the couples with only his eyes. He was enjoying himself. Marcus and Victoria looked of two lovers on their wedding knight. Jess and Jimmy both smiling like children finding their first true love. Phillis and Charles like parents chaperoning the nights' festivities. A father and daughter dancing their night away. And Elizabeth and Gabriel, two worthy opponents meeting upon the dancefloor as allies.

"Is this what I've been searching for?", Scott asked himself aloud. "Is this the life we were meant to find at the end of the road? I wonder... If not, then I should wish I never wake up from this dream. This is worth living for."

He laughed to himself holding out the black bottle to the scenery in front of him. "I could die for this", he said before he drank again.

The song ended, the partners all stepped away bowing to each other. The crowd clapped and cheered. The next song started and the audience begin to find their own partners and join the group that decided to stay. The King and Princess walked back up to their chairs.

Susanna was approached by a knight and accepted his offer to dance. The King sat in his great chair looking down at Scott, searching for his next question.

Scott opened the conversation first. "I understand the rules of royalty, however...", he paused searching for the way to ask.

"Just ask your damn question, boy", the King spouted.

"Does your daughter have a prince she is waiting for?", Scott asked.

The King laughed out loud. "The issue we face here is that the only time our people find mates is when the other Kingdoms like ours, pass by."

"There's more Kingdoms like this?"

"Several. They stay hidden in the clouds or anchored between mountains and all usually centering around the equator because of our cold blood."

"Makes sense."

"We will not make the mistakes of our creators, inbreeding, immoral acts of malice against each other. That is not the way of our people. If you fancy my daughter as she seems to fancy you, don't break her heart. If I don't kill you, her mother will. And let me tell you, her mother is one of the best warriors I've ever seen."

"Where is the Queen if you don't mind me asking?"

The King took a drink. "She is off on a campaign to the north, as it would stand she is actually fighting over the very ruins your kind were developed in. If you ever have a chance I suggest you travel there. Whatever answers you could ever want to know lay hidden in those old domes."

Scott nodded. "I just might one day."

"As much as I know about your particular kind, Scott… I've always been curious, what is it you believe in?"

Scott lit another smoke. "I can't speak for us all, but it's said that the Black Dog will walk the battlefield leading the worthy dead to the endless battlefield. A paradise where we cannot die, and there is plenty of enemies to kill. We fight alongside our fallen until the battles over, then we go home to our loved ones whom wait with the best ale and food. We lay with our lover, and at times it's said they too fight alongside you."

"Interesting! There hasn't been a dog in existence for many, many years", the King replied.

Scott laughed. "Is that so, I've seen him once, it was years ago, the bastard had 6 eyes, and smoke poured from his mouth as he exhaled. He was huge and covered in blood and blackness. He disappeared just as fast as he appeared. I thought he had come for me."

"A warrior's deity through and through", the King spoke in a dreamy voice.

"We also believe that Mother Earth is a goddess whom we must protect at all costs in this afterlife. For if she dies, then all is lost."

"We, too, believe in Gaia that she is the goddess of our paradise."

Scotts face seemed to have changed, almost nothing behind his eyes, like a void that was unending. "Even with all the wrong I have done in this world, I believe that I lived it the way I was meant to thus far, and that I will end up on the endless battlefield one day… If it'll have me."

The King raised his glass, Scott did as well, clanking them together.

"You're an interesting creature, Scott."

"As are you, great King."

The two drank.

Scott continued. "Look at this Kingdom, your people, I don't mean to pry, however…" He gestured to the scene before him, lit cigarette between his pointer and middle finger. "The reason for all of this, the way the world turned out, surviving ad flourishing, continuing to evolve in a way never witnessed by anyone…. Your subjects are happy, they are good natured and loyal. They are strong and just and the children have a bright future. If anyone would dare to attack you they would be met with the severest of defeats ever witnessed. I thank you for allowing us to be here and offering this as a home, but I feel that this is far better than anyone like me could have ever deserved."

The King leaned over placing a heavy hand on Scott's shoulder. "You and your people survive this, bring my baby girl back to me. I won't be able to ever repay what you think you don't deserve. Succeed or fail, you've already have given the people here more than they could have asked for, you could end up stopping a genocide by you wanting to help us. If that isn't deserving enough, then I am not a King."

"Great King…", Scott started. "Like it or not, war is coming like nothing you and I have ever seen before."

"Maybe, but there is no war tonight, boy", the King replied.

Susanna interrupted the two. She placed a gentle but strong hand on Scott's other shoulder. "You two have been talking for too long. It's my turn now."

The King sat back hands up laughing. She pulled him up and out onto the floor into the center of the twirling partners. She placed his hand at the small of her back, her arm around the back of his neck, her hand in his. They were close, her tail almost vibrating from her excitement.

"God! you're are gorgeous." He spoke softly considering her big eyes.

"You're okay for a human, I guess."

"You guess huh? For someone who tried to kill me, you seem awfully attracted to me."

"Psh, me, attracted to you, never", she joked.

She spun herself away from him, he spun her back into him. She was facing away, pressing her butt into him. Her tail wrapped around his leg like a snake. She leaned into him as they pressed their faces against each other. He breathed into her ear. She spun away against giving him such a seductive look as they meet pressing against each other. Their lips almost met as he looked down at her.

Scott obviously was not very rhythmic compared to the Princess. She led the dance, he merely attempting to keep up. But it was elegant, like two lovers dancing for the first time.

Marcus and Victoria spun by. "You old dog", Marcus said to Scott.

Scott and Susanna laughed to themselves as the world around them began to fall away. They were the only two out on that dance floor. A single beam of light followed them around as they danced slowly to their own beat. They were all alone out there. Nothing but their own music, their own step, their own rhythm to follow. A devil dancing with his goddess. They were perfect everyone thought. APrincess and a Gun Walzer, the inheritor of the earth and the weapon to pave her way into the future.

Scott ended up bumping into someone throwing them off. He held his hand up checking if they were okay apologizing. Susanna put her hand on her face laughing at him. She then took him by the hand pulling him off the dance floor out onto an empty balcony. However,

Scott stopped. He noticed Jess and Jimmy, slowly dancing to their own beat, leaning in closer and closer. Susanna leaned against Scott watching as well, her tail slowly wrapping around them.

Jimmy leaned down and kissed Jess deeply, the moment seemed to last forever.

"As you should", Scott spoke in an almost whisper. Marcus waved at him and pointed to the two with a huge grin on his face. Scott nodded.

"Come on", Susanna said pulling him along. "Leave them be."

Jess and Jimmy pulled away and continued their dance slowly, her leaning against him embracing him.

Noticing that the balcony was occupied, she decided to take him out the other side. They ended up walking down the main hallway leading to a covered waterfall that spills into the massive multitier of giant dragon baths. She walked ahead of him now down an open walkway overlooking much of the kingdom and the night sky. A small open gazebo stood at the end where the water fell from. He was watching her every movement, the intent behind her walk, the elegance in her every step. She was every bit of a princess. He could smell the lavender in the air as he followed.

She turned around walking backwards enticingly, seductively, leaning forward winking. "Why did you hesitate?"

"When?", he asks defensively.

"When I was about to beat your ass on that wall."

"I saw despair in your eyes, like someone searching for something they truly love. I've never seen such beauty and sadness all at once."

She turned slowly around and continued walking coyly looking back. She was drunk, he could tell.

"You're the most beautiful woman I've ever seen before, in my entire life."

"What did you just say?", she asked angrily.

"Nothing…" he laughed.

"Why did you come here?", she asked.

He was behind her, arms around her.

"To find you", he whispered.

"I'm not that special", she pulled away, but he held on tighter.

"I wanna see what your soul tastes like."

She turned into him, looking deeply into each-other's eyes. Her eyes were glossy for some unknown reason.

"You're lying", she said.

"No, I'm not… I will devour you, my love."

They kissed.

The night continued onward calmly and slowly. Guests had left. Even the King had retired for the night. Jess and Jimmy left by themselves. Marcus and Victoria were shortly behind them. Victoria was blushing bright red. Phillis left Charles thinking over something in shock.

Charles was after her with intent behind his haste. He stopped to talk to Marcus for a moment. "Goodnight, us Dragonares can't keep up with the legendary drunkards."

Marcus laughed. "Goodnight to you as well. Don't let that old woman break you off, old man." Marcus joked.

Charles shook his head. "You vile beasts." And quickly disappears out the archway.

Elizabeth and Gabriel were sitting and talking at the table. A few lovers were still dancing the night away even after the orchestra had started packing up their instruments. Marcus and Victoria continued out the archway themselves disappearing up the stairwell towards their rooms. Victoria and Marcus stopped slightly up the stairwell.

"Where is the Princess and Scott? They disappeared early on" she asked.

"If I know Scott, he's found what he was looking for this whole trip. He's probably enjoying the princess as we speak. And I'm sure, she is enjoying him as well."

Victoria suddenly grabbed his face and pulled him up for a long deep kiss. He was quiet, the two quickly retired for the night upstairs. The moon was bright and the stars gleamed true. The night came to an end with a bow and a kiss or the soft moans of love under the covers in the dark. As calm as the night was ominously beautiful, the night rested before the break of day.

Chapter 14

A Storm Upon the Wind

Scott walked up the stairs dressed in his normal combat attire with his hands in his pockets. His pistols were sheathed and personal blade at the small of his back. He moved like the smoke bellowing from his cigarette. His eyes were dead almost black from the murderous intent behind them. He stopped at a large red doorway. Its heavy black hinges and large handle were beautiful molded into a vine-like décor. He raps on the door three times.

"Gaaaaaah...", came muffled from behind the door followed by a thud.

Marcus picked himself off the floor, naked and answered the door. Scott was leaning down like a predator, his menacing stance almost shocked Marcus completely awake. He was squinting still from the light, lipstick marks stained his face and neck. He smelled of sex. Scott's face split open with a sinister grin, the cigarette clutched between his teeth.

"Come on, get your ass ready..." he said taking the smoke out of his mouth. Turning to walk away he continued. "Tell Victoria too. I can hear her breathing in there. The ship is already loaded, we leave in an hour."

"Ship?", Marcus asked groggily.

"Yeah, think we are driving back? Fuck no! We have air remember?"

Marcus caught a beer that Scott seemed to produce from nowhere.

"Where does he keep these?", Marcus asked.

Scott disappeared up the stairs to wake up the others. Marcus shut the door. Victoria was now sitting up holding the blanket just above her breasts.

"Good morning, sleepy head...", Marcus said seductively. "Now, where were we?" She let out a yelp as he jumped on top of her and they started wrestling under the covers giggling to themselves.

Scott was just about to knock on Jimmy's door when Phillis's door opening caught his attention. He waited, observing out of the corner of his eye, as he leaned back against the wall Charles was backing out of her door. Phillis's strong arms pulled him back in.

"I had an amazing last night. You're not so bad after all, Colonel", Scott heard Phillis say.

Charles walked down the steps towards Scott. His hair was a mess, shirt unbuttoned, belt undone. Scott was grinning. "She break your old ass off?", Scott asked loud enough for even Phillis to hear. She slammed her door.

"Fire Grapher, my ass..." Sc,ott said to him as he continues down the stairs. Charles hand combed his hair and doesn't pay the Gun Walzer any mind. "Shoulda been called the Beast Tamer!",he laughed sinisterly.

Phillis's door opened and a vase went screaming through the air above Scott's head bursting against the curving wall.

"I might have deserved that", Scott laughed.

He looked down at Charles. "Are you limping? Fuck, she tamed your ass then", he said out loud laughing even harder this time.

Phillis, wrapped in her towel, threw a bottle of wine. It screamed towards him and he caught it turning like second nature.

"Get your asses ready! We leave for the docks in 45 minutes."

Jimmy's door opened.

"You alright Scott? That sounded heavy. Whatever that noise was."

"You good?", Scott asked.

Jimmy looked at the sinister man. Jess was standing behind the door peeking around Jimmy.

"We are fine."

"Good! I'll meet you two downstairs in 45 minutes. I'll show you to the air docks."

Scott talked to himself as he walked down the stairs opening the bottle he had caught.

The Air Docks.

The docks were simple wooden walkways suspended between the lowest outer castle walls. Nothing but forest below them, the crew stopped on a stairwell to take in the sight. The city wall was held up by giant beams jutting out the side of the mountainous piece of earth that floated silently. They continued down the multileveled stone stairs towards the main loading docks and walkways that connected all the docks.

Many cranes and cables took crates from one end of the docks to the other. Some vehicles drove supplies down the docks to certain air ships. It was bustling like usual. The ships, a mix of ancient sailboats, blimps, some hoovering fighter jets, some small planes with several propellers that suggested that the craft could fly in any direction it chose.

It was a sight to behold as the group walked out towards their ship. A sailboat bottom suspended under an oblong blimp. Propellers jutting out the rear end. Heavy machines guns facing towards the surface around the hull of the ship. Guns on the deck and forward and aft bow. It was rickety but strong.

As the group passed by, the people completely stopped what they were doing to bow. It was odd, but it seemed they had the gratitude of everyone in that kingdom. The group came to the ramp leading up to the air ship. The King and his daughter awaited the group. Guards lined the deck around them. The group stopped in front of the King before they headed onto the ship. The King steps forward and bows. Everyone on the deck bowed.

The group returned the bows and started heading on deck. Elizabeth was stopped by Gabriel who kissed her hand. "May your sword and shield be ever ready at your side, Baroness", Gabriel said aloud before stepping back into his rank. She leaned in and kissed his cheek. And just as quickly as the moment came, she was headed up the ramp. Gabriel stepped back into his rank.

Marcus stopped in front of the King. The King put his large hands on Marcus and Victoria's shoulders. "I wish you all safe return. Hurry the hell up and come back home."

The two nodded and continued up the ramp.

Jimmy stopped in front of the King. "Great King, we will bring your daughter home. I promise."

"You, Jimmy, are a great man and it has been my pleasure to have been allowed to meet you in this lifetime. Come home soon, lad."

Jess and Jimmy both walked up the ramp followed by Phillis and Charles. Scott was standing in front of Susanna, the two could have cared less about anyone around them.

"I wish you could come with us", Scott said to her.

"Me too, I would have been locked up if I tried to come. So I thought I'd see you off instead", she giggled.

She raised off her toes rubbing her nose against his. "Come back to me", she said pushing herself back.

"Yes, my dear", The Gun Walzer replied with a real smile.

She leaned against him, looking up pressing her pointer finger into his chest. "Or I'll kill you."

"Only if you'll have me", he replied.

She smiled. "As I should." They both laughed.

Embracing each other deeply, he pulled away. She almost jumped grabbing both sides of his face to kiss him. They parted ways and he walked to the end of the ramp ready to board. However, the King blocked his path holding out his hand.

Scott accepted the heavy hand shake.

"Don't get yourself killed out there. It's not yet your time for the Black Dog to walk you into your eternal battlefield."

Scott laughed as did the King. "Keep 'em safe! We'll be back. It takes a lot to kill us."

"Keep your head down and your powder dry", the King replied.

Scott grinned. "My old man use to say that to me when I was a we' lad."

"Your old man was certainly a wise one", the King replied.

"He is the worst enemy anyone could ever face, even as old as he is now."

"Let us hope he doesn't become ours than."

Scott looked back as he walked up the ramp, waving as he disappears onto the ship. The ramp retracts. And the ship starts to rise. The group are overlooking the Kingdom as they flew the castle walls. A huge banner unraveled from the middle level wall. The huge tapestry read in capital letters:

"HURRY THE HELL HOME!"

Scott lit a cigarette as the group slowly ascended into the clouds.

"Marcus", Scott called.

"Yes, you old devil?"

"Open the box up. We have about 12 hours before we can really attack these assholes. So let's start handing out the good shit", Scott exclaimed.

Marcus started undoing banding around wooden crates. The crates came in all sizes. The lids came off revealing packing shavings. Marcus pulled a long object from a long rectangular box, wrapped in a black cloth over to Victoria. Scott threw a huge thick bladed claymore to Elizabeth.

Everyone gathered around the two to see what they had. Victoria removed the black cloth, revealing a long spear. The end of the hilt was like a spear head. Its pole arm was wrapped in a tight leather binding.

"It's beautiful Marcus. Thank you", she said as walking away from the group whipping it around. She thrusted it forward, creating small gusts of wind. The spear point almost disappeared from everyone's sight.

Elizabeth gripped the long handle of her sword slowly unsheathing it. "It is said that the ancient weapons were the epitome of weapon development from each of our territories once upon a time."

The hand crank started a whirling mechanism in the long blade as she swung it around. It whistled through the air.

"Are these weapons reaped from the ruins?", Elizabeth asked.

"No, no. We only found one thing. And it almost blew us all up. These are gifts from Dr. Hamel", Marcus replied.

Elizabeth spoke as the blade began to glow red. "Do you know what this ancient weapon is known as?", she asks, her voice almost in a trance.

"This is the centripetal cleaver. A weapon that vibrates the very blade so that it separates the molecules in the very matter it touches cleaving the target without effort." She sheaths her new sword.

"Thank you both. I shall die with this gripped tightly in my hand."

Scott turned his head around slowly with a grin on his face. "As you should, my Lady."

It was quiet while the group watched the two Gun Walzers pulling two heavy cases from the side of the mess of crates. Marcus sat it aside and then continued rummaging around the other case. "Ah!", he yelled running over to Jimmy handing him a thin, medium-sized metal case. He opened it and quickly his eyes were wide with joy. Jimmy turned to Jess.

"Look at what they got me! You see these ones?" Jimmy was so excited as he started explaining every single type of explosive tip and what each of the special heads performed when they hit their targets.

Scott opened the case Marcus had sat on the ground pulling from it an unstrung recurved bow. He handed it to Phillis with the wire. Her eyes were wide with disbelief. The shelf was for a left hand, right hand draw. However, the arrow sat on the right side of the shelf like the archers of old. The bow itself was sharply designed of some unknown extremely hard material.

"Oh", Marcus said pointing at Jess. "We have something for everyone. Hold on."

"You guys got me a real Chimera Hunter", Phillis says walking over to the two Gun Walzers and hugging them.

"We're sorry though...", Marcus choked out of Phillis's hug that was around his neck. "It was the only one we could get. So, we thought it was fitting that you should have it Phillis. And Jimmy should have the warheads."

"Thank you both", she then went to restring it not paying attention to anyone.

"Oh wait", Scott said digging through another box. "Here it is", he said holding up a tensioning engine that looked like it pulled the bows leaves in so it can be strung. Scott handed it to Phillis and then started pulling ammo boxes from another crate.

Marcus pulled out two short assault weapons both sporting large magazines, folding stocks, monolithic rails with forward pistol grips and an assortment of ambidextrous controls. The charging handle lay forward of the ejection port. Reflex sights halfway down the 1913 rail. The barrels were thick and octagonal with short, fat suppressors at the ends.

"Impressive weaponry!", Charles exclaimed.

"Well what did you two make off with?", Phillis asked excitedly.

"Well, since you asked so nicely", Marcus replied. Scott and Marcus began setting their own ammo to the side and pulled out two medium length rifle cases each.

Marcus and Scott opened their cases as Marcus pulled his rifle out. The gun as very like a M1 Grand. However, the stock was sharply designed coming to a blunt angled point just past the heavy barrel. The magazine was short, but longer than his previous rifle. The iron sights were large and the ejection port was to the side of the weapon instead of at the top. The charging handle was ambidextrous, sticking out from both sides of the bolt. The buttstock was short and angled down more and the pistol grip was more ergonomic and meant to be wielded with one hand.

"This is my new rifle", he announced. "This is the 13mm by 60mm Gundrill. Well, that's what they call it. I haven't been able to figure out if it actually drills anything other than my enemies in the face", Scott and Marcus both laughed at his joke.

Marcus began to swing his new toy around like a sword. Then taking aim with one hand, he pulled it back, racking the heavy bolt till it locked. He extracted the magazine and inspected the chamber.

"It's really nice. I'm pretty sure it was designed to fight hand to hand with for when we are out of ammo. Like most of the weapons from this era."

The group was impressed and then turned to Scott who pulled his new weapon out. "This is it. Nothing too special… just a little shorter. Whatever this material is made of is pretty bad ass. It's hard as fuck." He pulled out his heavy cleaver from the small of his back and chopped the side of the monolithic heatshield over the barrel and magazine tube. The blade sparked off the weapon. He looked at the blade with an irritated twitch of his right brow.

"Fuck, why did I do that?", he growled to himself.

His shotgun had a similar stock and grip like Marcus's rifle, but the receiver was like a semi-auto shotgun. It continued into a downward angle encasing both the barrel and the shot tube. The bottom of the heat shield was blunt, but came to a point along the bottom. The weapons were menacing because they were designed to be used as bludgeoning weapons when the users ran out of ammunition.

Jimmy raised his hand. "Scott, why does your weapon have no sights?"

Scott shrugged his shoulders. "Don't know… not like I need them anyway, my friend."

"Well what's special about them?", Jimmy asked.

"They can fire the Moon Cutter cartridges, Jimmy", Marcus replied.

"What are those?", Jimmy asked.

Scott turned around, showing Jimmy the end of one of his black shot shells. The casing was some sort of black metal with a glass optical lens.

"Whoa, what do those do?", Jimmy asked.

Scott stuck them into his pocket. "An artifact, banned long ago after they were created. Only a few even exist. I'm kinda surprised the good doctor was able to part with such treasures. But they fire a super-heated beam of light that cuts through anything. Only issue is that if you don't know what's behind your target, you could destroy far more than you intend to. Legend says though that the beams can reach the moon."

"They were destroyed because someone tried to shoot one into the moon and cut it apart", Charles interrupted Scott.

"So they say. Either way, these will be a last resort", Scott laughed.

The two moved the broken crates away and started breaking open two more. Two large metallic cases were revealed from the crates. They set the heavy cases with much effort from in front of Elizabeth and Victoria. They pushed two buttons on the side of a small touch screen panel. Pressurized steam released from the cases. Inside each of the cases was a small form-fitting robotic armor designed for the two Knights.

"We have no idea how they work. But we recommend that you figure it out soon", Marcus said.

"Why is that?", Elizabeth asked.

Scott took out one of his under-barrel revolvers. They looked slightly newer than his previous ones. He picked a helmet out of the case closest to him. Holding it out, he pointed his pistol at it. The loud crash of his 454 blasted out. The group took their hands off their ears and to the entire group's surprise, not even a scratch was found on the oddly designed helm.

"These rounds are pretty much about the epitome in armor piercing munitions. They were designed to defeat all of you."

"Our armor is designed to stop those rounds", Victoria replied.

Scott pointed his hand out. "Care to prove me wrong."

Victoria looked at Elizabeth. Elizabeth nodded. "Hand the Gun Walzer your helmet, Lady Victoria."

She does as Elizabeth had commanded. Scott held it out and fired another round. Sparks flew. The group removed their hands from covering their ears. Scott tossed the helmet back to Victoria. The round had ripped through the front leaving a massive three-inch diameter hole out the back.

"I don't know what this material is, but it is probably the strongest thing I've ever seen."

Victoria nodded. "Point taken, Gun Walzer."

Scott leaned against the crates. He lit a smoke. "Ah", he spouted, blowing smoke with his words. "We also have an assortment of plate carriers for the rest of you. They should all be the right sizes too. They stop pretty much everything. Oh, except for Phillis's bolts. Her arrows will pierce through your armor. So don't get in her way."

Phillis looked at both of the two Gun Walzers. "Thank you...", she started stopping their joking among each other.

"For what?", Marcus asked.

"For all of this. You two are the only reason we even made it this far. Regardless of what you two are...in my eyes, you are good men", she spouted genuinely.

The rest of the group agreed with her statement. Scott's hand went up stopping everyone.

"We thank you all for your kindness. But please remember, you may not think the same way after this little adventure of ours."

"Why is that, Gun Walzer?", Victoria asked.

Phillis answered for them. "Because if they become sober during this…or if they have to be sober during this we can be nowhere near them. Everyone will become an enemy to them. Nothing will sate their bloodlust. If they are lucky, they accidently drink themselves back into their tolerable states. Otherwise, we will have to leave them behind."

Scott pointed at Phillis with an emotionless look on his face. "Regardless of what happens…" He started as he walked over passing out black bottles of the wine he and the King enjoyed just this past night.

"Remember, that we are mercenaries and nothing more. War is our only true love and it will be the death of us one day", Scott said genuinely.

Everyone pulled the corks off the bottles. Scott and Marcus held them high as everyone else clanked into theirs.

"To you all…", Scott said with a look of malice across his face. "I wish nothing more than to be there in your greatest moments across this distant battlefield. So that I may witness you pay your weights worth in suffering to the Black Dog as he walks you into the endless battlefield. If I had one wish, I'd do it all over again with all of you. May we meet upon the endless battlefield. Friend or foe, it has been nothing but an honor to suffer with you all."

Then the group found it, all at the same time, the perfect reply to end Scotts toast.

"As you should."

Chapter 15

The Best of Us

The night became angry as the wind rocked the ship with angry gusts. The stars hid behind storm clouds as the ship descended through them. Crashes of lighting brought loud rolling thunder with them. The group peered out of the bottom of the ship as the wind thrashed around them. Items and tools and cables clanking and slamming into the hull made it all the more harder to hear each other as they broke through the storm clouds.

Before them lay their old kingdom. The same one who had cast them out into the forest to serve as bait. It seemed like they hadn't seen their land in forever. It was almost foreign to them. The mass of shapes began to take form as they descended ever closer to the ground. They were just over head a stronghold in the Dragonares territory and coming fast.

Charles pointed as he stood holding onto a cable next to Scott. "That's the weapons testing facility right there!", he yelled.

Scott looked back to the group behind him. "Remember, the Princess is our only priority. If we are separated, then we meet at the extraction point. If that is compromised, the secondary…well, if that one's fucked too…then, we're fucked!"

They all nodded. Scott could see the fear in some of their eyes, but it only brought a smile to his face as he laughed looking down at the building below him.

"Let's go die for something real!", Scott roared.

The ship stopped hovering abruptly, then started rapidly ascending. The group dropped out all at the same time from the bottom of the ship. They made their way through the many pipes and chimneys, hopping over pipes and eventually making it to a stairwell that led inside the building.

Once inside, the two Gun Walzers led the group. Charles pointed out directions as the two cleared down the tall stair wells flight after flight.

"She will be held in the basement, more than likely class S containment", Charles said to the group.

Finally, Scott heard something below him. He looked back at the Old Guard Knights who looked more like futuristic robots than knights. He pointed towards the door above them. The group held their position as Scott and Marcus started moving down the stairs, leaping to the next level. The only noise anyone could hear was the sound of their clothing flapping for a second or so.

Two heavily armed guards stood on both sides of the door talking to each other. Scott and Marcus sheathed their weapons behind their backs and then pulled their blades. They both leaped, almost flying, down on top of the two unsuspecting guards. Scott's blade pierced straight through the soldier's plate carrier. Marcos spun slicing the second soldiers head almost clean off. Heavy pulses of blood gushed out of the soldier's neck as his body jerked and fell against the wall. Scott stared into the eyes of the soldier as he followed the soldier falling back slowly down the wall. Once he couldn't see the light, Scott pulled his heavy blade from the soldier. The lifeless body jerked and twitched as Scott stood slinging his heavy blade throwing a thick trail of blood across the floor.

The door required a key code the two noticed. After searching the corpses neither of the soldiers before them possessed such a card to open the door. Scott and Marcus looked at each other. Scott knocked on the metal door listening to the clanging as he continued randomly searching for the sound he wanted. He looked at Marcus, the two stepped back and Scott kicked the door in. The door ripped from its hinges and bounced off the ground destroying something then lodging into a far wall. Scott and Marcus were already in the room clearing corners and everything they could find.

"This is far too easy, brother", Marcus stated.

Scott lit a cigarette as the rest of the group ran down the stairwell. "Indeed, they were waiting for us. I wonder how, maybe some sort of radar system. But even so, this place is clear. Two guards for one door protecting such a treasure." Scott almost growled to himself as a low rumbling started shaking the ground.

The room was massive, suggesting that it is some sort of training facility. An overhead viewing control room could be seen to the right side. Massive sliding ballast doors to the far back of the facility. Speakers were in the top corners with cameras suspended by cables above them. It was a training facility. Targets on one end, fighting dolls and dummies on another. Several obstacle courses were set up around the massive room. A small quarter mile track was on the outer edges. And in the center of the room was a square room with glass walls. Light poured down from luminescent fixtures overhead. A bed, table, a computer on one end. A tray slid across the floor towards the heavy sliding doors, bits of food left over.

Scott walked over to the glass cage. He knocked on the doors lightly. The metal was so dense his knuckles almost made no sound.

"How the fuck do we open this?", Marcus asked searching for a panel or locking mechanism with no luck.

Jess, Victoria, Elizabeth and Phillis all came up to the Gun Walzers. Phillis patted Marcus on his shoulder. He looked as she pointed up to the control room. Charles was standing in plain view of the control room looking down searching for the door release.

Jimmy was looking at the terrified girl. She was huddled in the corner on her bed with her head buried in her knees. He could hear her sobs as he walked over to the entrance. He pulled a bolt out and drew back as far as he could. The arrow flew into the center of the doors lodging halfway in. He began to pry the doors open with the arrow. He heard the heavy hinges breaking as the wrenched it apart. Scott and Marcos grabbed hold of both sides to help. The two ripped the doors clean off the hinges.An air raid siren begins to wale in the distance.

Marcus and Scott looked up at Charles. "What the fuck?", Marcus shouted.

Charles responded with his hands in the air saying something was along the lines of... "It wasn't my fault."

"What did he say?", Scott asked Marcus.

"I think he said, "It wasn't my fault..."

Scott laughed. "It was probably ours when we forced the doors open. Fuck it! Let's get ready."

The scared little dragon was almost completely white. She skin was changing into the exact color of the room. She was blending into her surroundings as Jimmy got closer. She was growling and hissing at him now. Her pupils opened up almost completely. The red and sapphire was almost blacked out at this point. She resembled a scared feline Jimmy thought.

"Get away from me!", she screamed swiping at the window with one hand. Bright sparks flew from her scratching shards of thick glass from her walls. Jimmy didn't flinch. The girl started to calm as she made eye contact with him. Her pupils began to thin revealing the sapphire iris and red eyes. Big and bright, beautiful Jimmy thought.

Her horns were black thin and long, jutting from the sides of her temples. They curved back and upwards. Her spines of dark blue were thick and feathery like sharp scales. The luscious hair came down to her feet and curled around her. Her black and blue tail and skin started to change back to the rainbow-like tint it once had. As Jimmy shifted closer to her, her skin seem to shine that gorgeous color with his point of view of her, as if it were following his very eyesight.

"Jimmy, come on man! We gotta go!", Marcus yelled to him.

The little princess was wearing a form fitting workout suit of some kind. All black with red lines along the outer seams.

"Hi there. What's your name? My name is Jimmy. And these scary people are my friends. But they are good people. What's your name, sweetie?"

"It's Kathrine."

"Nice to meet you Princess Kathrine. But we need to leave right now, sweetie."

"You're not here to make me do any more tests?"

"No honey. We are here to take you home", Jimmy said softly.

She leaped into his arms sobbing tears of joy.

"It'll be okay Princess. I won't let anything happen to you ever again", Jimmy said picking her up.

She pulled away to look at him.

"Promise?", she said sniffling.

"Promise."

"You good, Jimmy?", Scott yelled from outside. The rumbling had gotten much louder, suggesting it is right outside the main doors.

Suddenly the heavy ballasts doors slid open. A loud pulsating alarm sounded in the corner and a small, spinning yellow light flashed. When the door opened, the sun shined in and with its rays rained in heavy machine gun fire. It sparked and bounced off the metal walls. Jimmy turned, kneeling protecting the Princess. He looked up after it had stopped and realized that the glass was bulletproof. Not even a scratch, just splashes of metal turning to dust as the bullets hit. The walls stopped moving as Scott and Marcus stuffed the heavy metal doors into the threshold tracks, stopping them from fully opening.

A loud speaker sounded out as Scott and Marcus leaned against the door peeking out into the field. "You have two options. Give the girl up and die a quick soldier's death by firing squad. Or don't, and die miserably on this field."

Scott laughed. "Fuck you!", he said out loud.

Marcus was wide eyed as Victoria and Elizabeth slammed into the wall, their armor sparking against the metal doors. He looked over to Scott who was calmly lighting a smoke with an evil grin on his face as he checked his under-barrel pistols.

"What is the depth of their forces?", Victoria asked.

"Take a look."

She peered around. Scattered on the field before them lined row by row were hundreds of men standing in formation. Black Uniforms, no identifying marks. They were accompanied by three gigantic tanks and three mechanized robots. She leaned against the wall next to Marcus pulling the cigarette from the corner of his mouth and taking a drag. Choking she handed it back to him. To his smiling surprise, he took it back trying not to laugh at her.

"Hey bud?", Scott called to Marcus.

"Yeah?", Marcus answered.

"You ready?"

"Fuck it! Let's do this brother", Marcus replied.

"Drink up. It will make you sober in about two maybe three minutes."

Marcus pulled a small flask from his pocket. Shaking, he opened it, staring at it for a second, he looked back to Scott.

"You not drinking?", Marcus asked shakenly.

Scott laughed. "I've been sober for years now brother. I don't need to drink for control. I just drink to tolerate."

"Wait, what?", Marcus was shocked, as was everyone else who heard him. Scott looked out into the field once more talking to himself as he formulated a plan. Marcus was shaking and shocked. He didn't want to become sober.

Phillis sat her hand on Scott's shoulder, "You've been sober this whole time? But how? How are you able to function? It's impossible! You looked drunk when we met you. You drink all the time."

Scott smiled. "It's pickle juice."

"But why?", she asked.

"Who knows? Sometimes you can't be truthful to stay true to yourself."

Phillis was baffled. Scott paid her no mind.

Victoria put her hand on Marcus's hand to calm him. "It will be okay. We won't let you get out of control, I promise."

"I'm a little afraid, I hate to say", he said through a nervous laugh.

Scott watched as Victoria kissed Marcus on his lips intimately, slowly. "Go do what you were born to do. I'll be waiting for you when you come back."

Marcus knocked it back, pulling it from his mouth, coughing a little and squinting from the tart nature of the substance. "Is this pickle juice?" Marcus asked.

Scott looked over with a matter of fact expression on his face. "Yeah. Why do you think it's banned throughout our side of the Kingdom? Pickle juice makes us sober almost instantly."

Scott continued checking his weapons as Marcus just had his whole world turned upside down in a matter of minutes.

"Battalion! Weapons tight. Kill all of them, but be sure not to kill the creature. She is your only concern… everyone else is fodder. Separate and capture that girl!"

Scott pulled two pins and chucked the two smoke grenades skipping across the concrete. The two grenades burst throwing quickly expanding plumes of smoke in all directions. The soldiers opened fire and the tanks started pounding the heavy doors with their 200mm cannons.

Scotts face split from ear to ear in an evil grin. He laughed aloud, cracking his fingers and clawing through the air like a mad man. "Let's go skull fuck some unfortunate souls by bullet and blade." He laughed to himself again.

Scott stood in front of the door crouched into a sprinting position with a look on his face that worried Marcus. As the smoke reached in, Scott disappeared dragging smoke with him. The Gun Walzer shot out of the top of the plumes of smoke over the formation. He drew his shotguns rapidly firing shells over the formations of men. The rounds exploded on impact killing on average ten men with each shell. Scott landed on top of an unfortunate soldier crushing him into the grass and instantly killing him. He stepped up swinging his shotguns like swords, shattering rib cages, cracking helmets, sweeping soldiers off their feet. Then shooting them in the chest, he sent the lifeless bodies flying into another group to explode.

Marcus was soon out, sprinting to the right flanking the element firing with his rifle. Killing one, the round cut through three other men, wounding them. He lopped off arms and legs at the joints with horrific accuracy. Reloading in a blur, the fire was almost faster than the machine gun fire that sporadically chased behind Marcus. He stopped turning and then charged the fearful soldiers. He batted one into the air, shot another, lopping off the soldier's leg from the thigh. He barrel-tapped another in the face, breaking his jaw loose. He fired several more shots before spinning and landing his rifle into another unfortunate soldier snapping his neck.

Scott threw several smoke grenades into the scrambling formation of frantic soldiers. The grenades exploded sending plumes of thick clouds covering the masses. He flickered and disappeared into the cloud. Screams and gunfire started coming from the frantic men. Some went flying from the cloud skipping across the field lifeless sliding to a stop. Scott slid from the smoke a soldier clutched in his strong hand choking, kicking, and clawing at the Gun Walzer's arm. He threw the soldier into several others violently and sent a hail of bullets from his revolvers killing all twelve of his targets before the Gun Walzer skipped backwards into the cloud of thick smoke.

The three mechanized dolls spun up and started charging into the cloud firing their heavy Gatling guns. A hail of rockets slammed into the cloud exploding sending body parts and debris in all directions. Scott flickered across the field sliding to a stop. He continued to reload his revolvers and holstered them. He drew both his shotguns from their sheaths. Taking aim, he volleyed the first mechanized robot just taking flight a few inches off the ground. The robot exploded slamming into the grass. Its engines were still firing and propelling it towards Scott. The Gun Walzer stepped to the side keeping his eyes trained on the other two. The robot exploded behind Scott as he started walking towards the two surviving machines.

Several soldiers had made their way towards the opening of the entrance. Stopping suddenly as Victoria and Elizabeth walked from the opening standing on either side. Victoria with her spear and sharp shield and Elizabeth scraped her heavy blade on top of the concrete.

"You bitches think you can stop all of us with those obsolete weapons? Men, shoot those whores." One of the soldiers yelled. He picked up fire. The rounds bounced off Victoria as she slid towards him thrusting with her long spear. She pulled, the lifeless body flew past her sliding across the concrete to a bloodstained stop against the heavy doors. The soldiers started violently twitching. Just behind Victoria Elizabeth shoved her shield into the concrete and in a blur, she ran to Victoria's right, button-hooking left and slicing across. Blood splattered in a large moon shape behind the confused soldiers. Then again as her sword rested on the concrete with a heavy clank. The men all fell in half.

"We will make our stand here!", Elizabeth roared.

"Aye, my Lady", Victoria replied.

Marcus plowed through rank after rank, dropping grenades, lopping limb off from every soldier he shot at. Not killing them, but simply making them die slowly. Marcus slid to a stop, stomping an unsuspecting soldier behind a barrier into the concrete. The soldier's chest was crushed. Blood spilled onto the white cement and grass below. A soldier stabbed at him. Marcus caught the man's hand crushing his fist to mush around the handle. The soldier fell to his knees screaming in pain trying to wrench what was left of his hand free. Marcus shot another one running to aid the poor soldier, killing him instantly. Without missing a beat, Marcus kicked the soldier in his chest, ripping the soldier's arm completely off.

Marcus burst into laughter as he picked the arm up to inspect his handy work. He took off sprinting, coming to a sliding stop where he beat another soldier to death with the severed arm. Marcus was covered in blood as he began to stomp the lifeless soldier's head into the grass. Horrified onlookers began to run away. Marcus reloaded his rifle and body came flying at him from his left. Marcus stopped the screaming man by stomping him into the ground, then shooting him as he pinned the soldier's face down to the ground.

Marcus saw Scott uppercut a soldier into the air and quick drew his pistol killing the soldier before he could even start falling. Then Scott flickered away from even Marcus's sight. A mechanized robot strafed just a few inches off the grass circling Marcus. The heavy machine guns started spinning on, Marcus ran straight at the machine just as it began to fire. The bullets chased him into the air. Marcus landed on the top of the robot beating the machine's head with his rifle. The rifle broke as the head shattered to pieces. He pulled his blade. The machine as now flying sideways towards the testing facility. Marcus ripped the chest piece from the upper torso sticking it into the grass. The horrified pilot shielded his face as Marcus pressed his pistol into his hands pinning them to his face. Marcus fired killing the man. The robot crashed into the side of the building.

Marcus rolled springing to his feet. He sprinted and attacked the nearest person to him. Victoria picked her shield up. He knocked it away effortlessly with his hand. The shield sparks across the concrete. She blocked with her spear, but he grabbed it and kicked her in the chest. She lost her grip. He stuck the spear into the concrete drawing his pistol approaching her like a predator with great intent. She slammed into the thick metal blast doors. She looked to find his barrel in her face.

"Marcus! It's me! Victoria...", she frantically exclaimed.

Elizabeth spun in a whirlwind slicing men to pieces trying to get past her into the doorway. Scott noticed the ordeal unfolding at the facility. He shot another three men running away without looking. He took measure of the battlefield for a moment. An aircraft was now flying over the facility. Lines dropped from the opening of the belly of the craft. He drew his shotgun and fired. The grenade soared exploding as soon as it slammed into the cockpit. The craft caught fire, spinning and crashing into the top of the building exploding into a ball of fire sending a large smoke mushroom clouds towards the sky. Scott flickered, disappearing once more.

Victoria lifted her helms face shield. "It will always be yours to take", she spoke softly with absolute resolve and trust in her tone.

Marcus's hand started to shake as debris fell all around them from the fiery craft burning above them. Heavy metal remains of the craft bounced and slammed into the concrete still on fire. Some bodies and some unrecognizable remains hit the concrete.

"Nope!", Scott yelled as he grabbed Marcus by the back of his plate carrier throwing the young Gun Walzer into the air. Marcus, without a thought, started firing at Scott. Victoria jumped out of the way. Scott's image faded as the bullets passed through nothing. Marcus regained his level landing hard onto the corner of a tank. The remote weapon took aim on Marcus. Marcus had the pistol trained behind him under his arm. He fired destroying the optical lens. Marcus leaped from the tank and ran back into the mass of disoriented soldiers still trying to rush the two Old Guard knights.

Two foot soldiers took up positions with launchers aimed at the tall doors. They fired off two missiles straight and true. With all that is happening upon the battlefield no one noticed until it was too late.

"Jimmy?", Phillis called.

"Yes, Phillis?", Jimmy yelled back.

Just before she could give her orders, the two heavy blast doors blew inward. Phillis happened to move out of the way just in time. The doors landed on both sides of Kathrine's glass holding cell. She was standing next to Jimmy holding his hand tight.

Phillis was unscathed by the falling doors.

Observing the war before them. Phillis fired bolts killing the men who were flanking the two Knights as Elizabeth slashed and cut through every foe. Victoria spun her great spear around in a beautiful array of movements striking and thrusting killing and knocking away soldier after soldier. The gusts of wind pushed and cleared away dust and dirt with ever movement of her great weapon.

Scott almost hovered over the grass with blinding speed punching a soldier who skipped across the battlefield and bouncing off a tank fast approaching the two Knights. He fired off his shotguns as he spun, sheathing them. He came to a stop his arms blurred as he quick drew killing 12 more men. And then he vanished again leaving behind a smoke grenade. Marcus could be seen chasing after Scott killing unlucky soldiers as he attempted to catch his mentor.

"Who are your friends, Jimmy?", the Princess asked.

"They are the greatest. You'll get to meet them all. But there is Elizabeth and Victoria who are real life Knights. Victoria is beautiful when she wields her spear. It's like watching a dance or music being played for the first time. And Elizabeth is the best swordswoman in all the land. She can cut anything with her great sword. And there is Scott and Marcus who are real gunslingers. Mr. Scott can be scary, but he is a good man. And Marcus he is the greatest. He's always nice to me and funny too. And then there is Phillis…she's like my mom. She raised me and taught me to hunt and use my bow. She can teach you too. And then there is Charles, he is very important and very smart. And Jess, she's my girlfriend. I really love her."

"Your friends sound wonderful, Mr. Jimmy", Kathrine said holding his hand. She watched the world unfold and burn before her. She saw the intensity in Jimmy's friends' eyes. The lengths they were going through to save her, the enemy they were facing. This small group was fighting against so many for one little girl. She was baffled, astonished by the anguish they paid to the world and to their enemies.

"Jimmy?", she started, only to be interrupted by the flash and bang. The taste and smell of carbon, the after math of the deafening ring.

"Kathrine, run!", Jimmy yelled out.

The gunshot was muffled within the glass walls as blood splattered before Jimmy up the wall. Eyes wide Jimmy spun around pushing Kathrine out of the way. Simultaneously drawing his bow, Jimmy fired his arrow through the man behind him. The arrow punched through his stomach, sticking into the concrete behind him causing the man to fall to his knees as Jimmy was shot two more times in the chest knocking him against the back glass wall.

"Why, Charles?", Jimmy choked.

Charles was on his knees, holding his stomach trying to stop the bleeding.

"Why would you betray us?", Jimmy choked. Kathrine, eyes wide rushed to Jimmy trying to stop him from bleeding. She was crying, tears pouring from her eyes. Charles shot himself up with his Madness. His wounds stopped bleeding and he could stand once more.

"Because you are the past and she is our future, you simpleton", Charles replied.

Kathrine rushed to Jimmy trying to protect him. Charles grabbed the girl by her arm and attempted to pry her from Jimmy. The boy wouldn't let go even with his last breath.

"Give me the girl!", Charles yelled firing his pistol into Jimmy's chest until finally he could no longer hold onto her.

Kathrine stopped crying. She clawed at Charles hand cutting his index, middle and ring fingers off.

"You little insect!", he growled as he attempted to get closer reaching now with his other hand.

"Get away from him!", she roared.

Her scream becomes so loud the glass cracks, shattering as her scream grew louder. Charles covered his ears falling to his knees turning away from her. A light began to brighten from within her mouth as she screamed. The humming that stared coming from her shook the ground as it became a constant roaring furnace. Sparks of light began to shoot out in all directions. A blue beam fired from the child's mouth blowing the building out and cutting through the kingdom. The ground began to glow red hot and exploded following the massive line across the kingdom. Debris and molten rock exploded in all directions from the blast. Many onlookers stopped in their tracks as debris from the building falls around them.

Kathrine fainted onto Jimmy. Charles stood looking out the hole with wide eyes. His jaws dropped as the sound of sirens all over the kingdom began to ring out. He turned and attempts to grab her once more only to find Jimmy had his bow in his hand holding it drawn on Charles.

"You don't get to have her", Jimmy choked.

"You've killed us all!", Charles barked.

Jimmy said nothing, holding his bow steady. Charles backed away and disappeared into the debris from the destroyed building.

Jimmy let out his bow dropping it to the side and held on to Kathrine.

"I'm sorry sweetie, but I won't be able to keep my promise after all. Goodbye, Princess." He kissed her on the forehead.

He tried to chuckle through the blood, "She looks like a butterfly."

His eyes closed and with his last breath kissed her forehead as he held on tight. The two lay there against the glass, stained in blood all around. Like rubies spilling over diamonds. She held on tight to his shirt as she lay against the young man.

Scott stomped a soldier's neck in, kicks another soldier completely off his feet while he drew his pistol shooting the broken legged foe in the face as he tumbled away. The ground started rumbling as just over the crest of the hill behind the facility, reinforcements were headed their way. Tank after tank, mechanized robots crested the hill. Its four giant red legs moved like a spider. The large sleek head outfitted with cannons and machine guns. The giant mechs legs could crush the tanks driving past it.

Marcus charged the reinforcements landing on top of a tank ripping the door off and dropping inside. The tank started straying from the formation running into another. Marcus jumped out just as the tank exploded. The giant mechs head traversed and fired its large cannon. The tank he was on exploded sending Marcus unconscious into the air. He slammed into the wall and fell face first onto the ground.

The formation started rolling over their own people. Screams rang out before they were silenced by the tracks of the tanks. Blood curdling cries were silenced as the large walking robot crushed soldiers still barely alive. The robots flying only a few inches off the ground burned living and dead soldiers with their rocket stabilizers as they slowly take up position between the group and the wall.

Victoria and Elizabeth fell back into what's left of the building as Scott dropped smoke after smoke in between the small army and the destroyed building. Finally the group was standing inside, and the scene they came to called all of their attention.

Jimmy was sitting up against the glass as he laid in blissful slumber. Holding on to Kathrine whom was laid against his chest clutching his bloodied shirt. His eyes were closed, his head was leaning against hers. She breathed softly against him not knowing what had happened. Jess was sobbing on her knees off to his side. Phillis had tears down her face. Scott leaned against the corner pillar lighting a smoke. He took in the whole scene around them. Phillis kneeled next to young Jimmy, fixing his hair. She noticed he was smiling as she leaned down kissing his forehead softly.

"My precious boy, you saved her. Just like you promised. Let's get you home." She dipped her fingers in his blood and wiped two streaks just under her eyes down her cheeks.

She passed by Scott.

"I'm going to find Charles."

"As you should", Scott replied.

She walked out into the open. The giant four legged mech aimed its massive cannon. Phillis started to sizzle and steam. Her skin darkened as her muscles seem to grow and become more defined. She drew. The bow stressed to hold itself together. Her fingers bled from the line. She was calm. The wind was calm, the unfortunate souls before her would bear witness to beauty only few have known.

"Hold your breath little soldiers, you're going to need every bit you can muster. For now, behold the Breathless Arrow." Scott voiced holding his hands out.

Scott waited patiently with a grin on his face observing her. Elizabeth and Victoria stood ready on both sides of him. Scott lazily pulled his pistol and killed a soldier emerging from cover about to take a shot at Phillis. Scott never took his eyes off Phillis as he killed the young soldier.

"We are going home", Phillis said.

She let it fly. The vortex of wind blew everything around her violently away. The arrow screamed for a second and burrowed through the giant four legged machines front right leg. Soldiers ran to get behind the tanks suddenly drop gasping for air. Then the drag caught up to them, blowing all of them towards the tanks violently under the path of the bolt. The machines leg exploded, ripped away from the joint. She drew once more firing into another tank. The insides of the tank appeared to have been sucked out the other side just before exploding. The tanks opened fire. Elizabeth and Victoria ran in front of her blocking the rounds. Sparks fly and rounds skipped off the shields exploding in the air and into the hill side.

Jess kissed Jimmy on the lips.

"Rest well my love", she voiced just above a whisper.

Suddenly the giant stone wall behind the Dragonare forces began to turn red. Liquidating and exploding. The whole battlefield seemed to have stopped. Turrets turned, robots turned and from the smoldering melted rock two massive Chimeras jumped onto the field. The baby ran straight for the building. The mother started ripping apart tank after tank, picking them up by her mouth and tossing them. She opened her mouth and fired a thick red beam across the formation of tanks and robots. The ground and machine after machine exploded. The robots took flight in all directions shooting and lobbing missile after missile at the gorgeous horned beast. Her heavily armored tail whipped and sliced through the robots chasing her like flies.

The baby leaped over the prism prison cell and slowly walked up to Jimmy. Jess gets in between the two. The baby snorts blowing her back. The beast bowed over him slowly sniffing the dead boy. And Jess could see the sadness in the Chimera's eyes as he nudged Jimmy. Scott patted the beast on the side as he began to walk out onto the battlefield. The mother Chimera was now being chased now across the hillside. The ground was trembling from the massive beast's strong legs at she sprinted away.

The baby Chimera sat back and began to howl. Its cries were deafening as he called for his friend. Jess was stricken with awe. Phillis fired arrow after arrow. Steam rose from her body more and more as she killed hundreds with every arrow. Destroying tank after tank, robot after robot from her Breathless Arrows. The dust and debris shot from her in all directions as she loosed her arrows straight and true.

Scott called to Elizabeth and Victoria. "Get Jimmy and the girl. That hole in the wall is our exit. I'm going to go get Marcus. But don't wait on us, get the fuck out of this shithole while you still can."

Phillis was out on the battlefield by herself now. She spotted Charles jumping out of the giant spider mech running towards another tank. Phillis drew and fired another arrow blowing the tank apart. Charles got sent across the field landing in the smoldering ditch from the Chimera's beam.

The baby Chimera lay down its long nose between Jimmy's legs. Jess was pulling Jimmy's strong arm away from Kathrine, with much difficulty she could free her. She took the girl into her arms and placed Jimmy's arm back onto his lap. Elizabeth kneeled next to Jimmy, being careful not to touch the great beast. She slowly picked him up onto her shoulder. The beast perked up, its ears shooting straight up backing out of the glass prison. Elizabeth walked out.

"Jess, can you carry her?"

"Yes", she choked through her lump in her throat.

The baby led out as Elizabeth, Jess holding Kathrine, followed by Victoria.

Scott took a knee on top of Marcus's chest. The young Gun Walzer violently started swinging as he came to. Scott popped open a flask and grabbed Marcus by his jaw slamming his head into the ground. He shoved the flask into his mouth dumping the contents down the flailing, choking Marcus. He kicked and choked as Scott pinned him to the ground with one hand.

"Stop struggling you little bastard", Scott laughed out loud as he continued to torment Marcus.

Scott jumped up and stepped back. Marcus grunted as he got onto his hands and knees. "Fuck…you…", he said drawing his pistol. Scott kicked it from Marcus's hand and then kicked Marcus up onto his feet. Scott blocked Marcus's futile attempt to counter, stepped and palm struck Marcus into the wall. The giant stones cracked from the impact.

"Come on young man. Test your grit against this old man", Scott yelled with a smile on his face.

Marcus sprung from the wall and threw a fury of blows and kicks. Scott dodged and blocked without care. Scott ducked and slammed into Marcus with his body. Simultaneously, he elbowed Marcus in the face and, with a blinding snap, backhanded him. The young Gun Walzer was rocked and thrown off balance. The force of the blow weakened his knees. Scott, with great intent, walked up onto Marcus who held out his hand as he slowly got to his feet.

"I'm back! I'm good", Marcus slurred.

"Get the fuck up and go help them. They are about to leave this shithole. I'm going to go check on Phillis", Scott replied.

Marcus searched the smoldering battlefield taking in the destruction across the torn scene. He took a winding path to catch up to the group. Once there, the group stopped and he slowly walked up as they face him. Victoria walked towards him quickly.

"I'm sorry, if I did any-", Victoria smacked him across the face.

He was surprised. But then she lifted her visor. She was happy he was okay and he could see it.

"Don't scare me like that again", she said softly.

He nodded.

"Let us take our leave", Elizabeth broke the moment.

Marcus noticed Jimmy. His face twisted into sadness as he tried to keep his composure.

Charles woke up on his back. He sat up to find Phillis fast approaching with a single arrow in her hand. She dropped the bow as Charles quickly attempted to scurry away. She was on top of him pulling him up, tears in her eyes steaming off her skin just as they formed. Her body was on fire. Charles could feel the heat from her as she slowly stuck the arrow into his plate carrier. Wide eyed, horrified and almost yelling, Charles attempted with all his might to stop her from pushing it through his plate. His hands burned as he tried to stop her from pushing it deeper.

He let out a blood curdling cry as the arrow pops through the plate into his chest. She passed it straight through his chest. The choking and gurgling man coughed blood onto her face could do nothing. She showed no remorse as she continued sticking it through. He punched and beat against her, to no affect what so ever, she continued, true horror was written upon his freakish and jerking actions.

Suddenly she passed out. Her body was burning, steam slowly rising off her skin. Charles quickly crawled away from her until he hit something hard behind him. The frantic man looked up to see Scott looking down. His eyes were almost black. Hatred was written all over his face. Charles quickly rolled over crawling away from the devil standing over him. Scott slowly followed, pulled his blade from the leather sheath on the small of his back.

"You will not leave this field alive", Scott spoke sternly.

Scott walked around Charles, circling him spinning his blade around his finger.

"She could save us! She was the answer to all our problems. We are the ones who should exist on this planet. Not them! And you, you betrayed your own kind!"

Charles as on his knees now. His hands shaking as he reached for his injector. He shot himself up as Scott pulled his smoke from his mouth. Charles stuck himself with another injection and another. His body was jerking violently as it healed itself. Charles was grinning as his body was growing in mass.

"I will wipe you and your kind from the face of the earth!", Charles laughed as the veins in his head started to bulge. He ripped the arrow from his chest throwing it to the side. On his feet now, he was ready to charge Scott.

"Not by your hands", Scott replied catching his blade from its last spin.

Scott stood lazily ready. The heavy wet steps from about 30 soldiers surrounding him came to a dead silence as they reached their positions. Charles was ready, Scott spun his blade ominously.

"Kill him!", Charles roared. The soldiers opened fire. Machine guns rattled from several positions and rockets screamed towards him from all directions. Charles pulled his slung rifle and began to fire while walking into where the thick white smoke had filled the area.

Scott had used his last few smoke grenades. The plumes have spread and covered the area encompassing the soldiers and Charles now. It was dead quiet now. The soldiers peeked over their positions to see if they had hit their target even once. But alas, they see a figure still standing there, and then it was gone. A man screamed off in the distance. The body slumped to the ground in a heavy wet thud. Another scream in the smoke, the sound of a weapon being cleaved in half was followed by a limb hitting the ground. And the figure was gone as the screams muffled under a heavy boot.

Charles looked in all directions attempting to make out anything from the thick smoke.

Scott landed behind him. "You can't kill a ghost, Charles."

Charles turned and fired randomly killing a soldier running away.

Scott landed behind him again. "You killed the best one of us."

Charles turned as Scott palm struck him under his chin, lifting Charles into the air. Scott drew and fired hitting Charles in the chest. But Charles's body was healing fast. The massive hole was sealed up in seconds. Charles hit the ground hard and he was back on his feet in a flash. Scott slid into him swinging his shotgun like a sword. Charles narrowly parried the blow, sending sparks and metal shavings from the weapon. Scott disappeared into the smoke once more.

"This smoke won't hide you forever, coward!", Charles screamed.

He began to fire randomly at silhouettes of soldiers running away. He did not care. He continued to kill his own men as they attempted to escape the Smoldering Ghost. A rocket fired off nearly hitting Charles. The explosion sent the Dragonare rolling out of the slowly dissipating smoke to a heavy landing onto scraps of metal and bodies. Charles stumbles to his feet. He could see a dark figure moving about and disappearing. A soldier was sent flying across the field missing from the right knee down. The body hit the ground finally rolling lifeless into a burning tank. Another is sprinting towards Charles direction. Charles quickly fired and killed the young man.

"Useless, all of you! Worthless dogs", he ground his words through his clenched teeth.

The smoke was finally blown away. Charles spotted Scott holding a limp soldier by his shirt. Charles picked up and fired at Scott. Scott slung the lifeless soldier at Charles. The bullets ripped into the soldier, the soldier slammed into Charles with blood splattering in all directions. Scott turned to see another soldier taking aim with a shoulder fired rocket launcher. Scott whipped his blade slinging it like a boomerang. The rocket soared towards Scott. The blade struck into the soldier's left side. Scott backhanded the rocket as if he were swatting a fly. The rocket spun and flipped out of control smashing into the stone wall behind him exploding. Scott walked towards Charles who was now back on his feet. He took aim, pulled the trigger, but the weapon as empty. Scott was in front of him now, his image flicking into a steady form. Charles tossed the weapon and drew his pistol firing from the hip. Scott caught his hand. His grip so tight as he was turning Charles right hand to mush. The pistol was cracking and bending.

Charles grunting and breathing heavily, pulled his thin dagger and thrusted to no avail. Scott had caught the blade with his right.

"All your might, all your strength, all your drugs, your plans, your very life, it amounted to nothing in the end, Charles. You're an imitation, a copy, a fake, nothing more."

Charles's eyes were wide, the fear had settled in completely now. Scott leaned over him with a grin. Charles began to weaken at the knees. Charles smiled. Scott was taken back for a moment as his face became stern.

"What's so funny?", Scott growled.

"Fake or not, we will both die right here, dog", Charles replied falling to his knees. Scott looked up and the scrap behind him was a mech. A timer was counting down rapidly on one of the console screens. Charles began to laugh. But Scott couldn't move. For what was looking down at him was keeping him frozen.

The beast was black and ominous, towering over the two, seated it was over 10 feet tall. Its thick coat covered in blood and ash and soot, matted formulating feathered spikes. Its grin was split across its face with hundreds of large shark-like teeth. Its head was that of a wolf, its six eyes stared down upon Scott. Only at Scott. Scott could do nothing. The beast spoke but its mouth did not move.

"Not yet", the beast said. Its voice harsh and threatening.

It looked, waving its ghostly tail off in the distance. Scott managed to look as well. To find Phillis, bow drawn. Charles looked as well. Scott turned back. The beast was gone. Phillis let the arrow fly. The bow ripped apart in her hand and the wire snapped. Scott flickered appearing right before Phillis sliding to a stop. The arrow cut into the ground slamming into Charles. He disintegrated from the force of the arrow. The timer hits zero. The explosion struck up a brilliant, white shockwave that knocked Phillis and Scott back. The mushroom cloud rose high. And the blast burned with the intensity of the sun. Phillis passed out again. He could hear her before she went out.

"What was that thing?"

Scott looked out onto the battlefield calmly.

"It was the Black Dog, Phillis."

Scott approached the group with Phillis over his shoulder.

"Where have you been?", Marcus slurred.

"Taking care of a loose ends, brother. Here take her. I'm going to go help this guy's momma. I'll meet you at the craft. Leave without me if you have to."

The group as Scott turned and disappears into the smoke towards the Mother Chimera defending herself from the pestering robots. Scott pulled his other shotgun sticking out of the dead soldier from earlier and draws his other. The group made it onto the cool melted rock of the wall. All but Marcus leapt out and head into the forest. Marcus watches as Scott and the Chimera dance around each other shooting the robots out of the sky. Rockets and machine gun fire chased them, The Chimera fired another beam completely decimating three mechs caught in her blast. Scott shot another two out of the sky.

"How do I become as great as you?", Marcus asked himself before leaping from the wall.

Finally, Scott sheathed his weapons. The Chimera was panting like a dog. He turned as she walked up to him.

"I think we can leave now, momma", He said as she towered over him.

The storm hit and she leaped over the wall back into the forest. Scott held out his hand as the rain fell. The fires smoldered out and the smoke began to clear. And just before Scott leaped down he looked back.

And there he was again. The massive black dog looked at him with his six red eyes. A small woman was standing next to it this time as it billowed thick black clouds of smoke with every breath. She was not human. She was like a tree in autumn. And holding her hand, was a young man who lifted his hand for a wave farewell. She slowly faded away with the young man. The black dog turned and faded into plumes of black smoke.

"I'll see you there, Jimmy."

Chapter 16

The Weight of His Soul

Scott landed onto the ship just as it picked up off the ground, cracking the deck under his feet as he landed like an animal. Jess was sitting next to Jimmy laid out on a table covered in a blue and gold embroidered blanket. Elizabeth, Victoria, and Marcus were sitting around him with their hands on his chest. Scott searched the deck with that empty look on his face. He was annoyed by their day and tired from their travels and a pain from their loss weighed heavy on all their hearts.

"Where is the girl and where is Phillis?", Scott asked as he light his cigarette.

"They are both sleeping in the captain's quarters", Marcus answered.

The rain bounced off the ship with heavy ticks and thuds against the decks cover. They picked up out of the forest and start heading home. Scott combed his hair to the side in a messy part. He was dripping wet from his travels to the extraction point. He sat back on the railing looking back, exhaling heavy plumes of smoke while peering off towards the wrecked Dragonare territory. Ships flew around with more reinforcements searching the area. The Chimera and her baby were safe somewhere in the forest under them. The group could hear their calls to the fallen friend even under the thick canvas of leaves and limbs.

Suddenly Kathrine came out of the captain's quarters, the door slamming hard against the wall.

"Where is Jimmy?", she demanded.

She found her answer as the group looked at her without a word.

She started crying as she rushed to his side laying over him. Jess hugged her and started crying herself. The rain fell harder as they carried onward towards the floating castle.

"You promised me!", she screamed. "You promised me."

Jess gripped her tightly attempting to comfort the princess. Kathrine turned and buried her face in Jess's chest as she rocked her. Tears poured from their eyes like the rain.

Marcus got up and walked over to Scott.

Jess took Kathrine away from Jimmy with difficulty and disappeared back into the quarters. The group can hear her cries. Victoria and Elizabeth both began to cry.

"Why did it have to be him?", Marcus leaned onto the railing.

"Because it's the way of the world, my friend. The price we pay for being who we are. He understood it just the same as you and me. He was more honorable than any of us. So let him rest because if anyone deserved to go to paradise, it was that boy." Scott replied.

"What now?" Marcus asked.

"We go home and we live on. Prepare for the next war and the one after that and then for those who will inevitably inherit the one after that."

"It's okay to feel something every now and then", Marcus replied.

Scott's eyes slid over glaring at his friend. He turned and shoved his finger in his chest. "He filled his fucking boots, we shouldn't be crying over this shit. We should be celebrating him, not sitting here sulking. So crack a fucking beer and watch some fucking scenery and remember who he was and how he showed his true fucking colors in the end when it boiled down to fight or flight. Mother fucker died with honor and protected the weak."

Victoria and Elizabeth were looking at him as he was towering over Marcus like a predator.

"He did his fucking job, and that's more than most, he paid his weight in worth, his sacrifice wasn't in vein and the faster you realize that, the faster you can find your own goddamn resolve, because he found his. She's in there right now because of him. So don't let me hear any more of this shit. Let him be the hero he already was long before any of us ever met him. By bullet and blade, remember mother fucker?"

Scott turned and walked to the front of the ship.

Marcus stood there pondering to himself.

Elizabeth picked up his bow and set it under Jimmy's hands. She slid the blue vale over his blissful face.

In the captain's quarters, Jess was wiping the blood off Kathrine's face as she sat on the sink. Her eyes were glossy and her cheeks puffy from crying. She was staring at nothing as Jess wiped away Jimmy's blood with the soft rag.

"Why did he have to die?", Kathrine asked coldly.

"I don't know, Princess."

"You were his girlfriend, right?"

Jess was surprised but she sighed in happiness. "Yes", she said holding her tears back.

"What was he like?", Kathrine asked.

Jess kneeled down, looking up at the little girl waiting patiently for her answer.

"He was the greatest man I've ever met in my life."

The rest of the trip Kathrine listened to Jess tell of who Jimmy was and how great of a man he will always be remembered as. Phillis sat next to Jimmy the entire ride. Scott kept watch as the rest of the tattered group sat with heavy hearts as the storm carried on. The ride home seemed to take longer with the weight of their loss.

Several hours later, Scott checked on Phillis sitting next to her. He offered her a bottle and then a cigarette. The two walked over to the railing leaning against it looking at where Jimmy rest. Scott lit her smoke.

"I never told him he was like a son to me", Phillis broke the silence.

"He knew...believe me. We all knew. You raised the best of men and he couldn't have been a better human being. He loved you very much. You should be proud of that man right there", Scott replied. Pointing as he does under his glare.

"I never had a chance to tell him I love him", she began choke and tear up.

She leaned into Scott dropping her bottle and smoke onto the deck.

Scott tossed his over board and put his large arm around her.

"He knew and he went as he would have wanted to go. And we would be so lucky to go the way he did. Protecting, fighting with honor as a true warrior. He went to paradise and we will see him again. You can be sure of that."

Scott pulled her away, looking into her eyes. He wiped the tears away with his thumb. "Be happy for your boy. He was a hero and maintained a true heart. You and I will never be as great a person than he was. So let him rest as he should."

The sun was shining brightly as the morning broke, The airship was now in sight of the castle. Banners and cheers could be seen and heard from the entire Kingdom as they awaited the ships landing. Two fighter crafts ushered the ship into the docks. A long blue carpet, the King and Queen and Susanna were waiting at the beginning of it where the ship slowly docked. The group was ready on the deck. Phillis, Scott, Marcus, and Jess all carried Jimmy's body.

Kathrine ran down the ramp to her mother who was crying as she knelt down with open arms. The King wrapped around them with his great wings as he embraced his wife and child. Susanna leaned down onto them. Elizabeth and Victoria led the group carrying Jimmy down the ramp. The King stood to greet them. His smile slowly faded as he saw Jimmy upon the open casket.

"Your highness. May we present Jimmy, the Truest Arrow."

"Thank you all for your sacrifice. We will never be able to repay you", The King spoke. "He will receive a hero's pillar in the Gardens of Legend. And, however, you all deem fit, we will hold the ceremony tonight for his memorial."

Victoria replied. "Sire, he is the reason why your daughter was brought back to you safe and sound. He gave his life protecting her from a treacherous snake."

Kathrine looked out. "Father, we can never forget him. He was my friend."

The group continued walking down the pathway carrying their friend. The Queen stopped the group and leaning down, she kissed the young man on his forehead.

"Thank you. May you rest peacefully", she spoke softly.

"What was his full name?", She demanded.

Phillis answered.

"Jimmy Valentine."

"It shall be remembered for the rest of our existence for generations to come. You have my word as Queen."

The Queen bowed as did the King, Susanna, Kathrine, and the entire Kingdom as the group continued down the docks. Gabriel and three other knights joined the group as the King and his family now reunited walked behind Jimmy. Winston landed upon the wall to observe as well as he passed down the docks. Flowers began to snow from the great tree down onto the whole kingdom.

Dusk now, every able body in the whole kingdom was present for this moment. Lining the shore of the great river flowing over the side of the island. As the sun set, Phillis kissed Jimmy's forehead as he lay peacefully on the wooden alter in his small boat.

"Sweet dreams", she whispered before leaving the boat. Next, it was Jess's turn. She kneeled next to him, kissing him softly on the lips. Her tears fell upon his face.

"I love you Jimmy", she whispered over his lips. She quickly left the boat as well.

And then it was Kathrine's turn. She hugged him, tears rolled from her face as she held her cries back. She then softly kissed him on the cheek. She quickly ran to her mother burying her head in her stomach.

"He was the very example of it", Marcus said as they two men readied to push the boat down the river.

"Of what?", Scott asked.

Marcus replied. "Of your old saying."

Scott laughed quietly. "A bullet never lies and the blade's whisper is never sweeter. I think, in his case, however, it would be more accurate to say... The arrow never truer, and his heart never more loyal."

"Agreed", Marcus replied.

Scott and Marcus gently pushed the small boat from the dock. It slowly drifted away as they all watched. The whole kingdom held candles high as they watched a hero float away. Phillis sniffling takes her bow lighting an arrow and drawing.

Victoria and Elizabeth bowed behind their weapons. Scott and Marcus held out their drinks to the young man. And Phillis let the arrow fly. It hit the boat straight and true igniting the oil. The boat rose in flames as it drifted down the still waters.

Kathrine continued to cry as she peered with one eye. Jess stood next to Phillis, tears rolling down her face as well. Marcus and Scott rose their bottles to Jimmy as he drifted further and further away. In his honor, they drank.

Suddenly the entire kingdom let floating lanterns drift into the night. They all for some unknown reason followed him as he drifted further and further from their view. The flowers from the trees were still snowing down as the sun set. Jimmy's flame was gone. Only the lanterns remained lighting the way for his soul.

"He made it to paradise", Marcus said to Scott.

"As he should. If anyone ever deserved it. It was that man."

"We're gonna miss you, Jimmy". Marcus whispered.

Chapter 17

The Incoming Storm

"Practice went good today. Phillis has been showing me how to use a bow and I'm getting really good. One day I will be as good as you. Everybody misses you. They tell me lots of stories. My training is really hard. Even Uncle Marcus and my big brother Scott are teaching me how to shoot but I'm better with a bow. You were right. Uncle Marcus is really funny and Scott is scary. But he makes my sister happy, so he must be a good man. They take me on drives all the time too. I have a lot of fun with them."

Phillis was watching as Kathrine was showing Jimmy her bow. Winston was laying around the statue and the princess as she talked to him. His statue was magnificent. It was made of a blue gem, carved with perfection. Jimmy stood holding his bow with a Chimera standing behind him looking out into the distance. His hand was stretched out in front of him as if he were offering help. Just how Kathrine remembered him. The masterpiece was placed in the center of a garden dedicated to the great man. The large steps led up the giant round tower on three sides. Trees and beautiful flowers surrounded the perfectly green and thick grass blanketing the floor of the memorial.

The group walked up stopping only to observe with Phillis.

"I see she is out here again", Susanna stated.

Phillis turned, placing a finger over her lips.

Kathrine drew her bow. "I made this. Phillis helped a lot. I'm still learning, but she is a really good teacher. Marcus and Scott say that you are in paradise protecting everyone. How is it up there? Will I get to see you again? I hope so. Jimmy Jr. has gotten big. Aunt Jess says he will be big and strong like his dad. Victoria and Marcus are going to have a baby soon too. I can't wait! Mr. Scott and my big sis are getting married soon. Okay? That's it for now. I love you Jimmy." She ran up and hugged the statue and then jumped on Winston's back. Winston and the Princess flew off with a heavy gust from the dragon's wings.

The group continued up the steps to Jimmy's statue.

"Has it really been a year?", Phillis asked.

Victoria was wearing a black dress, very pregnant, but still proper and elegant. She bowed her head. Elizabeth drew her sword and kneeled behind it. Phillis touched the statue's hand. Susanna sat a reef of flowers at the base of Jimmy's statue.

"And what, pray tell, has those two fools engaged, that they would miss our day of honoring our Truest Arrow?", Elizabeth asked.

Susanna answered. "They are preparing to leave for a few days. Something to the north has my mother concerned and she's is only sending them and the rest of the Gun Walzers who came here to aid us."

Victoria answered as well. "Marcus kept his oath. He did not mention his resolve in this matter. I just pray that they return soon", Victoria rubbed her stomach softly.

Jess came up the stairs seeing everyone already waiting. She held a three months old little boy in her arms wrapped in a blue blanket. She was dressed in a simple blue dress. Her hair was long and braided, tied with a bow at the end. Joining the rest of the group, the women talked and giggled as they sat on the comfortable benches circling Jimmy's memorial. The rest of the group left except for Jess and Jimmy Jr. who was fast asleep in her arms as she looked up at the handsome statue.

"We are fine. Just so you're wondering...everyone is fine."

Jess walked away as the sun begins to set.

Marcus and Scott sat on the small wooden docks looking off into the sunset glaring off the water from the cascading pool at the edge of the castle. The same pool Jimmy was sent home down.

"Has it really been a year?", Marcus asked.

"Yeah. It seems it was just yesterday that we met all those weirdos", Scott replied.

"Well Jimmy, I'm sure the little princess has told you all about how we are doing down here. But we just want you to know...we are protecting them. We won't let anyone harm them while you are getting paradise ready. We all miss you brother. Your memorial is pretty awesome. Kathrine had it carved straight from her memory. And I gotta say, it looks pretty damn good. Your son is starting to look like you too. It's pretty peaceful here. You belonged here more than any of us. We will never forget you and how your honor and sacrifice saved an entire kingdom and a princess. You're a real fairytale hero, Jimmy. Take care, brother", Marcus held up a black bottle elbowing Scott to lift his as well.

"Here's to you my friend", Marcus said. They both drank.

"I'm sure we are going to get an earful for missing visiting his memorial by the old ladies whenever we get back from this", Scott stated.

Marcus and Scott both laughed.

"Well Jimmy, take care brother. We'll see you soon", Scott said standing up. Marcus stood as well. They both poured their bottles into the water.

"You ready?", Scott asked.

"Oh yeah", Marcus said checking his chamber on his rifle.

They two got to the docks and stood there peering over the horizon as an ominous, rickety ship descended. Its rustic metal and heavily armored design added to the puffs of smoke backfiring out of its old pipes jutting out the back of the ship. Its blimp was patched together and the flag flying was Scott's old unit flag. The gun cog symbol flying true. The shotgun crossed with a knife and thin cog encompassing where the weapons crossed.

"I'm relieved that they decided to come", Marcus said looking up at the old ship.

"Somethings coming", Scott said.

"Where, now?"

Scott shook his head lighting a smoke. "On the day Jimmy died, I saw it. The black dog twice. Once while I was about to kill Charles. And once just before I had left. And something else, a woman. But not a human. She was like a goddess."

Marcus was taken back. "But why?"

"I don't know. He wasn't there for the lives we took. He was there for me. I felt it deep down. And he spoke, he said. 'Not yet.' And then he was gone. Faded away into nothing."

"What, not yet... that is real fucking helpful?", Marcus asked looking at Scott intently.

"I think it has something to do with everything happening. The reports are of floating masses of land that had torn themselves from the surface. The sounds of explosions that seem to come from everywhere. The beasts in the forest have become unsettled. The earthquakes and storms coming from nowhere. The kingdoms are all on verge of war. The wars were happening on other continents. Something's coming and I don't know if we are going to be ready for it when it gets here."

Marcus looked back up towards the ship.

Scott continued. "You ever wonder why it was called the Fossil Forest, Marcus?"

"I have no idea. Just that this forest covers the entire world except for the bodies of water, of course."

Scott held up his finger making his point as he spoke. "How would we know where we're going if we don't know where we came from?"

"I don't follow", Marcus replied.

"You see...the greatest mistake of the generations, after the fall of mankind, was that they tried to do what every society before them did. They teach children what they decide will produce slaves. Ill-informed, weakness, hatred and fear. They call it the Fossil Forest because they hoped no one would dig up the past. But the past has all the answers. It always has from war, the societies rising and falling. People don't change. They breathe in and exhale. A constant fluctuation of momentary desires and survivalist instincts. Due to the current situation one or many find themselves in. It was named the Fossil Forest, not because our ancestors didn't want us to dig up the past.... but to go after the greatest resources we have left on this planet. Not food or fuel or weapons. But simply the truth which is more devastating to society than anything you could ever possibly fucking imagine."

Scott turned taking a long drag off his cigarette.

"We are but a teardrop in the eye of the Universe. And how she weeps so."

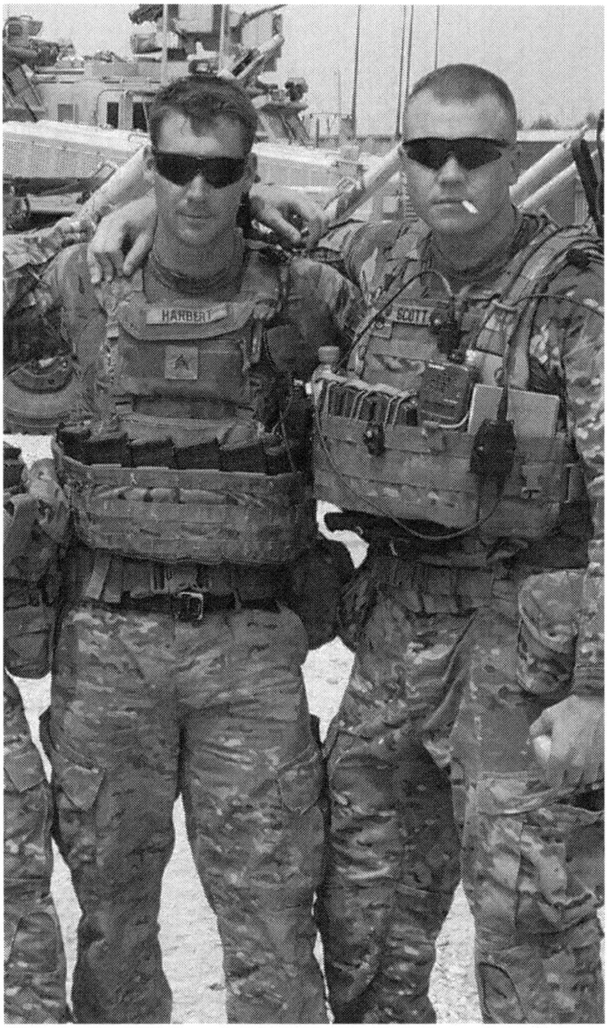
HARBERT
SCOTT

Made in the USA
San Bernardino, CA
29 June 2017